MW01287420

Kitchen Heat

A Restaurantland Romance

Kathleen McFall

Clark Hays

PUMPJACK PRESS

ISBN: 978-1-7345197-9-2
Copyright © 2023 Kathleen McFall and Clark Hays
All rights reserved
Library of Congress Control Number: 2023914158
Cover design by ebooklaunch.com
Pumpjack Press
Portland, Oregon USA

Also by Clark Hays and Kathleen McFall

1

EXT. HOLLYWOOD MOVIE SET — DAY

(February 1996). A seasoned Hollywood
REPORTER interviews a debut SCREENWRITER
about her hot new film.

"Kassi Witmire, tell me all about your new movie *Kitchen Heat*. You've finished the second month of shooting and it's getting unusually great buzz for a new screenwriter."

Kassi leaned back and tried to steady her breathing. She centered her mind on his large, odd handlebar mustache. He looked like a character in an old-time silent film, the dastardly villain who ties the damsel in distress to the train tracks.

But he was not a villain. The reporter, Mark Hessian, was from *Filmmakers Quarterly*, one of the most influential magazines in the industry. He was the last interview of her media junket day, and the most important.

Of course, right on cue, Kassi was having a minor panic attack despite her best efforts at mustache distraction. She could feel the heat starting on her chest and creeping up her neck, approaching her earlobes. If it made it to her scalp, it was all over. The sweat would turn on like a faucet and the biggest moment of her life would be ruined.

"It all feels like a dream," Kassi said.

Not a great response, she thought, but at least she managed to formulate a thought and say words out loud. A catastrophe averted equaled success in this case.

"It's unusual for an Oscar-winning director to sign on to a small art-house project," Mark said. "With a debut screenwriter, no less."

Kassi nodded. That was the understatement of the decade, she thought, and not an actual question.

"I can't tell you how excited I am to be working with Jane. She's an amazing director."

Okay, that was good. She was calming down and her breathing was slowing. This would be fine.

"The buzz around town is that your script captures what it's really like to work in a restaurant, that it's authentic. The pace, the artistry, the chaos."

The sex too, she thought, assuming he'd added that in his head. He would eventually get to that question. They all had. The sooner the better. Sex sells.

Kassi fake-laughed and slipped into an alternate persona like the public relations coach taught her yesterday in a half-hour speed training session mandated by her agent. *Pretend you're an actress and it will all go fine.*

She settled on what she hoped was a combination of her favorite film characters: Louise, Susan Sarandon's confident and wise waitress character from *Thelma and Louise*, and bubbly Cher played perfectly by Alicia Silverstone in last year's movie *Clueless*.

"Mark, you hit the nail on the head. Perfect description. It is indeed chaotic work, and that frenetic energy shapes the people who are thrown together in a restaurant. It's half fun, half soul-crushing, always boomeranging between boredom and pure adrenaline. There's no middle ground."

"Sounds like you have some real-world experience in food service," he said.

Kassi took a sip of water. "I've worked in plenty of restaurants in my time. Most recently, at the Rose and Thorn in Portland, Oregon. I wrote the screenplay while I worked there."

"Writing scripts is hard work," said the child seated next to her in a miniature director's chair.

"Is this your agent?" Mark asked.

"I'm her daughter. My name is Samantha, and I'm four. I'm writing a script too." She was holding a tattered notebook in her lap decorated with stickers of horses and butterflies.

"I see," Mark said. "Has it also been fast-tracked into a major motion picture?"

"Not yet," Samantha said, returning her attention to drawing in her notebook. "But it will be."

"I'm sure it will," he said. "How are you and your mom liking Hollywood?"

"It's a little bit lonely. Mommy drinks more wine here. And the food isn't very good. Not like Cooker makes."

"Okay, honey," Kassi said, feeling a neck flush threatening to rise again. "Why don't you let me answer the questions for a little while?"

Samantha's nanny wasn't on shift for another hour. Kassi had no choice but to bring her daughter to this interview. She hoped the crayons would distract her enough.

"Sorry," Kassi said.

"No problem at all." Mark smiled and glided seamlessly, graciously, to the next topic. He must be a dad, Kassi thought. She warmed to him.

"Insiders report there's a killer love story at the heart of the screenplay, very hot, maybe even skirting an NC-17 rating, along with several supporting characters, restaurant workers and customers, who fall in and out of love, and in and out of bed. Are restaurants really like that?"

The sex question. There it was. Kassi looked at Samantha, who was now, thankfully, totally ignoring them, immersed in her coloring. She wanted to get through this part of the interview quickly, while her daughter's attention was focused elsewhere.

She needed to handle this question perfectly. Sex was a pivotal element of the movie's plot and of restaurants more generally. For better or worse, sex in restaurants was something Kassi knew plenty about. Still, she stayed in her Louise-Cher persona. It was easier to talk about sex if you pretended to be another person.

"Mark, restaurants are like that, honestly. Not just sex though, it's love and romance too. It's partly tied up with the long hours, the nutty pace, the drinking after shifts to bring down the adrenaline, not to mention the high turnover, which means there's almost always someone new being added to the already-steamy mix." She uncrossed her legs and leaned in.

"On top of that, there's the sensual, intimate nature of cooking and serving food, of nurturing people. Even if you're not into the gourmet side of things, these are very personal acts. The icing on the cake, so to speak, is the way waitresses, and waiters too, need to sell themselves. You know, flirt with customers to increase their tips. Put all that together, repeat it day after day, and it's a romantic pressure cooker. Wait, that was a terrible pun. Don't write that."

"A romantic pressure cooker. I love it," he said, laughing. "You're making my job easier. Does the plot of the movie match your, shall we say, romantic experiences at the Rose and Thorn?"

She paused. Too long. It was noticeable and awkward. The flush crept back up her neck.

"No," she said at last. "It's just a movie."

"That's not what the rumor mill is furiously churning. Are you denying that the central romance and the hot sex are autobiographical?" He whispered the words *hot sex* so Samantha wouldn't hear.

"I made it all up, totally fictional," she said, this time too quickly.

Thinking back, Kassi now wondered if she had made it all up, if by writing about their love, by capturing it in a screenplay, she had somehow changed their reality, changed their outcome.

"I don't want to spoil the movie for my readers, but are you saying that the incredible ending, the one that has everyone talking, the big surprise, isn't your story?"

She smiled but shook her head, wishing it were otherwise. "That's why we love the movies, right?"

2

INT. ROSE AND THORN RESTAURANT — DAY

(Nine months earlier, May 1995). KASSI,
twenty-eight years old, enters the
eclectic restaurant. The dining room is
crowded but not with customers. She's
got competition.

"You here for the waitress job?" a dark-haired woman
asked. She was in her mid-thirties wearing a light-yellow
summer dress with white polka dots that perfectly set off
her dark complexion.

Kassi nodded. "Yes."

"Come in and quit blocking the door. We might have
actual customers trying to get in behind you."

The woman tore a ticket off a roll like a carnival barker
and handed the ragged stub to Kassi.

"Number twenty-seven. Sit at any of the open tables in
the back. Nick the manager will call your number if he
wants to talk to you." She looked Kassi up and down. "He
probably will. You've got experience, right?"

"Tons."

"Fill out this application." She handed Kassi a double-
sided form.

Kassi did a quick scan of the dining room. Up front

where she came in, there was a bulletin board thick with flyers for local rock bands, psychic readings, domestic abuse hotlines and birthday clowns. On the far side was an elaborate playroom for children, currently empty. In the middle of the dining room was a salad bar, bigger and more complicated than any Kassi had ever seen. The furniture was unremarkable—standard composite dining tables, a few booths, a glass refrigerated case with desserts, floor-to-ceiling windows that were mostly clean. All told, the place had a friendly charm. Welcoming.

A woman bumped into Kassi from behind. She giggled an apology as she pulled off her headphones and turned the volume down on a Walkman that was hooked to the strap of her ripped blue jean overalls.

A second woman came in behind her. She had long hair pulled into a high ponytail and was wearing a skinny black leather tie, a crisp blue blouse and a black leather skirt. She looked like an indifferent punk rocker.

"Here," the dark-haired woman said, ripping off two more tickets, after giving them both the once-over as well. "Numbers twenty-eight and twenty-nine. Fill out this application and please get the hell out of the reception area. Customers get priority."

Kassi and the two women moved to the rear of the dining room. Applicants one through twenty-six were already crowded around a half-dozen tables, each clutching a job application and ticket stub as if they were badges of honor.

"Hard to believe how many people need this job. President Clinton should fire Greenspan," number twenty-nine said as the three women sat together at a four-top.

"I don't know who that is but firing people is not nice," number twenty-eight said. "I've been fired and it's awful. Still, I sure hope there's more than only one open position because this is a ton of people."

Kassi felt a stab of fear. Her limited funds were running out. She needed a job badly.

Number twenty-nine started filling out her application. The woman with the headphones, number twenty-eight, smiled again at Kassi. She had red hair, a kind face and artfully applied blue eye shadow with matching dark-blue mascara. Kassi took the smile as an opening.

"Is the job situation in Portland so bad?" Kassi asked, fishing around in her bag for a pen.

"It's not great but this crowd size is probably more on account of the fact that the Rose and Thorn has an amazing reputation," the still-smiling number twenty-eight said. "A really good place to work."

"How so?" Kassi asked, emptying her purse onto the table. Keys, a notebook, Vaseline, a stuffed octopus, a package of baby wipes, fish crackers in a plastic baggie, two expired bus tickets and a handful of dirty popcorn.

No pen.

"I'm Kassi, by the way," she said, sweeping it all back into her bag.

"Who comes to a waitress interview without a pen?" number twenty-eight said, giggling and handing a pen to Kassi. "Sorry, green is all I got. I'm Rosalyn. Most people call me Roz."

Kassi thanked her, took the pen and started filling out her form. Name, birthdate, places she'd waitressed before. How was it possible she'd already worked at six restaurants and she wasn't even out of her twenties?

At first, it was to make money for teenage things, then four more restaurants over the four years it took to put herself through college to earn her impractical degree in film history. Those were the years she figured out how to make good money waiting tables, how to move fast and work the customers. Still, while she was good at it, she gladly gave it up after the wedding, happy her serving days were forever behind her. She was wrong. Kassi was back at it right after her marriage collapsed.

Even though she didn't much like hauling food and making nice to customers, she knew waitressing had saved her, keeping her and her daughter from being homeless, or worse. So far, it was the only thing she was any good at, and she was grateful to have the skills now when she badly needed them.

Still, the chance of getting this job today didn't seem high. The six restaurants where she worked were all back east, so tough to verify her past employment, and she had circled *days-only* in the availability section of the application. She couldn't afford a night babysitter and Kassi wasn't going to leave Samantha with Barry any more than necessary. But mostly, she wanted to be around to tuck her little girl into bed.

A waitress who doesn't work nights is a waitress who doesn't work, she thought. She looked around at the sea of hopeful faces and considered leaving. Maybe it made more sense to try the temp agency, get a secretarial job. Wouldn't pay nearly as well as working for tips but it would be steady, and not nights.

"You're not from around here, I take it," Roz said.

"That's so obvious?"

"You talk kind of fast."

"Is talking fast bad?"

"Not bad, just different. East Coast different. People 'round here talk more slowly," Roz said, emphasizing her slow lilt for effect. "What brought you to Portland?"

"I needed a change," Kassi said, avoiding the real reason. She moved to Portland because her estranged husband got a job here and Kassi felt she owed it to her daughter to take one last shot at reconciliation, however unlikely it was. Two weeks after she uprooted them both and moved across the country, it all went to hell.

Her mother had warned her.

"What makes the reputation of the Rose and Thorn so great?" Kassi asked.

"You know anything about Portland?"

"Only that it has a lot of roses so that's why they call it the City of Roses, and it rains all the time."

"Yeah, that's true," Roz said. She giggled again, not nervously, but as if laughter was the natural way to finish her sentences. "This place is super well-known in Portland, at least in certain circles. It's a safe place for gays and lesbians, and battered women, other victims of mostly male violence. Anyone can hang out here if they need a ride or help or whatever. No one will hassle them and no one gets kicked out until they have a plan or a place to go. And it's real pro-woman. Like, the owner is a single mom and she tries to hire single moms whenever she can."

Kassi brightened at that piece of information and wrote in caps at the top of the application that she was the single mom of a preschooler.

"Also, the food here is good for you, more or less," Roz said. "Organic and healthy, with stuff for macrobiotics and vegetarians, all those weirdos with their weird diets. From a tip standpoint, in my experience, healthy weirdos are happy people, at least more so than most, and happy people tip better."

"Don't forget the legendary Hungarian mushroom soup," said number twenty-nine, as she finished her application and joined the conversation. "I'm Meredith." She stood and held her hand out to collect their job applications. "I'll run them over. Make a personal pitch. College isn't cheap. I need to work every angle."

Kassi and Roz gave her their forms but watched Meredith to make sure she didn't somehow "lose" theirs on the way over. All's fair in love and job searches, Kassi thought. Meredith took the high road though, delivering all three applications to Nick, the manager—a frumpy looking ruddy-faced middle-aged man in a brown sweater vest—with a flash of her killer smile and a wink.

As Meredith returned to their table, a woman—forty-something, stout with short gray hair, wearing baggy tan corduroy pants and a red and black plaid flannel shirt—burst through the swinging kitchen doors and stood for a moment, hands on hips, looking at everyone.

Glaring, more accurately.

"That's Molly, the owner," Roz said.

The manager jumped up from his seat and walked to her side, clutching the stack of job applications. Kassi watched them confer and look over the applications. The dark-haired woman who had been handing out numbers and forms earlier joined them. The trio huddled and whispered, occasionally looking up at the applicants.

"I don't care!" Molly shouted, quieting the entire room. "Just make it work."

She marched over to the salad bar where a bearded man wearing a white apron was spooning out fresh tomato wedges into the refrigerated serving container. Molly stuck her face above the sneeze barrier and peered in at the offerings, then turned and grabbed his shoulder.

"Dave, the cucumbers are so old they're transparent. Transparent!" she yelled. "Fix the damn cukes!"

Dave stood motionless for a few beats watching Molly leave. He turned and looked at the cucumbers, then back at the crowd of job applicants now staring at him. He smiled, his white teeth gleaming through the curls of his beard. "As you wish, my liege," he said loud enough for all to hear, bowing and tipping his hand toward the office. "Thine cucumbers shall not disappoint."

He drew some nervous laughter before he disappeared through the swinging doors into the kitchen. Kassi wondered how he kept beard hairs from falling into the vegetables.

"Okay, listen up," the man holding the applications said to the crowd. "My name is Nick, and I'm the general manager. Hold your number in front of you so I can match applications with applicants." He walked around the room, sizing up every applicant, smiling, nodding, making a quick comment here and there. Kassi felt like she was in a server zoo.

When he got to their table, Kassi looked him straight in the eye with what she hoped was a "hire me, I'm great" expression as he gave her the once-over. She tried to imagine what he was seeing. A woman, mid-twenties. Thick, shoulder-length curly blond hair, unruly and frizzy. Pale blue eyes. A slightly crooked nose from an adolescent kickball accident. A goofy smile whenever it happened to surface, which was rare these days.

Nick stared a little too long. Was she his type or something? That would probably be an okay thing under the circumstances, if a little icky.

His gaze fell to Roz, and then Meredith.

His gaze lingered on them a little too long as well.

Meredith had long, straight brown hair and Roz was a redhead. Okay, maybe he didn't have a type.

Now he was nodding. Why was he nodding?

She followed his eyes to her chest and then he glanced sideways at the other two.

Boobs, that's what he was going for. All three were about the same boob size. On the big side for their smaller body frames.

Gross.

She was used to it, all women were to one degree or another, but it never felt anything less than terrible.

"Numbers twenty-seven, twenty-eight and twenty-nine, stick around while I clear out the place," Nick said quietly to them. He turned to face the crowd. "You can all go now. Sorry you didn't make the cut this time. We'll keep your applications on file for a month in case anything changes."

He turned back and smiled again at Kassi, Meredith and Roz, as the less lucky, or less booby, applicants filed out, a few glaring at the trio.

Kassi felt a surge of relief, even as she was disgusted by the fact that her breasts seemed to matter more than her experience, but she needed this job. She wondered if the reputation for being a cool, woman-friendly place was all bullshit.

"You're the one with the kid, right?" Nick asked her. "Lucky for you, Molly has a soft spot for single moms."

So, big boobs *and* a broken marriage got her the job. Nothing is ever black and white in the restaurant business.

"Come on, grab your stuff and let's go. I'll show you the kitchen, introduce you to the crew and get you the paperwork you'll need to fill out," Nick said.

They stood and the dark-haired woman who met her at the door earlier caught Kassi by the arm. "You better be worth it," she said with a whisper that managed to be terrifying. "Nobody else gets nights off."

Kassi nodded. "I appreciate it."

"Don't try to take advantage. I'll be watching you."

Kassi shook her head. "I won't. I promise."

"Ione, my office," Molly called from the hallway.

"Wow, you're getting nights off. How did you swing that?" Meredith asked.

"By having an amazing little daughter," Kassi said,

throwing her bag over her shoulder. Along with a shitty soon-to-be ex-husband, but she kept that to herself.

"Your new friend there is Ione, the floor manager," Roz said. "She's gorgeous, scary and polyamorous."

"Poly what-orous?"

"Polyamorous. She has multiple simultaneous ongoing relationships, some of them in groups. She's really open about it."

Nick was holding the doors into the kitchen open, waving for them to hurry up.

"Nick will undoubtedly ask each of us out in the coming weeks," Roz said, ending on her now-familiar giggle. "He's kinda a horn-dog."

"How do you know so much about this place?" Kassi asked.

"My ex used to work here," Roz said.

"Your ex sure knows a lot about the sex lives of these people," Kassi said.

"That's why he's my ex. Care to guess how many of them he slept with?"

They all followed Nick into the kitchen. He introduced them to Dave, the bearded salad chef, who bowed again. "Our salad bar is the best in the city," Nick said. "Two people staff it and both are named Dave. This is Dave-one, our lead."

On the other side of the kitchen, two men stood with their backs to the grill. One was standing behind a post and it was hard to make out his appearance or see what he was doing.

The other man was chopping mushrooms, his knife a gleaming blur rattling out a staccato rhythm as the mushrooms fell apart in thin slices under his attention. He had shoulder-length brown hair pulled into a ponytail and was lost in the focus required of the moment. He was wearing running tights that emphasized his muscular legs and a chef's jacket with the sleeves rolled up, showing his chiseled forearms.

"Wow, look at that ass. Is he as hot from the front as he is from the back?" Meredith whispered to Roz.

"Yeah, he is. That's Clay, the chef. Another great reason to work here," Roz said.

"What did your ex say about him?" Kassi asked.

"Surprisingly, nothing. Clay is a man of mystery when it comes to workplace romance."

"Clay and Gilroy, meet the new hires. Kassi, Meredith and Roz," Nick said, nodding at each in turn.

Gilroy spun around and the three women waved. And then Clay looked up and turned, and Kassi felt her breath catch in her throat. He was the most beautiful man she had ever seen.

3

INT. ROSE AND THORN RESTAURANT KITCHEN –
SAME DAY

A commercial kitchen. Gleaming. Busy.
Lots of chopping, laughing and risqué
banter between CLAY, GILROY and OTHERS.
The scene begins *a few minutes before*
KASSI, MEREDITH and ROZ enter.

"Did I tell you about the weed?" Clay asked, glancing over at Gilroy, a line cook.

Gilroy was a little on the heavy side but carried it well although he carried a pencil-thin mustache less well. Gilroy spent his non-work time reading philosophy and writing poetry. Bad poetry.

"Weed? I didn't think you were into that."

"I'm not. Makes me paranoid. When I was coming in yesterday, Russell was right in front of me," Clay said.

"Was he already stoned?" Gilroy asked.

"Probably. Anyway, a baggie full of weed fell out of his pocket when he opened the door. He didn't see it, so I grabbed it and gave it to Dave-one. He sold it back to Russell and split it with me."

"That's hilarious. How much did you get?"

"Fifty bucks. Added it to my food truck fund."

"Fifty bucks? We're in the wrong business."

Gilroy was chopping garlic for the line, enough to fill two ceramic ramekins. He'd barely finished chopping two bulbs in the time it took Clay to slice up a half-flat of mushrooms.

"I don't know why you don't run the mushrooms through the mixer," Gilroy said, gesturing at the floor mixer squatting next to the steam kettle. "So much faster."

"Because it doesn't cut them so much as mangle them. Plus, they're cut too thin that way, totally disappear in the pasta." He grabbed a clean rag to wipe the blade of his chef's knife. "Besides, I'm fast and I like showing off."

"Have you seen the new waitresses?" Gilroy asked.

"Nope, not yet," Clay said.

"Another great batch."

"Nick is anything if not predictable. If Molly ever figures out his hiring criteria, she'll fire him on the spot, plus maybe give him a swift kick in the balls. Goes against everything she stands for."

"Yeah, well, how do we know those aren't Molly's preferences, too?" Dave-one asked as he used the edge of his knife to sweep a stack of newly sliced cucumbers into a salad bar container. "Could be Nick is just following orders."

"She's in a relationship and her partner doesn't look like that," Gilroy said.

"Doesn't mean you can't enjoy the view," Dave-one said.

"Okay, new topic," Clay said. "One that won't get us all fired."

Along with his genuine love of cooking, Clay found the banter one of the best parts about working in a restaurant. The confined space of the kitchen, the relentless pace, the teamwork needed to get good food out fast, the whiplash stress of rushes mixed in with long boring stretches of prep time or cleaning all added up to an unusual camaraderie, a mostly fun work benefit that made the time pass quickly.

Even so, it was up to the chef to keep the banter on the mostly non-offensive side, which meant figuring out where that line was. One person's joke was another person's bruise.

"Me, I'm with the French on this topic," Dave-one continued, heading for the door into the dining room with his fresh cucumbers. "The perfect boob size fits into a champagne glass."

"Like I said, new topic," Clay said.

"It's not offensive, it's just an international fact," Dave-one said as the door swung shut behind him.

"I recognized one of them," Gilroy said. "Roz. She was the girlfriend of, what was his name, the one who OD'd in the bathroom a couple months back."

"Frank. I remember. That was a bad day," Clay said.

"Pretty sure it's her. Red hair. She was always a little too friendly with you. Used to drive Frank crazy."

"I think the drugs drove Frank crazy, not Roz," Clay said, reaching for another flat of mushrooms.

"Well, hey now, speak of the devil," Gilroy said, turning around as the kitchen door swung open.

"Clay and Gilroy, meet the new hires," Nick said, entering the kitchen with three women.

Clay cleaned his knife again and placed it on the cutting board, then wiped his hands. He turned and started to say something but lost himself at the sight of tangles of blonde hair, bright blue eyes, perfect lips, a slightly crooked nose and an easy smile. His stomach did a somersault and his knees wavered.

"Kassi, Meredith and Roz," Nick said, nodding at each, "meet Clay, our chef, and Gilroy, a lead line cook."

"It's a pleasure," Clay said, taking Kassi's hand and feeling an electric tingle of warmth in his palm. "Welcome to the Rose and Thorn."

He held her hand for too long, saw her eyes go a little wide, and then dropped it as if scalded and quickly shook Meredith's hand, and then Roz's. Gilroy, his own hands sticky with garlic, held them up and smiled apologetically.

"I believe we already know Roz," Gilroy said.

"Yeah, you do," she said. "Nice to see you both again. I'm stoked to start here."

"Been a while. How's Frank?" Clay asked.

"Better. Cleaned up. Moved back home with his parents, working in a hardware store or something. Said restaurants were too stressful. And he's leading twelve-step groups on the weekends, so staying clean."

"Good for him," Clay said.

"Yeah, I'm glad for him, also glad to be single again," she said, casually dropping the hint for Clay.

Clay picked up his knife from the cutting board. "Well, I need to get back to it. Reservations are piling up, so looks like we'll have a full house. Gonna be a long night. We generally do server tastings on the specials just before shift-start. If you have any questions about the menu, let me know."

"Only Meredith and Roz will be working nights," Nick said. "Kassi is exclusively on day shifts."

"Oh yeah?" Even Clay knew that was unusual.

"She's got a kid," Nick said.

Clay watched as Kassi shot a quick, defiant look at Nick, then returned her eyes to Clay. He dropped his gaze to her left hand. No ring. Didn't mean for sure she wasn't married, and probably she was with a kid and all.

"See you in the afternoons then," he said.

"Looking forward to it," Kassi said with a half-smile.

The three women and Nick returned to the dining room and Clay and Gilroy returned to their prep station.

"Damn, Kassi is gorgeous," Gilroy said.

"Yeah, too bad you have a girlfriend. You remember Angel, right? The one you're joining the Peace Corps with?"

"*Thinking* about joining the Peace Corps," Gilroy said, "and not for me, bonehead. For you. I thought you were having a stroke there for a second. It's time for you to get back out there. Past time. We're all starting to think Crystal maybe broke you for good."

"Don't you have some shrimp to de-vein?"

Gilroy nodded as he scraped the garlic into the ramekins and then called out, "Jon, board swap." The dishwasher poked his head around the corner. "I need a seafood board."

Jon nodded. He was gangly and thin with oversized glasses and jittery energy. He brought out a blue cutting board and swapped it for the green one.

"Thanks," Gilroy said. "Did you play today?"

"Yes," Jon said. "Four games. One draw, two wins, one loss." His way of talking made the words all seem too close together, like tiles with no grout.

"Not bad."

"I can teach you."

Gilroy shook his head. "Chess is not my thing."

"Anyone can learn. You'd be almost average in six years."

"Gilroy won't be alive in six years," Clay said. "If the smoking doesn't kill him, Angel will for not quitting."

"How about you, Clay?" Jon asked. "You seem kind of smart."

"That means a lot coming from an alien robot who crash-landed here from planet Geek."

Jon smiled and went back to the dishpit. Gilroy started de-veining the shrimp, flipping the gritty, stringy guts into the trash.

"Who's on the line tonight?"

"Russell. Rob called in sick."

Gilroy shook his head. "Russell is fast, but he's got a mean streak. Especially when he's stoned."

"The vodka-minis in the reach-in should help with that," Clay said.

"We're seating our first table," Kristoph called through the door. He was tall, bottle-blonde and wearing pink tights under cut-off jeans and an orange leotard top. With almost four years at the Rose and Thorn, Kristoph was the senior waiter. He already had Roz in training mode, shadowing him.

Clay looked up at the clock. "We're not open for dinner yet. We've got fifteen more minutes."

"Friends of Molly," Kristoph said. "Sorry. It's a big table and they're asking a lot of questions about the menu. Going to be a rough one."

The kitchen crew heard grumbling as Russell clocked in. "Hello boys," he said, stuffing a handful of little vodka bottles under the line in the refrigerated reach-in. "Ready to rock and roll?"

Russell would be working the grill, spending the night churning out grilled cheese sandwiches, quesadillas, tofu burgers, pastramis and more. It was mindless but kinetic, requiring perfect timing to prevent scorched food. Luckily, it was a task that could be accomplished while functionally inebriated.

Gilroy would be working the oven, finishing all the baked items like the rosemary chicken, enchiladas and flatbreads, and he was also plating. Clay was on the sauté station. He was always on the sauté station, the prerogative of being the chef. His focus was the popular Greek pastas, sautéed shrimp and the specials, like tonight's pork medallions with marsala sauce, plus the endless orders of pasta Alfredo off the kid's menu.

The first ticket rattled through the kitchen printer. Kristoph came into the kitchen and showed Roz how to tear it from the printer, call out the order and then reach through the window to hang it.

Ten adults and two children. One quesadilla with no salsa. Three Alfredos, two pork specials, hold the garlic on one, a Greek pasta, hold the Kalamata olives, three grilled pastramis, two with sautéed onions and one without mustard, and a couple of grilled cheese sandwiches with chips.

Dave-one rolled his salad cart into the kitchen, heading for the prep counter. He was mumbling to himself. "Gonna be out of lettuce in an hour, and they're already hitting the soup." He ladled out a big saucepan full of Hungarian mushroom soup to restock the soup bar and started it warming on the countertop burner.

"I will never understand the attraction," Russell said. "You can literally feel that shit hardening in your arteries. That soup is just savory flavored cream."

"Like you're a paragon of healthful eating," Clay said, flaring a splash of marsala to make the sauce for the pork.

"I eat plenty healthy," Russell said, flipping the pastrami. "I just have a chronic vitamin V deficiency." He reached down for a vodka-mini, cracked it open and guzzled it. "That helps."

"Molly ever sees you with that, she'll fire you on the spot," Clay said.

"I'm an aging gay man with an alcohol problem. She loves saving people like me."

"You're a cynical asshole is what you are," Gilroy said,

garnishing a plate for the first pork, and spooning in mashed potatoes and broccoli from the steam table. "I say that lovingly."

"A cynical asshole with a resilient liver," Russell said, plopping the pastrami on the prep counter. "Clay, hand me your knife."

"Not a chance."

Russell reached for one of the dull kitchen knives and chopped the sandwich in half with a practiced motion.

Gilroy moved it to a plate, spreading it open so the cheese sagged in strings across the divide, then added chips and an orange slice twisted just so to create a slot for a sprig of parsley.

"Order up," Clay called and rang the bell once for Kristoph.

The specials ran out at eight o'clock. Gilroy wrote the number "86" over the list on the kitchen blackboard and yelled out to Kristoph to spread the word to the wait staff.

By nine o'clock, they ran out of energy and patience.

Then, of course, a late table came in at nine fifty-five, five minutes before closing. A four-top.

The kitchen was mostly broken down and cleaned up by then. Clay sent everyone home except Jon, and he finished the last order on his own. He sent Jon home at ten forty-five.

By then, other than the four customers, all oblivious to the fact they were keeping the staff from going home, the only people left behind were Clay, Kristoph and Roz. They sat at the bar waiting for the late diners to finish.

"What'd you think of your first night here?" Clay asked Roz.

"It was busier than expected, but I think it'll be fun."

"That's bullshit, honey," Kristoph said. "It's not fun, but with that hair, your skin and your rack, you'll clean up."

He pulled a wad of bills out of his apron and handed her two twenties. "Thanks for helping me out. You earned it." He dropped five dollars in a jar labeled Community Fund.

"Who gets it this week?" Clay asked, nodding his head toward the jar.

"Jamie, the weekend waiter. He's raising money to go to D.C. for a protest next month to demand more AIDS research money."

Clay dug a five-dollar bill out of his wallet and dropped it into the jar. The late table stood to leave. Finally.

After helping Kristoph bus the dishes, Roz held up her twenties. "Want to go have drinks? My treat."

"My cat would never forgive me," Kristoph said, pulling on his jacket.

"I'll take a rain check," Clay said. "I've got to get up early. I'm working tomorrow's Mother's Day brunch."

"I'm going to hold you to that rain check," Roz said.

"Make sure she gets to her car okay," Clay said, holding the restaurant door open.

"Sweet of you to worry about me," Kristoph said, blowing a kiss.

Clay locked the door behind them and went back into the kitchen. On his way out, he stopped by the shift board. Kassi was also on the schedule for the Mother's Day brunch.

4

INT. THE ECONOMY MOTEL ROOM - NIGHT

KASSI talks on the phone. A half-empty
bottle of Ernest & Julio Gallo red wine
is next to her. Rain strikes the window,
lit up by flashes of neon from a seedy
bar across the street.

"I got a job today!"

Kassi was on the phone with her mom while watching
Samantha play with two plastic horses on the floor. She
wondered when the carpet was last cleaned and worried
the brown stain behind the couch, which she had tried in
vain to remove, was old blood.

"That's wonderful honey," Gina said. "Is it something
good?"

"Yes. I mean, it's waitressing but it's a cool place. The
people seem nice."

"I guess that can tide you over for a little while," her
mom said. "As it always has."

Kassi felt her disappointment from three thousand
miles away. There was an awkward silence.

"Right. It will give me some time to find the perfect
job," Kassi said at last. "Finally put my film degree to use."

"Shouldn't you be in Hollywood then, or New York?

Or here with me, where so many people love and support you?"

"Samantha loves me, she's right here." Kassi heard the defensiveness in her voice and wished she could pull the words back.

"Of course, she's your daughter. I'm just worried, that's all. Are you working on your screenplay at least?"

"No, I haven't had time. And truthfully, I've decided it's kind of a childish concept. Very, I don't know, film school pretentious. I need to come up with something accessible, sexier, more entertaining."

"I thought it was your best start yet," her mom said. There was a pause before she asked her next question. "How are things with Barry?"

Kassi sighed. "Terrible. It's not going to work out. It was never going to work out. I don't know what the hell I was thinking."

"You were thinking of Sam, that's what you were thinking," Gina said.

"We had a bad interaction last week. Really bad. It's over this time."

Her mother was silent for a few seconds. Kassi figured her silence was probably because she had heard her daughter say those four words too many times before. *It's over this time.*

Finally, her mom asked, "Are you okay?"

"Yes." Kassi wasn't sure that was exactly true, but her mom probably knew she wasn't telling the complete truth, so it wasn't a complete lie. More like a transitional lie, a delay to give Kassi more time to accept reality.

"And Samantha?"

Sam was still playing happily, rearing the two horses, and trotting them around the dusty carpet while making little neighing sounds.

"She's fine. She didn't see any of it."

"Are you moving ahead with the divorce now?"

The situation filled Kassi with a burning combination of shame and guilt, as if she failed some kind of test the world had imposed on her but she wasn't sure what test exactly. Like being a mother and a woman meant it had to be her fault that she couldn't save her marriage. Still, failure or not, it was time to move on. She wouldn't let herself be treated that way anymore, not now or ever again.

"Yes, I am."

"Kassi, please come home."

"I can't. Not yet. Even though Barry and I are through, we're here now and I need to let Sam see her father. It's the right thing to do."

"He can come to Pennsylvania to see her. You're too nice about everything. And to my mind, he doesn't deserve even that. He moved across the country and just expected, demanded, that you follow along, then pretended he had changed when you and Sam visited to check things out three months ago. He tricked you into moving because you're a decent person and—"

"Mom, please stop. No lectures. Not tonight."

Gina softened her voice. "Okay, I hear you. But honey, what if he treats Sam the same way? I don't think abusive husbands make good fathers, not when their daughters grow up and start to rebel a little."

"I understand what you're saying, believe me, I do. But he is her father," Kassi said. "I have to honor that. He's been good with her so far. It's just me he despises."

"I'm so sorry, honey."

"Mom, it's okay. I've made up my mind. I want to try and make it work in Portland for me and for Sam. A fresh start."

"I'm coming out there then."

"Not yet. Let me get my own place first and get settled."

There was another long silence.

"I'll call you every night," Kassi said. "I promise."

"Maybe not quite this late," Gina said. "Don't forget the three-hour time difference."

"Fair enough. I need to go feed Sam now. Love you."

"Love you too."

Kassi cradled the phone back into the receiver. "Ready for a little something to eat, tater-tot?"

Samantha smiled and nodded. She looked like a miniature version of Kassi, with blue eyes and wild, curly blonde hair. She was a joyful child who loved to sing to herself, talked to her toys kindly, and often laughed out loud for no apparent reason. Her happiness was the most important thing in the world to Kassi, and she was grateful Sam seemed to come by it easily and naturally.

Kassi microwaved leftover mac and cheese, put four baked potato wedges onto a paper plate with a splash of ketchup and watched as Samantha dug in happily. Not the healthiest dinner but options were limited given the tiny kitchenette—a mini-fridge, a toaster oven and a sputtering microwave. Even under the best of circumstances, Kassi was not the greatest cook, and the Economy Motel was far from the best of circumstances. She poured some red wine into a coffee cup and drank a third of it in one gulp.

After Samantha finished eating, Kassi cleaned up and they played cards, Go Fish, until Sam's eyelids started to droop. Kassi helped her into her pajamas and watched as she brushed her teeth, then tucked her into the double bed they shared. She laid down next to her and started reading *Blueberries for Sal* out loud. She was about halfway through when Sam fell asleep.

Kassi slipped out of bed, careful not to wake Sam, and slumped down into the battered chair next to the window.

She sat in the darkness, the sputtering neon lights from the bar across the street the only illumination in the room.

The phone rang and she picked it up quickly to preserve the silence. "No, she's sound asleep," Kassi whispered. "No, I'm not waking her up. You'll see her in the morning when you pick her up, and please don't be late. I start a new job tomorrow." She held the phone away from her ear as Barry bellowed an angry retort. "Stop it please, Barry, this is so pointless," she said, before hanging up and unplugging the phone from the wall.

She refilled her wine and turned the TV on low, flipping through the channels until she found an old black-and-white movie. She remembered it from film school. *In a Lonely Place*. A Bogart movie. A screenwriter framed for murder.

"This seems appropriate," she said, settling back into the chair.

"You get to a lonely place in the road ..." Bogart's character said.

"And you begin to squeeze," Kassi whispered.

5

INT. CLAY'S HOUSE - NIGHT

The walls are bare, the room is spare, the fridge is mostly empty. CLAY enters, agitated from the busy night at the restaurant, and from meeting KASSI.

Clay tossed his keys on the kitchen table, opened the fridge and reached for a beer.

He was hungry but there was nothing to eat, and he never cooked for himself unless he was testing a recipe. He opened a tub of hummus, sniffed it and rummaged in the cabinet for some stale crackers.

Even after all this time, it still felt weird to come home to an empty house.

As he snacked standing up, he flipped through the notebook on the counter until he found the list of potential names for his food truck and added an idea that came to him earlier—Burritows—then immediately crossed it out with a laugh. He plopped down on the small couch and turned on the TV. An old movie was playing. *In a Lonely Place*.

"Can't beat Bogart." He put his feet up on the scarred coffee table. The film was almost over, and he timed his beer to last until the credits.

He moved to the bedroom and sat down on the edge of the bed. It was the only new thing in the house. After what happened, the thought of sleeping in anything but a pristine bed was too much. He dropped a chunk of money, way too much, for a good mattress. One of those fancy fluffy things. Probably a rip-off, but he was in a hurry with no time or motivation to comparison shop.

But tonight, the thought of trying to sleep, even in his soft, overpriced bed, knowing he had to get up early, made him anxious. Instead, he pulled out a pair of shorts and a crumpled T-shirt from beneath the bed and grabbed his gym bag.

Outside, he walked the six blocks to the health club. The streets were deserted and the streetlights were glaring down on the empty sidewalks, making it feel like he was walking through the Bogart movie.

He showed his card to the indifferent staff person and looked around the cavernous equipment-filled warehouse. Music was pulsing, louder than he liked. The club was open twenty-four hours, and tonight it was more crowded than he'd anticipated given how late it was, nearly midnight. A lot of people must be having trouble sleeping.

A woman was jumping rope by the squat rack. Cyndi? Snyder? Lucinda? He couldn't quite place her name. She was fit and toned, her shoulders and abs and legs ripped—and rippling—as she worked out. She was in a two-piece stretchy purple number that drew a lot of attention. She stopped when he walked by, sweat glistening on her smooth skin.

"Hey, Clay, nice to see you. You're in late. Again."

"I need to burn off a little energy."

"Let me know if you need help, someone to spot you. Or anything really," she said with a grin. "It's Cyndi, by the way, in case you forgot."

"I didn't forget. And thanks, I may need a spot later. I'll track you down."

"No need. I'll be watching. Just give me a sign."

He headed toward an open bench press. A familiar figure was on the leg curl machine nearby.

"Couldn't sleep either?" Kristoph asked.

Clay stretched out on the bench, doing ten quick reps with just the bar to warm up, then stood and slipped a forty-five-pound plate on each side, clipping the collars in place. "Nah. How long you been here?"

"At the gym? About an hour," Kristoph said. "At this torture machine, about the same amount of time." He tilted his head toward the row of stair-step machines in the cardio area. "I like the view from here."

Clay looked across the room. A man, early twenties probably, headphones on, was working hard. "The one in the muscle shirt?"

"Correct."

"He's cute. Maybe I should move to a different bench. I don't want him to think, you know, you and I are ..."

"Oh honey, you scream straight. You're dreamy, and I wish I could turn you, but you'll always just be a fantasy. Him, on the other hand, I feel a real connection."

Clay laughed and stretched out again, doing ten more reps. He added two more forty-fives to the bar.

Kristoph smoothed his long, blonde hair behind his ears and did two reps on the leg extension.

"Are you ... do you have that on the lowest setting?" Clay asked.

"Don't judge. I hate working out. I'm just here for the mingling."

Clay added a twenty-five-pound plate to either side of the bench press.

"Spot me?"

"I can stand there and look fabulous," Kristoph said, "but there's no way I can help with that. What even is it, like a thousand pounds?"

"A little over a quarter of that. You can call for help if you need to."

Kristoph let the weights on the leg machine clatter down loudly enough so that the hunky man on the stair machine looked up and smiled in his direction. "We have lift-off," Kristoph whispered. Then more loudly, "I'm happy to spot you for the six-hundred-pound bench thing you're doing."

Clay shook his head and pushed off a set of eight reps.

"Push it," Kristoph shouted. "Push it good!"

When he settled the bar back in the rack, Clay sat up. "Okay, enough of that. Go talk to your new friend."

Kristoph wiped down the leg machine. "I'm not your only fan here tonight. That girl with the bouncy boobs hasn't stopped looking at you since you got here. You should ask her out."

Clay shook his head. "You know I'm done with dating."

"Okay, so skip the dating part. Let's focus on the getting you laid part. It's been too long. Like two years? It's not natural. Your thing will atrophy."

Clay grinned but otherwise ignored Kristoph.

"What about the new waitress? Roz. I saw how she looked at you."

"She's sweet, but not my type."

"What type is that? Pretty and available? How about Kassi? I saw the way you looked at her."

"That's not ... I didn't look at her. Anyway, she's married. With a kid."

"You got the kid part right, but no hubby. She's on her own."

"You sure?"

"I hear she's separated."

"Technically, that's still married, and usually means working on getting back together."

"You have a terrible poker face," Kristoph said. "I saw that little sparkle in your eye just now."

"You are imagining things. But how do you know she's sort of single?"

"Am I imagining how curious you are right now? That's why Molly hired her."

Of course, Clay thought. That's what Molly does. She rescues people. "Enough with the chatter. I need to tire myself out enough to make peace with having to work brunch tomorrow."

"You too? Mother's Day is the worst. Why do people go out to eat with their mothers? Doesn't anyone see the value of a home-cooked meal? Seriously, it's going to be a long day." Kristoph sighed and then smiled at the man on the stair machine. "But first, hopefully, a long night."

Clay did three quick pec fly sets, watching Kristoph and his new friend leave together, then moved to the heavy bag. He wrapped and taped his hands, slipped on the gloves and began raining blows on the scuffed surface of the bag.

The bag jumped and wobbled and swung wildly under his punches. When his arms were tired and his energy finally waned, he sat down cross-legged on the floor and unwrapped. The skin on his knuckles was split in a few places and blood was smeared in.

"Gosh, that looks painful," Cyndi said. She put her arms around the bag to stop its swing. "Could you teach me to punch like that? Without making my hands bleed?"

"I don't know," he said. "It's rough on your hands. But yeah, I probably could."

She pulled a slip of paper out of her gym bag. "Here's my number. Call anytime."

It was almost two in the morning by the time he got home. He needed to be back at the restaurant in less than six hours. He tossed Cyndi's number in the trash, got another beer and turned on the oldies channel. While he flipped the channels, he wondered what Kassi was doing. Sleeping most likely, like any sensible person before a madhouse Mother's Day brunch shift. Then he wondered what she looked like sleeping.

6

INT. ROSE AND THORN RESTAURANT - DAY

The dining room is packed. Customers
line up around the block. The playroom
is full of screaming kids. Mother's Day
brunch is a madhouse. Commence flirting.

"Is Mother's Day always like this?" Kassi asked. She was wearing the black pants and white shirt required of all servers, with a shiny black polyester apron with deep front pockets tied snugly around her waist. Kassi leaned into the serving window to pick up another tray full of omelets, French toast and eggs Benedict.

"From what I've heard," Roz said. She giggled, but not as brightly as usual, as she filled her tray with specialty espresso drinks. "There's a place in hell for customers who order soymilk lattes in the middle of a rush."

"Mother's Day is always, always bad," Kristoph said, wrapping silverware sets in napkins as he waited for a fresh pot of drip coffee to brew. "This one is worse than usual though."

"Why?" Kassi asked.

"Clay is here instead of the normal egg guy."

"How can it ever be bad that Clay is here?" Roz asked, arranging the hot drinks to precisely balance on the round server tray. "Hold on, there's a normal egg guy?"

"Yeah," Kristoph said, glaring at the reluctant coffee pot. "Well, he's not normal, but no one here really is." Both Roz and Kristoph paused to look at Kassi as if seeing her for the first time.

"Except maybe you," Kristoph said. Roz nodded in agreement.

"Anyway, Greg, the egg man. The Greggman. He's an egg wizard and looks it. Heavyset white guy, kind of shaped like an egg, with a pointy, scraggly beard. To be honest, Clay may be cute but eggs are not his area of expertise. He's a culinary artist, and eggs require speed and technique, not creativity."

The coffee finally replenished, Kristoph snatched the pot and led the way. Roz hoisted her tray and, followed by Kassi, they all returned to the dining room madhouse.

"Hey kiddo, watch out!" Kassi said, nearly tumbling over a child about Sam's age wandering alone. "Come on now, back to your parents." A mom wearing jeans and a flannel shirt scooped up the child, who wrapped his arms around her neck as she carried him back to the playroom.

For a second, Kassi let herself wonder what she would be doing with Sam if she wasn't working. Instead, Sam was with her father. Kassi had no illusions about him giving Sam a card or helping her make her a gift for Mother's Day. That wasn't Barry's style. But she had a job, and that was something she didn't have yesterday, so life was looking up.

"Not bad, newbie," Ione shouted as she hauled a tub of dirty dishes into the kitchen. "You're holding up pretty well for your first day."

***

In the kitchen, Clay was struggling as the backup egg guy. It wasn't the pace, it was the details. Cooking eggs was a fussy skill, precise and repetitive, while sauté pans and soup pots and big, bold flavors were Clay's preferred canvas. He cursed the Greggman for the twelfth time that morning.

Greg used to work in Las Vegas on a breakfast buffet line at one of the big casinos, churning out underpriced two-egg omelets and every conceivable style of egg—over-easy, over-medium, over-hard, up, scrambled (wet or dry) poached and basted—at an unrelenting pace. During his interview with Clay at the Rose and Thorn, Greg estimated he'd cooked between five hundred and a thousand orders five days a week, fifty weeks a year for twelve years. That meant he cracked and cooked somewhere between three and six million eggs in Sin City.

The number of eggs dropped substantially after Greg started at the Rose and Thorn. He worked Thursday through Monday, which included every weekend brunch, except for two weeks off each year. He took one in the summer to smoke weed and listen to music at Jam Fest in the Columbia River Gorge, and another in the winter to smoke weed and listen to music on the beach in Cancun.

He was supposed to be working today, one of the busiest brunches of the year, but instead was holed up at home recovering. Last week, he was smoking weed and riding around Portland on his bike—along with a bunch of his stoned friends—and fell off, spraining his shoulder and fracturing his wrist.

Rumor was he was naked during the bike ride. Truth was they were *all* naked. Greg swore he'd be back up to speed in a couple of days, easily able to cook eggs, but Clay couldn't risk Mother's Day.

"What the hell is even up with brunch?" Clay grumbled,

flipping two eggs over-easy.

"Normal people want to do something nice with their moms and then be done for the day," Rob said. "Not overly complicated." Rob was a small scruffy-haired man with a quick smile and perpetual shadow of a three-day stubble. He was a great line cook, super fast.

"I don't mean today, I mean in general. What is brunch even for?"

"It's a white people thing," LuRon said. "You all like to be seen when you're eating."

LuRon was the only married cook at the restaurant, with kids. Two of them. Today, he was working the grill, carefully managing sprawling islands of hash browns, orderly rows of French toast and pools of buttermilk pancake batter to make into fluffy rounds for adults and bunny shapes for the kids.

"Not all white people," Clay said. "Not me."

"Most white people though," LuRon said. "Look out there, right now, and tell me how many Black people you see performing the brunch ritual."

Clay tossed a handful of grated cheddar on a pan full of scrambled eggs and divided them onto three plates. He tossed the dirty pan onto the counter where a stack of them leaned precariously. "I need pans," he called to Jon in the dishpit.

Clay took a quick look into the dining room through the porthole window on the right swinging door. Kassi was dropping off a check at a table and he watched her, smiling and making just enough small talk to keep them happy but not enough to fall behind. She looked up in his direction and he ducked.

"What did I tell you?" LuRon asked.

"It's solid white out there," Clay said.

"Totally, one hundred percent white, not one person

who looks like me out there," LuRon said. "Portland is already the whitest city in the country, but at brunch it's all white."

"Portland really *is* white. Why is that?" Clay asked.

"Don't get me started on the real history of Portland and all these people who think they're so progressive. We got too many eggs to cook today, but if you want to learn, go to the library and look up Oregon sundown laws. It's a place to start."

"Sundown?" Rob asked.

"Laws to keep Black people out of the state," LuRon said. "Oregon may not have been a state where people were enslaved, but they tried every damn thing possible to keep Black people out. You'll be shocked just how recently those shit laws were finally taken off the books. And the vote then wasn't even unanimous."

"White people are generally assholes," Rob said.

"You are not wrong about that," LuRon said. "There are some exceptions, I'll grant you."

Rob grinned as LuRon slid a bunny pancake onto a plate to which Rob added parsley whiskers and blueberries for eyes and a nose and moved the plate to the window under the heat lamp next to an order of scrambled eggs and another of tofu hash. He rang the bell twice for Kassi and pulled the ticket down.

"Two poached, two up and a huevos," Rob called from the next ticket.

"Dammit," Clay said. "Universal truth. People who order poached eggs are double assholes and people who order eggs-up are always high maintenance."

"Here's another truth. We're gonna need more salsa soon," LuRon said, tipping the plastic container so Clay could see it was running low.

"Who was prepping yesterday?" Clay asked.

"Jose. I'll have a word with him later."

"Hey, Dave-two, make some salsa, fast."

"What about the soup?" Dave-two asked.

"Forget that for now and get on salsa." Clay turned back to Rob. "Ring Kassi in here again. Those eggs are getting cold."

Rob rang the bell again, harder this time.

Clay broke two eggs into a soup cup and then carefully tipped them into the poach pan. The whites congealed like tattered sheets around the yolk, but then a stream of yellow fluttered up in the simmering water. "Dammit," he said, scooping them out, tossing them and then cracking two more.

Kassi came in and reached for the plates.

"When we ring that bell twice, that means you come pick up your food," Clay said, without turning.

"I was talking to my table," she said to his back.

"While my food was getting cold."

"I don't think you understand customer service," she said, blowing a strand of hair out of her eyes.

"I don't think you understand restaurants," he said, carefully fiddling with the two eggs.

Rob arched his eyebrow at her sympathetically as she left with the food.

"Why you being harsh with the new girl?" LuRon asked.

"I'm just pissed at these eggs. Not her."

***

After dropping the food at the table, Kassi paused by the dessert case. "Is he always like that?" she asked Roz. "He seemed so nice yesterday. Who does he think he is, talking to me like that?"

"The chef, I guess, and chefs tend to be temperamental

when it comes to their food," Roz said. "Also, he's cooked a lot more eggs today than he wanted to."

"Still, 'you don't understand restaurants.' That was mean."

"He looks even cuter when he's under pressure, don't you think? I am so ready to get with him. You've been warned."

"I'm not the slightest bit interested," Kassi said, taking a pot of coffee from Roz to make a refill run. One of her tables signaled at her with a stiff sort of wave that always meant trouble.

The poached eggs were too poached. Hard yolks. And the up-eggs were undercooked, with runny whites around the yolks. What she wanted to say was Why don't you save us all some trouble and just trade egg dishes? But she would never say that, that would be the kiss of death for any tip. "I'm sorry. We'll replace them immediately," Kassi said instead.

She grabbed the plates off the table and banged into the kitchen through the swinging door. "Table nine is unhappy with two of their orders," she said, sliding the plates back into the window. "Can you please make these orders correctly this time, or do my customers just not understand how restaurants work?"

Time slowed. Rob stood with his mouth hanging half open. LuRon turned to fuss with his grill, stifling a smile. Even Roz smirked.

Clay looked at her curiously, then started to laugh. "Fine. I deserved that. Comp their meals and I'll redo them. Rob, start fresh toast."

The customers were happy with the second attempt, and even happier that their meals were on the house.

***

Back in the kitchen, LuRon looked up and saw Dave-two chopping jalapenos, handling the peppers with his bare hands. "Son, where are your gloves?"

"I forgot them. Is that a problem?"

"Only if you touch your tallywhacker," LuRon said. "It'll feel like it's on fire."

"I did that once," Rob said. "It was excruciating. I had to, you know, take it out under my apron and keep splashing cold water on myself."

"You had it out at work?" Clay asked. "Please tell me that was not here."

"Um, pretty sure you weren't here, if that helps."

"It does not. New rule. Keep the mouse in the house at all times."

"I feel like I missed a good story," Roz said, walking in just as Clay spoke.

"You didn't," Clay said. "Trust me on that."

She smiled, picked up her food and left.

"I can beat that story," LuRon said. "One time I went home and Dara, she was all worked up like she gets, and she met me at the door and we, uh," he looked around quickly, "we got down to business. Turns out, you know, I had some of that pepper juice on my fingers and I accidentally lit her up. She still hasn't forgiven me, and that was three years back maybe."

"That's terrible," Clay said.

"Don't you ever tell her I said anything."

"Your secret's safe with us," Clay said, pointing at Dave-two, who was pulling on plastic gloves.

When the brunch rush was finally, blessedly over, Rob and LuRon went out back into the parking lot for smokes and Clay watched the line.

"Sorry I flipped you shit earlier," Kassi said. She was

boxing up leftovers.

"No, that's on me. I was stressed. I hate working brunch. I was not in a good place, and shouldn't have taken it out on you," he said.

She smiled, and Clay noticed it wasn't her waitress smile.

"Let me make it up to you," he said. "Let me fix you something to eat."

"I *am* hungry."

"What sounds good?"

"I don't want to ask you to cook any more eggs," she said.

"I'd be happy to. How do you like them?"

"Those eggs Benedict looked pretty amazing."

"Poached eggs. Perfect. I'll make you something extra nice. Do you like spinach?"

Kassi nodded.

"Tomatoes?"

"Love."

"Give me a few minutes."

When she came back, he handed her a plate of eggs Benedict on toasted English muffins with sautéed spinach and slices of grilled tomatoes, all covered by hollandaise sauce and next to a raft of hash browns.

"Wow. This looks amazing. Thank you so much."

"Enjoy."

Kassi took the plate into the back dining room, now closed off from customers, and sat down to eat.

Rob watched through the porthole window as she pulled out a notebook, flipped through the pages, taking a bite, then putting down her fork to write something, looking up to think, and then taking another bite.

"What do you think she's writing in that notebook?" Rob asked.

"I don't know," Clay said. "Maybe she's taking a class or something. But no matter what it is, stop spying on her."

"Maybe she's trying to come up with a mobile restaurant too," LuRon said. "Writing down crazy names like the French Fry Connection or whatnot."

"I regret showing you my list," Clay said.

"Maybe she's writing erotica," Rob said.

"Rob, she's not going to any of your weird bondage conventions," Clay said.

"How do you know? I haven't asked her yet."

"Wait, what kind of conventions?" Meredith asked as she brought in a tray of half-full ketchup bottles to marry.

"Bondage," Rob said, without a hint of shame. "Along with other kinks. Sex kinks, you know?"

"Interesting. Tell me more," Meredith said as she began turning bottles neck-to-neck.

7

INT. POWELL'S BOOKSTORE - DAY

KASSI and SAMANTHA peruse books in the
ROSE ROOM. The store is big, busy and
overwhelming. Kassi's future pops into
view, supported by a tiny, tiny theft.

"I found some books," Samantha said. She was holding a
half-dozen and looking up at Kassi hopefully.

"Honey, I said three books. You have twice that many."

"I couldn't decide," Sam said, smiling, but Kassi could
see storm clouds gathering behind her eyes. She needed a
nap. They both needed a nap.

They were at the local bookstore, the famous one, so
Sam could refill her bookshelf in Portland. Kassi rifled
through the stash of dollar bills in her purse. Mother's Day
had been good to her. At almost every table, she managed
to casually work in the fact that she was a single mother
and lament how she wished she were with her little girl.
Playing the sympathy card netted great tips, and she was
feeling flush for the first time since moving to this city.
Flush enough for an extra book for Sam.

"You can have one extra. Three plus one makes four. If
you fuss at me, you can have zero, so please pick four."

"But ..."

Kassi held up her hand. "I know this is hard, but I also know you're a big girl. We're leaving here with four books, which is one more than three, or no books, which is zero. You make your decision. I'll be over here in the grown-up section."

Samantha, head down, sat on the tiny chair in the children's book stacks gazing at her books mournfully.

Kassi glanced over the best-seller shelf. She was tempted by a used copy of *Bridges of Madison County* to read before the movie came out, and the new *Spenser* novel by Robert Parker looked fun. She loved the relationship between Spenser and Susan—and also his relationship with Hawk, her favorite character in the series—but decided to wait to borrow the books from the library. It was cheaper that way. She checked on Samantha, who was studiously sorting and re-sorting her stack of books.

She ambled over to a magazine rack and flipped through *Vogue*, taking in all the clothes she couldn't afford or understand, then put it back and picked up the latest issue of *Poets and Writers*. There was a profile of a vampire writer, an article about how to connect with agents called "The Perfect Pitch" and one on how to write "Villains Your Readers Will Love to Hate."

Kassi skipped through to the list of contests at the end.

Fiction, short fiction, poetry, nonfiction … her eyes settled on the screenwriting category. The Screenwriters Guild Inaugural New Voices Script Competition. The judging was led by some famous director she'd never heard of and the contest was only open to writers who had never sold a screenplay, giving novices an edge. Any genre. A full-length feature was required, along with a fifty-dollar entry fee. The deadline was August 31.

A little over three months. She'd started six scripts before and only finished one. And that one was because her degree depended on it, but she finished it fast, in a month. She knew, in theory, she could turn out a script in that timeframe. If she stayed focused and if she had an idea for a script. And a typewriter and a ream of paper. Along with a bunch of white-out. A babysitter would help too.

"Details, details," she muttered and ripped out the page.

The customer next to her looked aghast as she folded the page, tucked it into her back pocket and returned the magazine to the rack.

Samantha arrived with four books in hand and turned her sad eyes on Kassi.

"Did you make a decision?"

"Yes?" It was an unstated question about whether her mom had softened.

"I'm proud of you," Kassi said. "Let's go buy these four and go home. You can read while I talk to Grandma."

Sam looked over her shoulder at the left-behind books and waved a pitiful little wave. "Can we come back for the other books someday? I promised them I'd come back."

"Of course," Kassi said. "If you still miss them in two weeks, we'll come back for them and one more book. What do two books plus one book equal?"

"Three!" Sam brightened at the thought and was skipping happily by the time they left the store.

They hopped the bus on Burnside Street and rode back to their motel in north Portland. The aptly named Economy Motel was a brick two-story affair with a boarded-up pool in the parking lot and a mostly empty vending machine in the lobby. In its prime Kassi imagined the motel was frequented by traveling salesmen visiting Portland clients by day and hanging out at The Alibi Tiki Lounge, the neon-lit bar across from the motel on Interstate Avenue, by night.

Now the people who stayed at the motel were mostly

like her. Down on their luck, nowhere else to go, hoping they wouldn't be there for long. Still, it was clean (except the disgustingly stained carpet) and cheap, and the management left everybody more or less alone. She felt safe. Or safe enough.

Inside their room, she unfolded the purloined contest information and taped it to the fridge in the kitchenette.

"What's that, Mommy?" Samantha asked, sitting down at the linoleum table with her new books.

"A contest for a screenplay. Mommy is going to write one."

"What's a screenplay?"

"A movie, basically."

"What will your movie be about?"

"Good question."

Kassi poured herself a glass of wine and stared at the scrap of paper. She sat across from Sam, fished out her notebook from her bag, opened it and then drank some wine.

She thought about the one script she finished in college for a fifty-minute experimental film using Dada-ist techniques to capture the experience of books in a library. *Checked Out.* Her classmates laughed, and not in a good way. Her professor called it "alarmingly original."

But that was unlikely to be something the Screenwriters Guild would be interested in turning into a showcase movie. Plus, it wasn't a full-length feature, which the contest required. She needed something with drama, but entertaining, a little bit funny.

She could write about her fucked-up marriage. That had plenty of drama. Nah, she thought. Too depressing. And painful. She could write about a mother and daughter driving across the country alone. While she might enjoy that, she doubted the story had mass appeal.

"What do you think I should write about?" she asked her daughter.

Sam looked up from her book and pondered the question. "How about a mean mommy who has a little girl named ..."

"Samantha?"

"Yes," she giggled, "and the mean mommy wouldn't let Samantha get the books she wanted so ..."

"Samantha took her back to the Mommy Store and traded her in for a better mommy?"

"There's a Mommy Store? For real?" Samantha asked, genuinely shocked.

"That's what *my* mommy always told me," Kassi said. "Speaking of my mommy, I'm going to call her."

She reached for the phone. Her mother answered on the third ring.

"I was just thinking about you. We must share a—"

"—psychic connection!" Kassi said.

"I was going to say those exact words! How are you?"

"Good. I had the day off so Sam and I went book shopping."

"Tell my little munchkin that Grandma says hi," Gina said. "Are you still looking for a better place?"

"Absolutely," Kassi said. "I've been watching the papers. Rent is high in Portland though, likely I'll have to pay at least five hundred a month."

"I meant a better place to work."

"Oh, that. Not really. I need to make some fast money, and I can do that there, plus it's a little weird."

"Good weird?"

"Definitely. There's a super-handsome head chef, a line cook who is into bondage, another who drinks at work, and another who used to work in a Vegas casino cooking eggs. Our floor manager is polyamorous, the dishwasher is a socially awkward chess genius, one of the waitresses is working on her doctorate in psychology focused on sexual dysfunction, the owner is a lesbian single mom who might turn out to be the best of the bunch, and another waitress just left her addict boyfriend who OD'd in the bathroom a few months back."

"Wow, that is quite a cast of characters."

"Yep."

"I'm guessing the doctorate student and bondage line cook may have something in common?"

"I think that's already happening," Kassi said. "I may ask the dishwasher to teach me chess. Give me a hobby. And one of the other line cooks has kids, maybe a play date for Sam one of these days."

"Let's hear more about the handsome chef. How handsome?"

"Oh, Mom, crazy handsome. The waitresses all think he looks like Brad Pitt. But he's better than that, and taller too, doesn't look as boyish. He has broad shoulders, long hair and he's super fit. Sometimes he wears a single shark tooth earring but not when he's cooking, of course, and—"

"How old?"

"Right around my age, maybe a few years older, closer to thirty."

"Single?"

"I think so."

"Are you flirting with him?"

"No, no way. Just observing. It's too soon after Barry and who would be interested in me? A broke single mom."

"Kassi, please stop using that demeaning term. Single mom makes it sound sad or weak. No one ever calls men single dads if there's no woman in the picture. They get called heroic and people bow down before them. If anything, you're a super-mom."

"Thanks, Mom. I appreciate that."

"I guess I can see why you might want to stay there for a little while. The Rose and Thorn sounds like a movie."

"It does, doesn't it?" Kassi looked at the contest information stuck on the fridge. "Mom, I need to go. I'll call you tomorrow. Love you."

Kassi picked up the pen. In her notebook, she wrote *The Rose and Thorn*, then crossed it out. Then *Order Up* and crossed that out too. Then she tried *Culinary Confessions* and studied it as she topped off her wine. "No, not quite right either," she said, scratching it out.

She watched Samantha trying to read, listening to her sound out the words. "She went to a magical land …"

Bingo. That was it.

Kassi wrote down *Kitchen Heat: A Restaurantland Romance* and smiled.

She started writing, setting up the backstory.

Restaurants have their own customs and rituals, their own rules—spoken and unspoken. To outsiders, it's a world of magic and mayhem. But it's like any other country—filled with lovers and losers, dreamers and doers, scamps and scoundrels. Welcome to Restaurantland.

The words came fast and furious and when she put the pen down forty-five minutes later, she'd filled ten pages and Samantha was asleep on the floor. She got her into bed, folded the laundry, quietly did the dishes, added a few things to the grocery list, and then made lunch for Sam to take on her first day at the new daycare tomorrow. Finally, Kassi slipped into bed, turned on the TV with the sound down low and half-watched *All About Eve* as she continued sketching out a rough plot and character list.

She stopped writing and turned to face the TV at the famous line and whispered it along with Bette Davis. "Fasten your seatbelts, it's gonna be a bumpy night."

8

INT. ROSE AND THORN RESTAURANT - DAY

The dining room is half full. TESS
cleans the front window. KASSI stands
next to a table where an agitated WOMAN
glares and points at her food. Uh-oh.

"There's a hair in my tofu scramble," the customer said, pointing at it with her fork. The hair was wrapped around and through the small uneaten mound of tofu remaining on the plate.

"I see that. What color would you call that?" Kassi asked.

The woman looked up at her. "How is that possibly relevant?"

Kassi knew customers occasionally put their hair in food to get a comped meal. This woman's hair was red, very red, like the hair in the food.

Roz's hair was also red.

"Let me take this plate away and I'll be right back with a fresh one," Kassi said.

Irritated and feeling used, but mostly just pissed about likely getting stiffed on a tip because waitresses always took the brunt of unhappy customers, Kassi took the plate into the kitchen, pulled the hair strand off the tofu mound, and held it up to the light, gauging its full length.

It was shorter than Roz's hair, closer to the length of the customer's hair, but she couldn't be sure. Roz's hair wasn't all the same length.

"Order up!" Clay yelled, dinging the bell three times while watching Kassi through the window. "Order up for Roz!"

Kassi held the hair out in front of her and walked to the salad bar prep station, smoothing it out flat on a white cutting board, then bent down and again studied the strand.

"Kassi, we generally strive to keep hairs out of our food, not place them on the cutting boards," Clay said.

"This is not Roz's hair," Kassi said. "I need a new tofu scramble, even though she ate nearly the whole thing before noticing the hair that is not Roz's."

"What about my hair?" Roz said, bursting into the kitchen to pick up the order from under the heat lamp. She looked at the cutting board. "Definitely not mine. Wrong color. Did someone plant a hair again?" Roz checked her order to be sure it matched what she'd put in. Satisfied, she slipped the plates onto her tray.

"The woman at table twelve," Kassi said. "I've seen her before. Usually sticks with coffee, decaf, until today. I think she was scoping us out, waiting for a shift when you were working. She's a redhead."

"I like redheads. Is she still here?" Rob wiped his hands on his apron.

Kassi nodded. "I'm about to take her a brand new tofu scramble and a free piece of mud pie. The oldest one in the fridge."

Rob peered out the kitchen door into the dining room and, after spotting her, whistled. Within seconds, Gilroy and LuRon were behind him, elbowing each other like teenagers, trying to get a good vantage.

"She's just my type," Rob said.

"What, breathing and by herself?" LuRon asked.

"Do you dye your hair?" Kassi asked.

"I'll never tell," LuRon said, putting his hand on his hip and blowing her a kiss. Clay grinned from behind the grill.

"Not you," Kassi said. "Roz, do you dye your hair?"

"No, I don't, and while I'm glad to know you boys are such fans of redheads, would you please get the hell out of my way? Coming through with hot food."

They stepped aside and Roz pushed the door open with her hip. By the time it swung shut, the men were back in position, eyeing the woman. Kassi knew they were making assumptions because she was eating alone. Men always thought a woman alone meant she was lonely, and lonely meant needy. And needy meant they might have a shot.

It was bullshit of course but the trope was so well established in the male lizard brain, the certainty of being hit on kept most single women eating at home alone in their kitchens to avoid the annoying avalanche of hopeful male gazes and the inevitable offer to buy them a drink.

That would be a good topic for the screenplay. In fact, this whole scene would be, Kassi thought. She made a mental note to jot that down in her notebook later.

The way LuRon and Rob were egging each other on now, Kassi almost felt sorry for the scheming ginger shithead, but not quite. This restaurant wasn't going to get cheated on her watch; no one would put one over on Kassi Witmire.

"Look at this," she said. "Here, there's a dark end. That means whoever's hair it is for sure dyes it. Since Roz doesn't, it must be a plant."

"It's a free tofu scramble, Nancy Drew," Clay said. "With dessert thrown in. Just let the 'The Case of the

Mystery Hair' go. She's probably broke."

"Then she should ask for food or offer to do dishes or something. This is stealing. If everybody who is desperate starts stealing, the world will go to hell."

"Have you checked out the world lately?" Clay asked. "Look at all the shit going on now just in this one, the year 1995, I mean considering—"

"Oh, boy," LuRon said, suddenly turning around. "Well, I've seen enough."

"Shit," Rob said. "That killed the mood. Time to get back to work."

Clay looked at them questioningly and LuRon pantomimed a round belly. Touching Kassi on the elbow, Clay swept the errant hair into the trash and steered her toward the door.

"What are you doing?" she asked, surprised by the electric sensation of his hand on her arm. "I'm in the middle of something important here, I have to finish, she might leave ..."

She let him guide her anyway, enjoying his warm touch on her elbow. At the door, she peered through the window and Clay, nearly a foot taller, stood close behind, bending down to look out at the same time.

The woman was standing. Kassi had missed it when she was seated. Kassi sighed. She was pregnant. Easily six, maybe even seven, months along.

Clay put his hand on her shoulders and leaned down to whisper close into Kassi's ear. "Should we call the cops, Nancy Drew, or just load her up a to-go bag?"

She leaned back into the heat of his whispered breath, feeling the stubble of his cheek against her skin. She elbowed him lightly, in response to the Nancy Drew remark. He didn't pull away. Being so close was making her light-headed, the solid feel of him, the warmth of his body, his scent of kitchen smells mixed in with salt and pine.

He kept his hands resting on her shoulders and they both knew it was too long, the gesture was moving past something impromptu and light-hearted, becoming intentional. They stood that way for a few more seconds until he breathed deeply and stepped back.

"Let's get a bag ready for our pregnant thief," he said, moving back to the grill, behind the order window. "We'll load it up with some fresh veggies and stuff to last a few days."

"You are way too kind, but yeah, okay," Kassi said.

When she left the kitchen, the distance between them felt oddly painful.

An hour later, Kassi was alone in the dining room except for a lingering coffee drinker. She was working the long shift today, the dead zone between lunch and dinner with only one server. It was her favorite time of day at the restaurant, although it was unpredictable in terms of tips.

Usually, there were barely enough customers for one server to have a decent day during the dead zone, but every so often something random and wonderful happened— like an entire sports team coming in after practice or a Mary Kay makeup sales club deciding to meet in the restaurant. A packed dining room meant extra hustle but big tips that she didn't have to split.

Today, it was shaping up to be painfully slow. She wanted to spend the time hanging out with Clay, but there was no excuse to go into the kitchen. Besides, he was busy, cooking soup and prepping for the dinner shift. Maybe she could talk to him later.

Why did she even want to talk to him?

What she said to her mom was true. She was in no position to start something new. And why would anyone, especially someone as nice as Clay, want to get caught up in her shit?

She nodded at the thin archaeologist, the last customer, as he left. He came in most days for an afternoon coffee, always reading some huge, dry textbook while sneaking surreptitious glances at Kristoph. He was a decent tipper.

Tess, the shift manager, said Kassi could sit for a while to see if any more tables showed up. Kassi didn't get to see Tess much since their shifts didn't overlap often, but a real kinship was developing between them.

At the back booth, Kassi pulled out her notebook and began writing. She was trying to decide how the pregnant redhead might fit into the scene taking shape in her head, but then Roz was suddenly standing by the side of the table.

She smelled like booze. It was two o'clock in the afternoon. "I thought you went home?" Kassi asked.

"Can I sit? Pretty please."

"Sure."

"I'm going to the Humane Society now to pick up some kittens." Roz's words were slightly slurred around their edges.

"Maybe today is not a good day to adopt new pets," Kassi said. Or rather, maybe drunk is not a good time to adopt pets, she thought. Roz would end up with an entire litter.

"I need something to love, love, love and to help me stay sober, sober, sober." Roz giggled, but it trailed off.

"You know what, let me get you a cup of coffee, and you can tell me all about it," Kassi said, standing, hoping to stall her until she sobered up. "Like what you'd name the kittens."

"I was thinking Miss Muffin, you know, like ..."

As she was pouring the coffee, Kassi watched Tess seat a man in the front of the dining room near the window at what was considered the best two-top in the house. Good people-watching spot. But private. Far from the noisy playroom.

Tess pulled her aside as Kassi was adding cream to Roz's coffee. "It's your lucky day. He's rich and he likes to share his good fortune with the little people."

"Are we the little people?"

"Exactly."

"Big tipper?"

"Huge," Tess said. "As long as you fuss over him a little. His name's Walter but let him tell you that."

"He's kinda cute."

"Cute and loaded."

"Could you please take this coffee to Roz? She's not feeling great. Tell her I'll be back after I get this order, and to keep thinking of kitten names."

Tess sighed and said, "I know her AA sponsor. I'll try to get ahold of him."

Kassi walked over to the new table, aware of and mildly ashamed of the amplified swing in her hips. "Good afternoon, I'm Kassi. I'll be your server today. Do you know what you'd like?"

9

INT. ROSE AND THORN RESTAURANT KITCHEN –
SAME DAY

CLAY and GILROY are on duty. A small
black and white TV flickers above the
line. Clay's past pops into view, and
she is smoking hot.

"LuRon is never late," Clay said.

It was a slow night, so they were watching a Trailblazers highlights show on the small portable TV with the sound off. Clay's kitchen had a three-ticket rule. Any more than three tickets hanging at once and the TV went off.

"He's out in the parking lot," Dave-one said as he walked by.

"What?"

"LuRon. He's out in the parking lot in his car. His wife too."

"Are they ... what are they doing?" Clay asked. He knew they wanted another baby.

"Fighting, I think."

"Go tap on the window and tell him he needs to get his ass in here."

"No way," Dave-one said. "I'm not getting in the middle of that."

Clay looked at Gilroy. "Go out there and wave or something, just to let him know."

Gilroy shook his head. "Does it look like I have a death wish? You're the boss. You go."

"I guess it's slow enough for now," Clay said, relenting. "I'll give them their privacy, but if it gets busy, I'm heading right out there."

"Yeah, right, sure you will," Gilroy said, squawking like a chicken.

Rob was covering a prep shift and leaned on the counter surrounded by enchilada fixings. "That's why I will never get married," he said.

"Not because there's no one dumb enough to say yes, much less go on a second date with you," Gilroy said.

Meredith, bored by the slow shift, pulled her long hair back and tied it with a scrunchie and then leaned on the order window and smiled, listening to the banter.

"I don't date," Rob said. "I don't have time. I'm part of a supportive and loving community of like-minded sexual adventurers. All my unique needs are met on a regular basis. I never get bored or feel like I have to compromise."

"We all have to compromise in life," Clay said.

"I meant specifically in terms of sexual relationships."

"Don't you get lonely?" Meredith asked. "For a deeper human connection?"

"There is no deeper connection than sexual, especially when you're experiencing pain and pleasure at the same time. Double that when it's a masked stranger and you're tied up so you can't resist. That kind of intimacy is deeply satisfying."

"You're a freak, Rob," Gilroy said.

"Sure. But a happy freak who isn't always moping around with a relationship shackled to my ankle."

"I do not ever want to hear anything about you and

shackles," Clay said.

"Submission is the ultimate act of liberation," Rob said.

Clay shook his head. "That doesn't even make sense."

"I find you fascinating," Meredith said. "From a purely psychological perspective."

"Come with me to Bondage-Con next week and you will find hundreds of fascinating people, many of them wrapped in latex and tied to tables for your amusement."

"It's like a perverse petting zoo for humans," Gilroy said.

"Now you're getting it," Rob said.

Ione stuck her head in the swinging door. "Meredith, new table."

"Maybe I will go with you," Meredith said, smiling at Rob and returning to the dining room.

They watched her go, her long brown ponytail swinging behind her.

"Do not damage that girl," Clay said.

"I doubt she needs, or wants, your protection," Rob said, returning his attention to rolling enchiladas, plopping them into stainless steel boats, ladling tomatillo sauce over them and then sprinkling a handful of cheese on top.

"She's got a dark side," Rob continued, almost to himself and his voice practically quivering with excitement. "She's a freak like me, I can tell. Even if she looks just like the girl next door."

"No one is a freak like you," LuRon said, walking behind the line and pulling his apron on. "Sorry I'm late, man. Thanks for clocking me in on time."

"No problem," Clay said. "Everything okay? Dave-one said he saw you out back."

"Yeah, we got into a fight. A big one. Like, she was gonna take the kids and go to her aunt's house. I couldn't leave until we got back on solid ground."

"What did you do this time?" Rob asked.

"It's not like that. Dara and I've been married for what, eight years now. It's not like in the movies. You don't fight about any one thing. It's always a fight about something else. Every fight, no matter what the topic, no matter what starts it, is about one of four things: sex, kids, money or sex."

Clay laughed. "You said sex twice."

"Oh really?" LuRon arched his eyebrow. "I guess I double mean it."

He started cleaning the grill. "I'm kind of joking. There's like this whole other thing, independence or some shit. You fight about losing yourself, or part of yourself, in the other person. You don't even know it, because you're starting out with some stupid-ass thing and all of a sudden, you're neck deep in a death match about something you can't even explain."

"This is the best description of marriage I've ever heard," Rob said. "What started the fight tonight?"

LuRon smiled and then exhaled a long slow breath. "The fucking dishwasher."

"Did you say dishwasher?" Jon asked, poking his head out of the dishpit.

"Yeah man, your area of expertise. The dishwasher. Dara, she loads it like she's blindfolded or something. Like she's pissed off at the dishes and physics don't work. Glasses upside down, bowls pointing the wrong way, everything angled so the water can't get in them. Big gaps where nothing else can fit, so half the space is wasted."

"It's a scientific fact that women are not spatially minded like men," Rob said.

Meredith came back into the kitchen to hang a ticket in time to hear Rob's words. "My baby sister is an engineer, my older sister is an architect, and you are a caveman."

Her comment stopped conversation for a second or two, as if to provide the space for a retort, but when nothing was forthcoming, the banter fell back into place as if Meredith hadn't said anything. She shook her head and walked away.

"Half our marriage is me rubbing Dara's feet when she's tired, which is always, cleaning up gross things from the kids and rearranging the dishwasher. Anyway, she saw me doing that this morning, putting those dirty dishes right, and it got on her last nerve for some reason. Things got … tense. Next thing you know, I had ruined her life and was never going to make enough money and wouldn't share the housework and wasn't going down on her often enough and we probably were breaking up because we're only hitting it like twice a week now."

"All of that from poorly loaded Maytag?" Gilroy asked.

LuRon looked at him like he was special. "You don't even live with Angel. What the fuck do you know? The dishwasher is a fuse to a much bigger fight, and it's always right there."

"I'm still stuck on *only* hitting it twice a week," Rob said.

Kassi came into the kitchen to clock in. Barry had Sam tonight, so she agreed to sub for Kristoph who wanted the night off because the skinny archaeologist finally worked up the nerve to ask him out.

"Clay, help me out," LuRon said. "You were married, you and your ex ever fight about some shit like how to stack the dishwasher and it was about something else?"

"I didn't know you were married," Kassi said.

"Divorced almost two years now," Gilroy answered for Clay. "She broke his heart." He made an appropriately sad face trailing his finger down from his eye like a tear. "But our boy is healing."

"Way more information than Kassi wants or needs,"

Clay said. "But I will say that one of our many, many fuses was laundry. Crystal never did it. She'd save it up for a month until she ran out of everything and then try to stuff it all in the machine at once. Burned the motor out twice. If I tried to wash her stuff, she'd get pissed because I was doing it wrong and I didn't respect her, and I was trying to sabotage her acting career because clothes are part of her persona."

"I hope you're both not implying that women are somehow solely responsible for relationship troubles," Kassi said. "I guarantee you every woman in this place, straight or gay, has a story to tell about how their partners emotionally ambushed them. And for straight women especially, that often involves the threat of violence, which way too often becomes physical violence."

"I'm definitely not trying to say that women are the cause of relationship problems," Clay said, taken aback by how fast they had moved from jokes about dishwashers and laundry to domestic violence. Why was that the first thing that came to her mind?

"I stand by my earlier statement that marriage is whacked," Rob said. "All 'committed' relationships are pointless." He used air quotes.

"I'm kind of with you on that," Kassi said. "It's ridiculous how we drag all that unspoken stuff around. Good communication can help. And honesty."

Clay nodded. "That requires both people are committed to the same thing. If they can't be honest, don't want to be, or don't know how to be in a committed relationship, then what?"

"You look after yourself," Kassi said. For an instant, her face mirrored sadness and despair, but then it hardened into a forced smile. "And you get the fuck out."

Everyone went silent by the seriousness of her reaction,

but then Rob said, "Better yet, never get the fuck in unless you have a safe word, am I right?"

Kassi laughed. The kitchen mood returned to its baseline of jovial banter, with orders coming in and going out, but after an hour, it became clear a dinner rush wasn't going to materialize.

In between the scarce orders, the crew collectively mused about why the night was slow. Maybe the nice weather. Maybe the Rose Festival. Maybe the pollen. In the end, the only thing they all agreed on was there was no logic to what caused a slow night and that they all hated them. Almost as much as a busy night.

***

The night crept by at a turtle's pace and the tips were terrible. Roz was opening bottles of beer for her one table. Kassi was trying to look busy so Ione wouldn't send her home. The paltry hour wage and free shift meal were better than nothing.

"Did you know Clay's ex-wife?" Kassi asked, rolling silverware into paper napkins.

"Yeah, I know her. Crystal," Roz said. "Such a bitch. A gorgeous bitch, but still. High school sweethearts. She cheated on him, broke his heart. Pretty sure he hasn't dated since. Such a shame. Whoever ends that streak will be one lucky girl. I hope it's me."

They were close enough to the kitchen to hear LuRon shout, "Holy shit. Crystal's got a new commercial."

Kassi and Roz dropped what they were doing and went into the kitchen, elbowing their way to the TV now that everyone was crowded around it. Gilroy turned up the sound.

Crystal wore a miniskirt flared at the thighs, a low-cut

T-shirt and stiletto heels. She was slowly easing her way into the front seat of a sports car with lots of rock and roll audio and choppy fast cuts.

She winked at the camera, slid on mirrored sunglasses, tossed back her long black hair and suggestively licked her lips. In the reflection of the sunglasses, a muscular and shirtless young man in a cowboy hat was smiling and reaching a hand toward her. The car roared off, the speedometer thrusting up to one hundred in a few seconds.

"This fast break brought to you by Fleet Motors. If it's fast, it's Fleet," the announcer said, then the broadcast shifted back to the Fleet-sponsored highlight show from the second half of the Blazers' last season.

"Damn," Rob said. "She got even better-looking. Sorry, but damn. I thought she was blonde."

"She's an actress, man," Gilroy said. "That was probably a wig."

Kassi and Roz gave each other side-eye. "That's some serious competition," Roz whispered.

Kassi looked over at Clay. Clay was watching her reaction to the commercial.

"Your ex is hot as hell," LuRon said. "Like movie star hot. I'm not saying you should forgive her or anything, but if she ever wants a little on the side now that she's married to that used car dude, you ought to at least consider it."

Clay continued to look at Kassi, without acknowledging LuRon. The crew was riled up enough that no one noticed their locked eyes.

"Guys, you are talking about Saint Clay the Pure here," Gilroy said. "Patron saint of the celibate and all those who suffer in silence. He would never relax his morals for such a tawdry reason as hot naked fun times."

"You all can kiss my ass," Clay said, finally looking away from Kassi. "There's more to life than sex."

"There isn't," Rob said. "Well, maybe there is one more thing. Guilt. But guilt is a learned behavior and with effort, it can be unlearned."

10

INT. PORTLAND COFFEE SHOP – DAY

KASSI starts the day searching newspaper ads for affordable apartment rentals. By nightfall, KASSI and CLAY are in bed together.

"I'm tired," Samantha said. She was drinking a hot chocolate, her little hands wrapped around the paper cup.

"We have one more place to look at, baby," Kassi said. "It's just a few blocks from here."

"Can we go tomorrow?" Samantha asked.

"I have to work tomorrow."

"The next day?"

Samantha did look tired but the sweet, hot, foamy drink was helping.

"Wouldn't you like to have our own place so we can get out of that musty little motel?"

"No. I love it there."

"Yesterday you said it smelled funny and you hated it." Kassi was sipping a triple latte—she was tired too—and tracing her finger along a tattered city map, looking at the location of the last apartment on the list.

"I love it there today," Samantha said.

Kassi folded the map. "Tell you what, how about we look at this last apartment and then hop the bus to the

70

restaurant and get some fun food?" She wasn't too keen on visiting the Rose and Thorn today. She needed a break from the place, and she knew Clay had the day off so she wouldn't get to see him, but the staff discount on meals was hard to pass up.

"Okay, but I won't like the apartment."

Turns out, Samantha did like it. A lot.

Mostly because the tiny little second bedroom had a stained-glass window with a fairy and butterflies on it, and a closet big enough to hide in with its own light bulb and a built-in bookshelf.

"I love it, Mommy, I love it!" she squealed.

The apartment manager was a kindly older man with a gray beard trimmed close. He smiled at Kassi. "What do you think, Mom?"

"Apparently, we love it," Kassi said, smiling. That was an understatement. The rental was one of six apartments in an old converted Victorian home, with all its original charm, on the ground floor in a nice neighborhood. Best of all, it was a deal, and she would be able to afford it.

He nodded. "Great. You seem trustworthy. I don't need to check your references. Sign the paperwork and give me a check for the first and last month, plus a cleaning deposit equivalent to another month's rent. Altogether, that's fifteen hundred. I'll give you the keys today."

Kassi did a quick calculation. She was a hundred short, and that was with everything all in. She hadn't expected such a high cleaning deposit.

"I'm sorry," she said, shoulders slumping. "That's a little steep. We'll keep looking."

"But Mommy, I love it here," Samantha wailed.

"I'm sorry, honey. We'll find a better place."

"There won't be any better places," she sobbed. Kassi wanted to cry too.

"Your daughter is right," the manager said. "There won't be a better place. Tell you what, how about I waive the cleaning deposit. Will that work for your ... situation?"

Kassi started to say no. She hated relying on the kindness of others, but she was pretty sure their new neighbors at the motel were selling drugs, probably coke. Or at least using drugs, with many friends, at all hours. It was beyond time to get out of the motel. "Thank you, yes, that would be great."

"Don't disappoint me," the manager replied. "You do any damage, take care of it like a grown-up."

She nodded and, before she could stop herself, hugged him, surprising them both.

After the paperwork was signed and he handed over the keys, Kassi and Samantha stood in the apartment looking at their new home.

There wasn't much furniture. A few pieces left behind by the last tenant. A rickety kitchen table with three even more rickety chairs and a couch that sagged in the middle. No beds.

"First things first," Kassi said. "Let's get some food. Then we'll get some beds. Then get our stuff from the motel."

It was a short bus ride to the restaurant, even walkable without a tired child, which was great for the future.

Sam was an instant celebrity when they walked in. The staff started fussing over her immediately. Roz told her how pretty she was. Kristoph said she looked like a princess. Tess said she was the smartest girl in the world. Ione offered to braid her hair.

"I'm going to introduce her to the kitchen crew," Kassi said, bending down and scooping her up. "You stay in mommy's arms, okay? There are hot stoves and sharp knives and all kinds of dangerous things in the kitchen."

Holding Sam, she pushed through the swinging doors. Clay was there. Kassi felt an unexpected flutter of joy. He was talking to Roz and pouring a cup of coffee. He wasn't working. He was in jean shorts and an old concert T-shirt, his long hair down, his biceps swelling the tattered sleeves. Every time she saw him, she was amazed at how handsome he was. It never failed to catch her breath.

He looked up, surprised to see her, and more surprised to see her holding Samantha. He instantly stopped talking to Roz, causing her smile to fade, and made his way over to them.

"Who's this little cutie?" he asked.

"Clay, meet my daughter Samantha."

"Some people call me Sam," she said.

"Which do you like?"

"Both are okay. Are you the cooker?" Sam asked.

"You got that right," Clay said. "I am the cooker, and it's very nice to meet you. You must hear this all the time, but you look a lot like your mother."

"I do hear it," Sam said. Her curiosity roused, she lifted her head from its nesting spot on the curve of her mother's neck.

"Good thing your mom's real pretty, right?"

"You think my mom is pretty?"

"Well, not as pretty as you," he said.

"Hey," Kassi said. "I thought today was your day off."

"It is. I had some seafood orders to put in."

"That's why he gets paid the big bucks," LuRon said, flipping pancakes.

"What are you doing here?" Clay asked Kassi.

"Getting something to eat."

"We got an apartment today," Samantha said. "My room has a fairy window and I'll show it to you if you want. You can come see it."

"I'd like that," Clay said.

"We'll see about that. Sam, let's go meet the rest of the cookers," Kassi said.

"There are other cookers?" Sam asked.

"Nice to meet you, Samantha," Clay said, disappearing into the walk-in, clipboard in hand.

After they made the rounds, Kassi and Samantha took a table by the window and Kassi looked at the menu, even though she knew it by heart, while Sam colored the chubby, smiling dinosaurs on the children's placemat.

"I don't know what to order," she said when Kristoph walked up with a coffee pot.

"Sweetie, I don't think you need to worry about that. Clay was putting on an apron when I left the kitchen. Let me go check, but I bet he has something in mind for you."

"That's a little presumptuous."

"Then why are you smiling?"

"I'm not. I just …"

Kristoph patted her arm. "It's nice when people actually see you, isn't it? Be right back."

When he returned, he had a waffle covered with fresh strawberries and a mound of whipped cream for Samantha, a creamy tomato pasta with spinach and blistered cherry tomatoes for Kassi and a chocolate mousse topped with more whipped cream for them to share for dessert.

"How did he do?" Kristoph asked, sliding the plates in front of them.

"Mom, it's my favorite," Samantha said, eyes wide.

"Pretty well, I'd say," Kassi said.

"What are you two up to?" Kristoph asked. "Girl's day? A little spa treatment and cocktails?"

Kassi laughed. "Yes, with my four-year-old daughter. We're off to have cocktails and pedicures."

"Are we for reals, Mom?" Samantha asked.

Kassi leaned over to cut Sam's waffle. "We just signed a lease on an apartment so we're off to find beds, and hopefully figure out how to get mattresses home on the bus."

"You know who has a truck?" Kristoph asked, resting his chin in his hand as if puzzling out an ancient mystery. "Clay, and he just happens to be in the kitchen today on his day off."

"I could never impose," Kassi said, taking a bit of the pasta and then rolling her eyes. "Oh, so good."

"Yes, why would you ever ask someone so gorgeous to do you a favor?" Kristoph asked. "It's uncouth and needy." He smiled and made his way back to the kitchen.

Ten minutes later, Clay made his way out.

"How is it?"

"Yummy," Samantha said. She had whipped cream on the tip of her nose and maple syrup and strawberry stains on her cheeks.

"How about your pasta?"

"Really good," Kassi said. "You should put that on the menu."

"That's the plan. And the chocolate mousse?" he asked, nodding at the empty bowl.

"A little too good," Kassi said, patting her stomach.

"Great. What's this I hear about you needing my truck to move some mattresses?"

She shot a dirty look at Kristoph who waved at her gleefully from the back of the dining room.

"Yeah, I just, I mean, I don't need you or your truck but, well, we just … I need to pick up some beds or mattresses or something and we only have the bus so maybe they can be delivered."

"It's no problem," he said. "I don't have plans until later, and I do want to see that fairy window."

Samantha looked up at him solemnly. "It's magic."

"It's settled. Come get me in the kitchen when you're ready."

***

LuRon was sliding two plates with sandwiches into the window as Clay walked in. "Are you helping Kassi buy a mattress? That's some serious planning ahead."

"It's not like that," Clay said.

"It seems like that. Just ask her out already. Everybody can see you have a thing for each other, except for maybe Roz." He pretended to think about it. "Nah, Roz can see it too."

Clay shot a look at Roz, but either she hadn't heard or was pretending.

"We should start a pool on when you two finally do it," Rob said.

"I'm not doing anything with Kassi," he said loudly enough to get Roz's attention. She looked up from her pile of tickets. "Except helping her move some mattresses. The same thing I'd do for anyone here who asked, except maybe you Rob."

"That's good because she's still married you know," Roz said, as she stacked a tray of espresso cups still warm from the dishwasher.

The kitchen went quiet. "Really?" LuRon asked.

"She's separated, but you know what that means, especially when there's a kid involved," she said with a shrug.

"Again, I'm not interested in dating her, or anybody," Clay said. "Just helping a friend."

"Eh, forget all that marriage bullshit," Rob said. "Be sure to get the mattress you want, like firm, I guess. Or maybe you like it a little softer. More cushion for the …"

"Stop it," Clay said. "Just tell her I'm in the parking lot by my truck."

He left out the back door.

***

A few minutes later Kassi poked her head in the kitchen. "Where's Clay?"

"He's out back," LuRon said.

"You know he's only doing this because he feels sorry for you, right?" Roz said. "A single mom and all."

Roz's comment stung. Kassi swallowed an angry retort, then shrugged. "I'll take what I can get."

Clay was waiting in his truck, an old Chevy, and after buckling Samantha in between them—her chattering, singing and asking Clay questions the entire time—he drove to two different want-ad listings for mattresses, a twin with a metal box springs and a double futon mattress without the frame. Kassi bought them both.

"Let's go see this magic window of yours," Clay said.

At the apartment, after examining the butterfly-fairy window, Clay helped Kassi haul the mattresses inside. Samantha's was small so it was easy, but the larger futon was awkward and the apartment had nearly impossible angles at the doors.

They were outside the bedroom shoving on it and when it finally cleared, the momentum caused them to stumble in after it. Clay slipped his arm around her waist and maneuvered Kassi so that he would fall beneath her. They landed on the mattress with a thud, Clay on his back and Kassi on top facing him. She had her hands on either side of his chest, and he was holding her by the hips. Their faces were close, her hair spilling over him. She was looking into his eyes, surprised, and felt a surge of heat between them, and between her legs.

In the movies, this would be when we kiss, she thought. Her lips parted as if her body was in the driver's seat, and her eyes closed. Clay moved his head closer to hers, pulling her tighter against him.

But this was not a movie.

"What are you doing, Mommy?" Samantha asked.

Kassi opened her eyes with a start and rolled off Clay, both of them quickly standing.

"Nothing, honey, we just fell, silly us. The mattress barely fit through the door."

"Yeah, silly mattress," Clay said.

Samantha stared at the two of them silently, her little head tilted left.

"I should be going," Clay said.

Kassi nodded. "Okay, great. Thank you for today."

"My pleasure. I'll see you at work tomorrow. Bye, Samantha."

Samantha was standing in her magic window waving at him as he got into his truck.

11

INT. CITY BUS - DAY

The BUS rolls through overcast and drizzly city streets. KASSI struggles to write a sex scene for her screenplay. Focusing on a certain someone helps her creative juices.

"You are so beautiful. I can't keep my hands off you."

"Please, take me now. Don't make me beg."

His hand slipped between her thighs and she moved her legs apart. Desire shot through her with a ferocity that stole her breath away. She went weak in the knees, he held her up. He kissed her neck, small butterfly kisses from her clavicle up to her chin, and when his lips touched hers, she was ready, passionately kissing him back, their tongues darting and probing—

"Mommy, why are you making kissy noises?"

Kassi opened her eyes and saw her daughter staring at her earnestly. The woman in the seat across the aisle laughed softly and then looked back down at her book. Kassi noticed the bare-chested man on the cover, his long hair blowing in a smoldering wind. Fabio. The proto-Brad Pitt.

"Are you writing in your head again?" Samantha asked.

"Yes, honey, that's what I'm doing." Although not very

well, she thought.

Samantha started to make loud kissing noises, smacking her lips together. "I'm writing too." The woman was now openly laughing.

Kassi pulled the cord for the next bus stop, grinning at her dramatic daughter. It was impossible not to be infected by her simple joy. A minute later, the bus stopped at the corner and the doors whooshed open. "Have a good day, Sam," the driver said. "You listen to your mom, okay?"

"Will you give me more candy if I do?"

"Sam!" Kassi swung her daughter up to her hip as she slung the bag over her shoulder. "My little kissy-faced grifter, mind your manners."

The driver, a plump man in his fifties who reminded Kassi of a kindly forest mushroom come to life, smiled. "We'll see, little one, we'll see."

"Thanks for the ride, Marcus," Kassi said. "How's Belinda?"

"She's fine. We've got an anniversary coming up. I'm taking her to the coast for a surprise romantic weekend. Thirty years."

"She's a lucky woman," Kassi said.

Marcus was the regular weekday driver on the city bus route from their new apartment to Sam's daycare center. Kassi still didn't know anyone in Portland outside of the restaurant, other than Sam's father who barely spoke to her these days except to berate her or announce the logistics for Sam's time with him. Marcus was friendly to Kassi and Sam, and his ready supply of terrible dad jokes, puns and kind small talk was a refuge.

"You'll find your Prince Charming soon enough," Marcus said. "Now watch your step ladies and make today a great day."

"Thanks, see you next time," Kassi said.

The bus door whooshed shut behind them.

Stepping onto the curb, Kassi thought about what she had learned since moving to Portland, how it was the whitest city in the country and the racism that led to those demographics. She wondered what Marcus had to put up with on a regular basis. Maybe someday she would ask him.

The air outside was misty, the sky overcast. She put Sam down and held her hand as they crossed the street. They walked the two blocks to the daycare cooperative in the basement of a community center. When they reached the edge of the playground, Sam spied a clutch of new friends on the merry-go-round. She looked up at her mother with questioning eyes.

"Go on, I'll give Teacher Peggy your lunch."

Sam ran off without hugging Kassi and she felt the sting. But watching her daughter welcomed by the three little girls and hearing her peals of laughter as they twirled around with hands clasped on the bars made up for it.

Kassi passed the sack lunch off to Peggy, made just enough small talk about the weather to be judged one of the friendly moms, and then trudged back up the hill to the bus stop.

Two rides and one transfer later, she arrived at the restaurant. She was an hour early for her shift so she grabbed a cup of coffee and sat down at a table in the dining room. During the lull between breakfast and lunch, no one cared if she took up a table, there were plenty open, and Ione wouldn't hand out section assignments for the lunch shift for at least another thirty minutes.

Kassi pulled out her notebook and stared at the blank page. She was making progress on the script but was stuck on the first sex scene. Turns out sex scenes were tough to write. What she imagined earlier on the bus was awkward and clichéd, and she wasn't even at the part in the plot that involved the actual sex, just the initial delicious fumbling.

It didn't help that it had been a very long time since she'd had sex. Nor that the last few times—when her marriage was imploding—were awful.

She decided to auto-write, without thinking, and she scribbled out the scene leading up to sex, drank the rest of her coffee and then read it. How could it be improved? Only a thousand ways, she thought. She forced herself to be specific. This was a trade, a craft, no room for ego. Does it need more detail? She decided to try to envision the scene in her mind, like watching through a peephole, so she could simply describe what she saw.

Kassi closed her eyes. She watched as the still-unnamed male character slipped his hand between the female character's legs. The female character shuddered. She looked at the male's hands. What would Clay do next?

She opened her eyes. Shit.

Ever since seeing the commercial with Crystal last week, how hot she looked sliding into that sports car, the eye contact Clay held with Kassi afterward, and then the ridiculous tumble onto the mattress yesterday, Kassi couldn't stop thinking about him. It was non-stop. Infuriatingly and wonderfully non-stop.

She knew logically that now was one hundred percent not the time for a relationship. Her life was too messy. Plus, she needed to focus on writing a winning screenplay if she ever wanted to be anything other than a waitress. She'd never make the August deadline if she fell in love.

Love? She was getting way ahead of things.

Maybe Rob was on the right track. Maybe for the first time in her life she could have sex for fun, for the shared pleasure. That might help her get through this writer's block or whatever it was keeping her from getting the sex scene right.

"Ready for a top-up?"

Kassi looked up from her notebook, startled. Roz was there with the coffee pot.

"Sure," she said, sliding her coffee mug to the edge of the table. She was still irked by what Roz said yesterday about Clay feeling sorry for her because she was a single mom, but she tried not to let it show. "Breakfast shift, huh?"

"Working a double today," Roz said, filling the cup. "The end of the month is in view, and bills come due, you know?"

Roz smiled and wandered back to a paying customer leaving Kassi to think about her own finances.

Things were tight, no question. She needed a few good shifts but had to balance that against the cost of daycare when she was working, so the shifts had to be really good. She was doing the lunch-dinner gap shift later this week, and that might help. She looked at the clock.

Twenty more minutes to write.

Well, why not put Clay in the screenplay? It almost made her laugh. What would Clay do next?

She closed her eyes and put herself back in the scene.

Clay pressed into her. She could feel his hardness, and she gasped. He locked eyes with her as he pushed his hands under her shirt and gently stroked the sides of her breasts. Is this okay? She nodded, never breaking eye contact. She trembled at his touch. He leaned down to kiss her and when he did, she circled her hands around his waist, pulling him closer and—

"Gather around, I've got section assignments," Ione shouted, interrupting her fantasy.

Kassi shook the sex out of her mind, chucked her notebook into her bag and said a little prayer she would get the adults-only back dining room in the back. It was much smaller than up front, but more intimate feeling and tips there were at least thirty percent higher, even on a slow day. Plus, only one server there, so all tables were hers. But Ione had given it to her the last two shifts, so it seemed unlikely she would get it again.

"Roz, playroom. Kristoph, front. Kassi, back dining room ..."

Kassi stopped listening. Wow. She'd be able to cover daycare this week.

Kassi got busy in the back dining room laying out the utensils, stocking the water glasses and coffee cups, pre-pouring four pitchers of ice water, perking a pot of coffee and prepping another green-label one in case she had decaf drinkers. She tied her black apron around her waist, slipped the order book into the front left pocket and checked to be sure her three pens were working. One was dry. She walked the few steps toward the kitchen—the back dining room had its own kitchen entrance—to borrow one but when she heard her name, she paused, hand on the door, listening.

Roz was talking. About her.

"Kassi is a table hog and it's not fair."

"She's the best server we've got hands down, twice as fast of any of you," Ione said. "Come up to her speed and see what happens."

"It's not only that," Roz kept on. "She lurks around the front door and poaches people into her section when Tess is seating other parties. Like some kind of vulture."

"She does do that, the vulture-thing by the front door," Kristoph said. "I mean, it's cold and a little creepy, but you gotta admire her hustle. Girl's got game. You want more tables, turn up the speed and charm. Me, I'm happy to coast."

"Still, it's irritating," Roz said, "and petty."

"Come on. She's got real shit to take care of," Clay said. "I'd be hustling too if I had that kind of responsibility."

"It's on her that she has a kid," Roz said. "Ever hear of the pill? Or Roe versus Wade?"

"I can see both sides," Meredith said. "Table hogs do suck, but she's super nice, and her daughter is so cute. But I hear you, for sure."

As Kassi backed away from the door, Tess was leading a four-top into the back room. Kassi grabbed a water pitcher and went to work. She couldn't let this bother her.

"Hello, my name is Kassi and I'll be your server today. Would you like to hear the specials?"

As she began rattling off the ingredients in each, her mind drifted. Clay had defended her. Really defended her. She realized one of the customers was saying something.

"Pardon me?"

"I asked how much the salmon salad costs and can the chef leave off the dried cranberries?"

"It's seven ninety-five, and yes, of course."

Three hours later, Kassi's apron pockets were satisfyingly heavy with tips and the lunch customers were all gone. She was setting up the back dining room for the dinner-shift server and getting ready to do her side work.

The good sections came with the worst side work. The toilets. She grabbed the gloves and supplies. Usually, it didn't take long, especially during the day when fewer people drank booze. Less chance of vomit.

Roz was in front of the entrance to the men's toilet. "Hate to be the bearer of bad news," she said, smiling like she meant the opposite, "but there's some bad shit in here, literally. One of the kids had a little issue. He barely made it. Well, he didn't make it to the actual toilet, but at least he made it into the bathroom."

Kassi looked at the door hesitantly.

"Yeah," Roz said with a fake sympathetic grin. "It's pretty rough." She left Kassi standing there and walked toward the kitchen.

Kristoph walked by holding his nose. "I'm glad you had the back dining room today."

Meredith was busy counting her tips. She looked up and shook her head in sympathy.

Kassi sighed. No problem, she thought. It wasn't that long ago I was changing poopy diapers.

She opened the bathroom door and revealed a disaster in brown. There was shit everywhere—on the wall, the sink, the door, even hand prints, like it was all some sort of toddler performance-art show—except the toilet. The stench made her gag, and she slammed the door shut and covered her mouth to keep from vomiting.

It was clear Roz sent the little pooper to use the adult bathroom to punish Kassi. There was a kid-friendly bathroom right next to the playroom and the side work for it would have gone to Roz.

Kassi wondered if maybe she should be less aggressive with the tables. But she was a mom and the consequences of not making rent were huge. That was always going to be true, and she would do anything for Samantha, including hog tables, and clean up shit.

And then an idea entered her mind and it was so awful it had to be true.

She had blown her shot at a happy life by choosing the wrong man. Totally blown it. There would never be someone like Marcus, she would never celebrate a thirty-year wedding anniversary, no one would surprise her with a trip to the coast. Because of her disastrous choice, her life was destined to be nothing but cleaning up other people's shit, being despised by people who were supposed to be her friends, and forever worrying about money.

Was her mother right? Should she go back east where a single mistake wouldn't mean the difference between eating and not? Get an office job with health insurance. Because seriously, who was she kidding thinking she could write a screenplay, much less one that might win a prize? It was a fantasy. She couldn't even write a damn sex scene. What kind of writer can't write a romantic sex scene? A person who wasn't a real writer, that's who. Or a person who had never experienced real romance. She was hopeless, a failure on all fronts and she wasn't even thirty. A broke single mom in a strange city with a mean ex, no friends and no prospects.

"I heard you might need a hand?"

She turned around. Clay was standing there with a bucket and mop.

She shook her head. "No, I'm good. I got this."

"I don't know who said it, probably one of the ancient Greeks, but you should never look a gift mop in the mouth, especially when there's poop involved."

"It's extremely smelly poop."

"Did I ever tell you I grew up on a ranch in Montana? Spent most of my childhood shoveling horse and cow shit. Killed my sense of smell early on when I was young. Not-smelling shit is my superpower."

Kassi's lip trembled and she fought back the urge to cry. She felt ridiculous. What was wrong with her? She must be getting her period.

"That's a terrible superpower," she whispered, keeping her head low so he couldn't see how pitiful she was feeling. "Thank you though. It's kind of you to offer."

They were quiet and in their silence the bustle and noise and laughter from the kitchen sounded like water rushing between them.

Then Kassi looked up at Clay, wiped her eyes and smiled. He nodded. "Let's get to it before it dries into the grout."

He rolled the industrial-sized yellow bucket toward the bathroom door, using the mop like a tiller. There was a heavy smell of bleach coming from the water. He tied a bandana over his nose and mouth to keep the bleach-shit stench at bay and offered a clean one to her so she could do the same.

"Where did you grow up?" he asked.

"Now? You want to know about my childhood now?"

"You have something else you want to chat about? Like, how bad toddler shit stinks?"

"Okay, why not? I was born and raised in Pennsylvania. A little town called Reading."

"Isn't that where John Updike is from?"

"Yes. How do you know that?"

"I read the first Rabbit book."

"Did you like it?"

"It was okay. I liked the descriptions of small-town Pennsylvania life, but the main character, Rabbit, was kind of a dick." He wrung out the mop and started swabbing the floor. "Did you go to college near there?"

Kassi nodded, using paper towels to clean the door handle. "Yeah. I got a degree in film studies from Albright College, which I'm putting to excellent use here at the Rose and Thorn."

Clay laughed. "My degree is American history from Montana State, which also armed me well for my illustrious career in restaurants."

She stopped scrubbing for a second. "Why are you helping me?"

Clay stopped too. He put the mop back into the bucket and leaned on the upright handle, considering his words.

She wondered what was going on in his brain, his expression seemed almost pained. He stared intently at her.

Finally, he flashed another quick smile. "I need to get the restaurant prepped for the dinner shift handover and I figured you would take forever." Then he grimaced. "How much poop can be in one kid?" He pulled on rubber gloves and handed her a pair.

"Trust me, a lot."

"Spoken like you have some experience," Clay said. "Tell me more about Reading."

12

INT. THE HIDEOUT BAR - NIGHT

CLAY is seated at a scuffed-up bar talking to gorgeous, flirty MEL, the bartender. The room is cramped, dark and dimly lit. SOMEONE shows up looking for love, and it's not Kassi.

"The usual?" Mel asked.

It had been a long day, including the unexpected bathroom side job with Kassi, which oddly enough had been the highlight. When they finally got the poop cleaned up, she looked at the time, thanked him profusely and high-tailed it out, apologizing repeatedly that she had to pick up her daughter before daycare closed.

Clay had waved her off cheerfully and emptied the gross mop bucket himself.

That was more than seven hours ago, a block of time that he had mostly spent thinking about Kassi. And the fact that he was willing to mop up diarrhea just to be near her.

He knew his growing attraction to Kassi was ridiculous, bordering on obsessive even. But he knew it was only a fantasy, something a shrink would probably tell him was a distraction from his own life, a bid to duck his problems. Because no way would he ever get in the way of her trying to put her family back together. Friendship it had to be, friendship was the only option. She had a daughter.

After work, to clear his head, Clay had decided it was either another late-night gym run or a drink. He flipped a coin and the drink won.

The Hideout was a classic hole-in-the-wall dive with darkened windows, tattered booths and unsteady tables for equally unsteady patrons. Rock-bottom prices, including a buck for a draft Henry Weinhard's beer, the local brew master, and five dollars for all-you-can-eat hot dogs drew a regular crowd. But the best part of The Hideout was Mel. She was tall with long blonde hair and a quick, easy smile. She wore silver and turquoise rings on every finger, including her thumbs, and her eyes could turn to ice in a heartbeat.

Mel pulled him a beer and poured a double shot of whiskey—even though she would only charge him for a single—with one ice cube, and set them on the bar in front of him.

"Not that I don't love seeing you, and your tips are always embarrassingly good, but can't you drink for free at your own restaurant?" Mel asked.

"Only beer is comped. Tonight, I need something a little harder. Plus, I like the company here better."

"I'm flattered. And if that's your way of saying you're ready to give this thing between us a try, you know I'm past ready."

"Tempting, but I don't think your husband would appreciate that much." Clay dropped a twenty on the bar. "Or your boyfriend."

"I'm my own woman. And I'm serious. We have a real connection. You have to know I'm interested. If not, I've been flirting all wrong."

He took a sip of whiskey. "Your flirting game is fine, and I do like you, but you know she did a number on me."

"Clay, honey, get your heart straight. What she did was wrong, but she did it because of who *she* is, not because of who *you* are." Mel took his hand between hers. "That's the real crime here. Only nice guys can hurt like this. Run-of-the-mill assholes would blame her and move on. You deserve a second shot at love."

"Thanks for making me feel worse," he said, smiling. He pulled his hand free and took a swig of beer.

"I should warn you, she's been coming in."

Clay set his beer down slowly. "Who's been coming in?"

"Your ex. Could be stalking you."

"When?"

"Last night. The night before." She looked at the door. "And tonight, it seems."

Clay swiveled his stool and saw Crystal in the open doorway, lit from behind by the flashing neon. She was wearing a black leather jacket, unzipped and draped half off one shoulder, over a loose white T-shirt with a deep V-neck. A pencil skirt and clunky, cherry-red punk rock boots completed the look.

"Of course, she looks gorgeous," Mel said. "She has professional makeup artists and a wardrobe budget."

Crystal walked across the scuffed floor like she was Cindy Crawford on the catwalk. Two regulars were playing darts and stopped to stare.

"You're that gal from the TV," one said.

"If it's fast, it's Fleet," she said with a wink, then blew a kiss. Crystal strode across the rest of the room and with one final hip swivel sat down next to Clay. She dramatically removed her jacket, tossing it on the stool on her other side. She wasn't wearing a bra and her breasts jiggled and swayed under the soft fabric.

The two regulars gawked some more. Crystal was done with them though and focused her attention solely on Clay.

"I'll have what he's having," Crystal said to Mel.

"One broken heart coming up," Mel said.

"Funny," Crystal said. "You should consider a second career in standup. Might make enough extra money to finally dye those roots."

"Stop it," Clay said. "Crystal, why the fuck are you here? You know this is my favorite bar."

"Duh. I wanted to see you."

"Why?"

"We had some real good times here, good memories."

Mel brought Crystal's drinks.

"You have a sudden need to trip down memory lane?" Clay asked.

"I do, actually. Like, remember that time I wore the little skirt, and no panties, and you got me off under the table in the corner booth."

"I was drunk," he mumbled.

"Gross," Mel said. "Remind me to bleach that booth. No, forget that. I'm gonna burn it."

"Oh, and the dart game we played for kisses and the winner got oral." Crystal leaned in close. "Little secret, I lost that one on purpose. I've always loved your taste. Sweet and savory."

"I need to be anywhere other than here." Mel walked to the far end of the bar.

"Seriously, what's going on?" Clay asked.

She pushed her whiskey in his direction. "Take this. You know I don't drink this stuff." She took a tiny sip of beer. "It's been a while. I'm worried about you."

"That is not why you are here. So, what is it?"

"Nothing. Everything," she said with a mock pout. "It's just, well, the sparkle is fading a little ..."

"And you thought you'd get some on the side with me?"

"Don't act so shocked. It's not like I'm leaving him.

He's a good man, a good and rich man, and those ads from his car dealership are getting me some attention. I've got auditions lined up. Real ones. But he works so much, he's never around. I thought, you know, maybe you and I could figure out an arrangement. My way of making it up to you for all the bullshit I put you through."

"Let me get this straight. You want to have an affair with the guy you cheated on and divorced because your new husband, who finances your acting career, is working too hard?" Clay asked.

"When you say it like that it sounds tacky. But yes, that's exactly right."

"If you want to make up for fucking up our marriage and my heart, how about you send a Hallmark card or make a donation to sexaholics. Don't try to sympathy-bang me."

"It's not sympathy if I enjoy it."

"You're really something."

"I get that a lot," Crystal said. "But it's true. I do feel bad. I want to make it up to you. And also, you're a really good lover. Very kind and slow, when it matters most."

Clay drained the second whiskey and stood. "You have no boundaries, Crystal, you never did, and now you're just embarrassing yourself," he said. "Don't come back here, please. Not ever. That can be your gift to me."

"I know you don't mean that, Clay," Crystal said to his departing back. Clay didn't respond, just walked out the door and kept walking.

An hour later, he was in front of his own house. He went inside and sat in the dark for fifteen minutes. Seeing Crystal rattled him more than he cared to admit. It wasn't like he wanted her anymore, but hearing her talk so casually about what happened between them, like it was some sort of game, brought back the pain.

He stood and put the kettle on. A cup of tea might help. With another shot of whiskey mixed in. Just as the tea kettle started whistling, there was a knock at the door. He turned the kettle off and crossed to the door and jerked it open.

"Crystal, I told you …"

It was Roz, wobbling unsteadily on the porch.

"Clay," she slurred. "I'm so glad you're still up. I happened to be in the neighborhood and had nowhere else to go. Surprise!"

He stared at her, confused. "How do you even know where I live?"

"I might have asked Frank once and then written it down." She stumbled halfway inside, tripping over the runner.

He caught her, wrapping his arms around her shoulders, and she looked up into his eyes longingly. "So strong," she said. "Strong and pretty. I also might have had too much to drink but I needed to make sure, I wanted to be able to…" her voice trailed off. "I thought we could have some fun together. I like you, Clay, I've always liked you. I know you think I'm cute. Frank told me that to, you know, spice things up. He liked to imagine things, and I never minded pretending it was you."

Clay sighed. What a night. He couldn't turn her away, not like this. A cabbie couldn't be trusted and he'd had too much to drink to drive her home himself. He let his arms drop and she tried to slip her hands around his neck and tiptoe up for a kiss, but he pulled back.

"Roz, you're way over your limit. Sleep this off on my couch, and we'll never mention it."

She stared blankly, trying to understand, then started drunk-crying, tears running down her face. "Why can't you love me? Is it because I'm not pretty enough?"

She pulled off her sweatshirt in one quick move and she wasn't wearing anything underneath. She stood there, her pale breasts and delicate pink nipples revealed in the dim light, her long red hair falling like a frame around them. "Don't you think I'm pretty? Don't you want me?"

Her makeup was running, twin streams of blue eyeshadow and black eyeliner dripping down her face. To Clay, she looked like a pitiful little urchin in an old Dickens movie. Or a sad, colorful raccoon.

"You're a gorgeous woman," he said, slipping his hand around her waist and pulling her all the way inside so he could close the door. He guided her toward the couch. "Lie down here, please."

After stretching out on the couch, she closed her eyes, pursed her lips and pushed out her chest. "Kiss me, Clay. Take me. Take me now. I'm yours."

He held back a laugh at the slurring drama of her words. Instead, Clay pulled a blanket over Roz. She opened her eyes, confused. "What are you doing?"

"Roz, I like you, but not like that. We're friends. I don't want this to happen, and certainly not when you're drunk."

"It might happen another time though, when I'm not drunk?"

"You're not going to remember anything about tonight. You need to go to sleep now."

"It's Kassi, isn't it? Table-hogging bitch."

"Don't call her that," Clay snapped. "You know she's a good person."

Roz was crying again. "It's true. She is good. I love her like a sister. I wish she was my sister. I miss my sister so much. Did I tell you my sister is in prison? Oh wait, nobody knows that. Shhhh," she said, putting her finger to her lips. "I promise to be nicer. I shouldn't have been so happy about all that bathroom shit. The mom offered to clean it up. I'm a terrible person. A terrible, ugly, drunk person. No wonder you don't want me." She let out a ragged sob and covered her face with her hands.

"Lift your head."

She obliged and he tucked a pillow under her head. She held his hand to her cheek. "You're so sweet and kind," she said.

By the time he returned carrying a steaming mug of chamomile with honey, she was passed out and snoring. He tucked the blanket in around her, put the cup beside her on the end table, along with a glass of water and a bottle of aspirin, and went to bed.

He turned on the TV and Hitchcock's movie *The Birds* was showing on the public television station, the scene where Tippi Hedren gets pecked nearly to death by the flock. That fits the mood, he thought.

13

INT. ROSE AND THORN RESTAURANT - DAY

KASSI brews coffee. MEREDITH is nearby.
The restaurant is not busy. NICK is
working the cash register and working
KASSI too.

Kassi was stacking clean bus tubs when Roz and Clay
arrived at the restaurant together. Clay went straight to his
locker to grab a chef's coat.

"Thanks tons for the ride," Roz said, loud enough for
everyone to hear. "You make a mean cup of coffee and
your house is so cute, even if it is a mess!" She giggled and
nudged him with her hip. "It was a perfect night, thank
you, Clay."

Clay looked embarrassed but didn't deny it. Kassi
hoped her expression didn't show her surprise. Roz looked
at Kassi triumphantly. Kassi abruptly stopped what she
was doing, leaving two tubs on the floor, and left without
a word, escaping into the dining room.

At the coffee station, she tried to settle herself down
and collect her emotions. She shook her head, trying to get
the picture of him in bed with Roz out of her mind, telling
herself she was overreacting. "It doesn't matter. Not one
bit. They're adults, free to do whatever they want. What
difference does it make?"

"What difference does what make?" Meredith asked, walking up to the coffee station.

"Was I talking to myself? Like, out loud?" Kassi asked.

"Yeah. Kind of charming, actually."

"More like a deranged bag-lady. Or that woman getting munched by birds in the Hitchcock film."

"Was she talking to herself in that movie?"

"I think so?" Kassi wasn't entirely sure, she fell asleep halfway through the movie the night before. When Roz was, apparently, at Clay's house, with a different kind of pecking going on. "She was screaming, I guess." Like Roz was probably screaming last night. Kassi tried again to shake the image from her head.

"The psychology behind why some people talk to themselves is fascinating," Meredith said, turning to make a run through the dining room with the full pot of coffee.

Kassi felt a headache coming on.

The restaurant was clearing out from the lunch rush. She'd be out the door in less than an hour, thank goodness. Kassi didn't think she could take any more of Roz flirting with Clay. Not that Kassi had any claim on him, she knew this, but somehow, she felt like he was cheating on *their* flirting. How could he clean out a shit-filled bathroom with her in the afternoon and then sleep with Roz that very same night?

Walter signaled for his check. Enough, she thought, enough of that childish reaction. She would purge them both from her mind and get back to work.

"Having a tough day, Kassi?" Walter asked as she dropped the check on his table.

Walter, the big tipper, was coming in almost every day now. He said it helped lighten his mood after selling dumbbells to gym-rats and overpriced exercise bikes to retirees with bad knees all day. He only seemed to come in when Kassi was working and always ate alone. When it was slow they talked, and she was getting to know him.

He was a boxer back in the day. By his telling, he wasn't a great boxer and lost a lot of fights, but he was a smart boxer who got some endorsements and got out early, before suffering any lasting damage. He earned enough money to franchise an exercise equipment business and it was doing well.

To Kassi, he seemed bored. He also seemed interested in her.

That kind of interest was an occupational hazard of being a server. They all talked about it, even Kristoph. The wistful looks, the notes and phone numbers left behind on napkins, the out-and-out ass pinches and taps. When something that overt happened, you could get angry, and usually the manager on duty would kick the guy out—it was always a guy—but most of the time a customer's flirting was less obvious and mostly harmless.

Still, why did so many people think servers and bartenders were fair game? She figured it was because customers knew your pay depended on your private performance for them, even if it was an unconscious response. Whenever someone added flirting into the mix of your performance appraisal, you had to play the game because a little return attention drove the tips higher, and if servers don't make tips, they don't eat. Or have money for daycare. So, Kassi flirted back.

The sad thing was that after so many years of waiting tables, flirting with customers was sort of a habit for her now, an automatic-pilot setting. Sometimes, she even initiated the game. Some guy came in, occasionally a girl, and she could see their eyes sparkle when she introduced herself. She could calculate almost to the dollar how much higher her tip would be based on how hard she twirled a strand of hair or laughed at a dumb joke or, mostly, showed an interest in their lives. Sometimes, she did want to hear their stories and felt a certain pride that she could help alleviate loneliness for a minute or two, make people feel good about themselves. She told herself it wasn't flirting-for-tips so much as it was mini-therapy.

"Kassi?"

"Sorry, what did you say?"

Walter laughed. "I wondered if you were having a tough day?"

"No, just a little distracted." She smiled. "Please don't take it personally."

She watched as he opened his wallet and slipped out a twenty, acting like he was putting the cash under the plate innocuously even though they both knew she saw it.

"Hopefully that makes your day a little better," he said, standing. "I'll pay the check at the register on my way out."

What was she supposed to say? How grateful she was? She was grateful, and Walter was a good and kind person, of course, but such interactions sometimes made her feel like a food delivery prostitute.

Okay, she was probably going overboard here, she thought. Not probably, certainly. Cue flirtation mode. Survival of the fittest and all. She needed to keep those twenties coming.

"Oh, you didn't have to do that, but it sure is kind. I'll put it toward that new typewriter I'm saving for." Kassi flashed what she hoped was a *Pretty Woman* Julia Roberts-wattage smile.

Walter was her last table. She wiped down the coffee station, restocked the glasses and napkins, and refilled the handful of salt and pepper shakers that needed it. Thankfully, today it was someone else's job to clean the bathroom. Then she went up to the register to ask Nick the manager if it was okay to clock out and sit in the back dining room to count her tips.

"You bet, but could I see you in the office first for a minute?"

"Of course," she said, following him.

It was the first time she'd been inside the manager's office. It was tiny and cramped. Wedged in the back was a small desk covered with papers, old menus and food magazines. Half of the desk was taken up by a computer and printer, similar to the type Kassi had used in her college days. A tattered swivel chair faced the door. She guessed the chair and desk were reserved for Molly.

Along the wall was a narrow table with four inboxes, one each for Nick, Ione, Tess and Clay. A single folding chair faced all four. She saw a scribbled note in Clay's inbox taped around a zucchini. It was Molly's handwriting, which they all knew well because of the incessant sticky notes she left for everyone.

Nick pulled out the single folding chair and motioned for her to sit, then he leaned against the edge of the desk.

Why had he called her into the office? Kassi assumed he was about to either lecture her for table-hogging or fire her. A lecture she could handle. Being fired would be problematic. Her mind was racing ahead to what would happen, how she would handle things. She would need to find a way to break her lease and then ask her mom for a loan so she and Samantha could fly home and move back in with her. Would she keep working on the screenplay? How would she say goodbye to Clay but since he was sleeping with Roz maybe that didn't matter anyway, plus...

Dammit. Nick said something important, and she missed it. He was looking at her expectantly. It didn't look like the face of someone who had just fired her.

"I mean ..." she said, letting her words trail off.

"You strike me as artistic, the cultured type. That's why I'm asking."

"I do?"

Nick reached into his pocket and pulled out two tickets. "It's *La Bohème*. Doomed love. *The Oregonian* called it a lovely staging. I hate going alone and it gives us a chance to dress up and have some fun. Do you like to dress up?"

"You're asking me out?"

"Not on a date. Just to the opera."

It's not like I have anything else going on, she thought, and she did love going to the theater. It was the one thing she and Barry did together regularly when they were married. In public, at the theater, she knew he would behave; it was a safe place. Plus, maybe this would inspire her on the screenplay, and take her mind off Roz and Clay together.

"I can't afford it," she said.

"I thought I made that part clear. Everything is on me. I'm an annual subscriber, so the tickets are already paid for."

"Tonight?"

"Yes, and sorry it's so last minute. I was going with a friend, but she canceled."

"Sam is with her father tonight," Kassi said, regretting instantly saying that out loud. Not having a babysitter was always a built-in excuse to say no.

"Perfect. It's settled then. Pick you up at six?"

Nick wasn't ugly. Older than her by maybe fifteen years. A little soft around the middle but a nice man. A mature man. The kind of man who would not try to manhandle waitresses who worked for him while at the opera. Granted, he had probably hired her based on her bust size but that wasn't manhandling. Eye-handling maybe, but everyone did that, right?

"Just friends?"

"Just friends," Nick said.

He gestured toward the door and she stood.

"Go ahead and clock out now," he said, as she was leaving, and it wasn't lost on her that he asked her out while she was still officially on duty.

14

INT. ROSE AND THORN RESTAURANT - SAME
DAY

KASSI counts her tips. It's quiet and
gloomy in the back dining room, and that
suits her mood just fine. Until a
certain flirt-cheating HUNK shows up.

Kassi untied her apron and sat down at a table. She pulled the loose bills from the pocket and turned the apron upside down, carefully spilling the coins onto the table. She began sorting the stack of one-dollar bills so that the George Washingtons were facing the same direction. My little soldiers, she thought, counting them out with emphatic precision.

She was so engrossed she didn't notice Clay walking up.

"Hey, Kassi," he said. She looked up and nodded. He slipped into the other side of the booth. "How was your shift today?"

"Great." She was determined to play it cool, to act like she didn't care at all about him and Roz. "In fact, so good that I can splurge on some Goodwill kitchen stuff for my new place."

She had cleared almost sixty bucks, thanks to Walter's twenty. After the tip-out to Miguel, the lunch busser, and the kitchen crew, she would walk with forty-eight dollars and some change, which still needed counting.

"Kitchen stuff?"

"Thanks to you we're not sleeping on the floor, but I still can't cook in my new place. Well, to be honest, I can't cook even with a stocked kitchen, but at least I need to be able to make boxed mac and cheese for Sam, and the occasional broiled chicken breast with frozen peas."

"I happen to be pretty good in the kitchen department."

"I've noticed." She started piling the change into dollar-equivalent stacks.

"I'm off today, I just came in to, well, it's not important why. I can give you a ride to Goodwill."

"You sure that would be okay with Roz?" Crap, that was not playing it cool.

He looked up at the ceiling and then down at his hands and she had the most horrible thought. It was true. He had slept with her. On some deep level, she realized now she had convinced herself Roz was playing some sort of game because Kassi didn't want Clay to be like that, didn't want him to be the kind of man who had sex with a rotating cast of waitresses.

She felt her neck and cheeks flushing. To think she had flirted with him in good faith! They had cleaned up toddler shit together, fell on a mattress together. Not only had he flirt-cheated on her, but he also cheated on their fantasy-potential to have something together, which in this moment almost felt like real cheating.

Shit, this is ridiculous. How can this man be making me think such crazy things? *Flirt-cheated?* That isn't even a real thing. She picked up the three stacks of bills, swept the coins into a water pitcher and slid out of the booth.

"It's none of my business," she said, embarrassed. "I never should have even said that, I'm sorry." She turned and walked toward the front counter to change the coins and one-dollar bills into bigger bills.

"It wasn't like that," he said to her retreating back. "Kassi, wait."

She paused.

"Roz was … she had too much to drink. Way too much. She showed up at my place hammered. I couldn't let her leave like that. It wasn't safe. She slept it off on my couch."

Kassi turned around, feeling a sense of relief tinged with shame for misjudging him so deeply. "Isn't Roz in AA?"

"I don't know. Is she?" he asked.

"She is, I think, but she's struggling. Tess has been trying to help."

"Now I feel shitty for ratting her out."

His handsome face was contorted into a pained expression. He hadn't slept with her. He was protecting her from ridicule, at his own expense. She walked back and stood too close to him. She touched his cheek with her palm.

"I assumed the worst and you were just being kind."

"I didn't want her to get razzed," he said, brushing his fingers across her hand as it rested on his cheek. "I'm not into her, not at all, and I need to tell her that tonight."

"Tonight?" she asked, lowering her hand. Her breath was coming faster. She felt as if gravity was pulling them closer together.

"Roz left her wallet at my place and needs to come by to pick it up." He was looking deep into her eyes.

"That's the oldest trick in the book," Kassi said with a slow smile.

"Trick?"

"If you want to avoid things getting messy, tell her you won't be home tonight, that you'll bring her wallet in tomorrow. She'll magically find it in her purse." She pushed a strand of hair away from her face. "Now, how about that ride to Goodwill?"

Less than a half-hour later Kassi was rummaging her way through a bargain-basement box in the kitchen section of the largest Goodwill in Portland.

"Look!" She held up a cast iron frying pan. "Only two bucks! And what are you doing over there just watching? I thought you were here to help." She didn't wait for an answer, just dove back in and within a few minutes had a stock pot, a colander, two saucepans and a crepe pan piled up in her cart.

"You know how to make crepes?" Clay asked.

"Spinach crepes with cheese sauce. Oddly, it's the only thing I know how to make for real. Mom taught me when I was a kid from some article she read in *Good Housekeeping* when Julia Child was all the rage."

"Your mom sounds cool," he said, evaluating the pans in her basket. He pulled out the stock pot and pointed to its pitted base. "Get rid of this one, not worth the price."

"It shall be done," she said, setting it back in the bargain box. "Next up, napkins and glasses."

"Get them from the restaurant. We go through them like water through a sieve. Won't be missed."

"If you had suggested that before I had a kid I would have agreed, but now I need to be a good example, even when she's not around. That means no stealing." She grinned. "Being upstanding all the time is exhausting."

"Understood. Speaking of Sam, okay if I buy her a toy?"

"Maybe a book? That is if there are any good ones here, it's always a crapshoot," she said, but then her gaze slipped away. He followed her eyes. She was looking at an old typewriter.

She pulled her notebook from her pack and ripped off a blank page as she covered the few yards between her and the typewriter and then rolled in the sheet, pecking at the keys. "Wow, it's in great shape, and has extra ribbons." She typed *Fasten your seatbelts.*

He looked over her shoulder and then reached past her and typed out with two fingers *It's going to be a bumpy night.*

"*All About Eve*," she said.

"One of my favorites. I watched it the other night."

"Me too!"

"You should buy the typewriter."

"Too rich for my blood."

He started to say something and she stopped him. "Don't you dare. I've asked too much of you already. I don't need it. I don't want it."

Even though, she thought, I do need it and I do want it.

"Everybody is moving to computers now anyway," he said. "These old machines will be worthless soon enough."

"A computer would be great, or even a little Dell word processor would do, but both are out of my budget this month," she said. "After the kitchen is outfitted, I'll figure that part out next."

He nodded. "Makes sense."

"I saw a computer in the office today at the restaurant. What do they use it for?" she asked.

"Mostly inventory and printing out the daily menu, since the specials change so often. I imagine someday it will be linked to tickets, but Molly is resistant."

"Why?"

"She thinks computers will get in the way of personal connections."

"She's probably not too far off, at least if science fiction writers have it right," Kassi said. "They've been warning about computers taking over for years."

"Speaking of books, I'm going to check out the kid's books. Meet you up front in a few minutes?"

"Sounds good. I'll grab some glasses. They won't match, but who needs matching glassware? The cluttered thrift store look is the latest trend in home-décor."

At the counter, Clay caught a clerk's attention. "There's an old typewriter back there I'd like to put on hold. Can you keep it quiet though? I want to surprise my friend. I'll be back later today. Name's Clay." The clerk scribbled *Hold for Clay* on a paper scrap and headed back to the typewriter.

Just then, Kassi walked up to the check-out, lining her treasures up on the counter, watching carefully as the register clerk—a young woman with purple hair—rang them up. She was so focused on the transaction she didn't notice there was no book for Sam.

"That will be twelve-fifty," the clerk said.

"The cast iron was on sale," Kassi said. "It had a green tag. And the crepe pan."

The woman looked at the two tags. "You're right, sorry about that. Make that ten-fifty."

They trundled the bags to his truck while Kassi bragged about her Goodwill score, proud of how frugally she was able to live.

As they pulled out of the lot, Clay offered to pick up Sam from daycare and take them both home. Kassi was grateful, she was already running late.

They drove across town, chatting idly, each feeling a sense of elation at being with the other but neither willing, or able, to admit why they were laughing so hard about how many favorite movies they had in common and why the air smelled so sweet and why their simultaneous spotting of a young hawk on a telephone wire seemed like a private miracle.

Clay pulled the truck into the community center parking lot and let it idle while Kassi went inside to get Sam. When they returned, Kassi boosted Sam into the spot between them and locked the seat belt in place.

"Hi, Cooker," Sam said.

"Hey, kiddo," Clay said, easing the truck onto Bertha Boulevard, and then driving down the road to the freeway entrance. On Route I-5, Kassi smiled as car after car whizzed by because Clay was driving way under the speed limit.

"You drive slower than my grandma," Kassi said after the driver of a yellow sports car honked and gave him the finger.

"I've got extra-special cargo," he said, not speeding up even a little bit.

"I do feel very safe at this speed," Kassi said. She felt a rush of warmth for his protective instincts. "Sam, tell us what was your favorite thing that happened at school today?"

For the remainder of the slow ride home, Sam's nearly nonstop chatter about the two chinchillas at daycare and how they weren't very good at leapfrog—they always seemed to get stuck—kept them both laughing and easily able to ignore the slew of irritated drivers.

When they were a mile or so from the new apartment, Clay stopped at a yellow light and turned to Kassi. "Maybe we could, you know, have dinner? The three of us I mean. I could whip you up something with your new cookware."

"Oh, that would be fun, wouldn't it Sam, and—" Kassi stopped talking and sighed. "I'm sorry, we can't tonight."

How could she have forgotten it was Barry's night with Sam, and that she told Nick she would go to the opera with him? That seemed like a million years ago. Why the hell had she said yes to Nick?

"Why can't we Mommy? I want waffles and whipped cream and Cooker makes them yummy. Please, Mommy?"

"We can't," she said. "Some other time."

"We have to listen to your Mom," Clay said, a forced lightness in his voice. Despite his kindness, she could tell by his expression that the rejection stung. He pulled up to the apartment and parked.

Barry, a tall man—about the same height as Clay but with a runner's thin build—with dark hair wearing a gray suit and mirrored aviator sunglasses, leaned against a classic BMW, casually evaluating Clay's beaten pick-up.

"Daddy!" Sam yelled. Kassi slipped Sam out of the seatbelt and helped her out of the truck. Sam ran over to her father. He scooped her up, twirled her around and they walked together toward the apartment. Clay got out and handed Kassi her shopping bag full of pans.

"I forgot he was coming over tonight," she said quietly. "I'm sorry."

"No worries. I completely understand. Enjoy your evening."

As he drove off, Kassi hoped he would ask her to dinner again and hoped even more that he didn't think she was having dinner with Barry. But maybe she deserved that based on how she spent her entire day certain he was sleeping with Roz. And was it any better than what she was really doing—going to the opera with Nick?

15

EXT. PORTLAND STREET - NIGHT

The evening is clear and mild. KASSI
waits in front of the apartment for
NICK. She's dolled up for a night at the
opera, still regretting her decision.
(Pro tip: Never date the boss, unless
he's the hot chef).

"You look amazing," Nick said.

She was standing outside the apartment in her one good
dress, a long, elegant form-fitting number in rich royal
blue. Perfect for weddings, funerals and now nights at the
opera. She had ironed her hair mostly straight, which
would last maybe an hour given the forecast of rain, and
was wearing makeup; not much and not artfully applied,
but enough to look mid-level glam, at least in comparison
to her resting state.

"You're sweet," she said.

Nick wore a charcoal gray suit with a lime-green shirt
and a dark-green tie with a gold tie-tack. It transformed
him, hiding his soft belly and compensating, a little, for
their age difference and his receding hair line.

"You look good in a suit," she said.

He fussed with the wide lapel. "This old thing? Thanks.
Truthfully, it's one thing I miss about New York. Always

something to do, some reason to dress up. New Yorkers take fashion seriously."

"I'm not too into fashion, and don't dress up often, as I imagine is fairly obvious."

"That fits right into the Portland scene. It's the land of flannel and jeans for everyone, even Big Foot."

"Big Foot?"

"No one's told you about Big Foot yet?"

She shook her head.

"Suffice it to say people out here think there's some half-man, half-beast thriving in the old-growth forests of the Cascade mountains, a legendary creature retaining its wild nature that has eluded all attempts to capture it."

"Like the missing link?"

"More like wishful thinking."

She shrugged and then raised the hem of her dress to show her footwear—Chuck Taylor high-tops. "I hope you don't mind. My good shoes have a broken heel."

He laughed and seemed genuinely pleased. "Perfect for Portland *or* New York. You pull it off well." He extended his arm. "Shall we go?"

She let him guide her to his car, a brand new 1995 fire-hydrant-red Chrysler LeBaron convertible with the top up. He held the door for her, then closed it and walked around to the driver's side. She noticed a mobile car phone, a rectangular boxy thing with an antenna, wedged in below the console. That was sort of cool, she thought. Kassi had only seen them in movies and on TV shows.

He slipped into the seat and when he started the engine, soft jazz was playing.

"Are you familiar with *La Boheme*?" he asked, turning the music down.

"No. I'm not an opera fan. I've been to one or two in Philadelphia, but I prefer live theater."

"I hope I can change your mind tonight," he said, steering away from the curb into traffic. "This is my fourth *La Bohème*. I'm excited to hear the soprano playing Mimi. She's world-class."

"I didn't know you were from New York," Kassi said, making conversation and watching the neighborhoods change, getting denser with more shops and people, as they got closer to downtown.

She wasn't thinking about New York, she was thinking about Samantha with her father. Whenever Sam was with him, Kassi's anxiety went up.

Nick was saying something and she forced herself to listen.

"... and I was the general manager there for several years, but then our chef opened her own restaurant and the partners brought in someone new. His vision didn't match up with what our clientele wanted, too radical, so they had to reorganize. Long story short, I decided to try something different. I've been in Portland ever since."

She wondered how much she'd missed. "How did you end up at the Rose and Thorn?" she asked, hoping that wasn't part of what he'd already covered.

"That's a good question. Let's grab a quick drink and a bite and I'll tell you all about it. Then you can tell me your story."

He parked in the public garage and they walked to a high-end steakhouse near the theater.

Nick had reservations for the bar and had pre-ordered their meal. Over red wine and wedge salads drenched in blue cheese dressing, he told her about trying to find a job in a local gourmet restaurant, but that the food scene in Portland was stodgy and limited to variations of vegetable sides to complement cedar-plank roasted wild salmon.

She tried to listen but kept thinking about Samantha.

And Clay. It was unfortunate, she thought, because Nick was being very gentlemanly, asking questions and keeping the conversation going even when she let her attention wander, which was often.

After a half-hour or so, they had covered his career, his roots in New York, her academic trajectory, her roots in Pennsylvania, his romantic life, including an amicable divorce from his wife who returned to the East Coast, saying Portland was too culturally homogeneous to bear, and she knew with tired certainty it wouldn't be long before he steered the conversation to her romantic situation.

As if on cue he said, "So tell me about your husband."

"Soon to be ex," she said. "We've been separated for more than a year now."

"Sorry, that must be hard. Did you move to Portland to be with him?"

"Not exactly," she said, dragging a wedge of lettuce through the dressing. "I moved here so Samantha, our daughter, could be with him. He got a dream job coaching tennis at Portland State. I didn't have much going on back home, so it seemed like the least I could do."

"That's kind of you."

"Just trying to minimize the suffering Samantha has to go through. I mean, I guess the childish part of me thought he might change and that we could reconcile, for her sake, but—"

Kassi had a flash of Barry, his face twisted by anger, screaming at her for some imagined slight the day after they arrived, while Sam was asleep in the back seat of the car. He had stopped yelling the instant Sam stirred, thankfully. He hadn't behaved that way in front of Sam yet, and she often wondered if it was a good thing or a bad thing that he could control his rage and chose not to do so with Kassi.

"—that's not going to happen. It's for the best."

She took a bite and a splash of creamy dressing landed on her chest. "Shit," she said, looking down at the stain already forming.

"Let me help," Nick said. "I have a better angle." He dipped a napkin into his water glass and began swiping softly at the stain, holding her arm with his other hand for leverage.

She watched the scene unfold like a screenwriter observing from above as he swabbed at the top of her breast. It was surreal, and at the same time she was thinking she would work this into the script.

He sat back and smiled. "There, barely noticeable."

She nodded and used a dry napkin to dab at the wet spot. "Thanks, I can take it from here."

He took her hand. "I'm enjoying our night together. I hope you won't think me too forward if I say I'd like to consider moving this into the actual date category. No pressure of course, but we seem to be having fun and I think we have quite a bit in common."

Kassi was glad she had an easy out. "I appreciate that. I am having fun but I *am* still married."

"That doesn't bother me. I have a good feeling about this, about us." He checked his watch before signaling for the bartender. "We should get going. Think about it, okay? Maybe, if you enjoy the opera, we could have a night cap at my place. I have an exceptional wine cellar. We can have a nice glass of pinot and explore this energy between us more fully." He threw his American Express on the check.

Kassi weighed what to do. She should immediately say she wasn't interested in him that way, and if it was anyone else, she would. She would be direct. Now it was all messed up. He could make her job harder. Or fire her.

She should have never put herself in this position. She impulsively said yes to Nick earlier because she thought

Clay had slept with Roz, and anyway, Nick promised it was just a friends-thing. She had known deep down that wasn't likely true, yet she willingly agreed to go on this opera date just so she could do something grown-up, be an adult for one night. And, if she was honest, to punish Clay.

Now she would spend the entire opera dreading the conversation at the end, rehearsing ways to get out of it without hurting his ego too badly. Otherwise, she might be banished to tip purgatory. Or worse. Losing her job would be a disaster.

They walked the few blocks to the auditorium. She was silent and he kept up a one-sided patter about wine and Northwest grapes and terroir.

Her anxiety was sidetracked by the crowd gathering in the Keller Auditorium grand lobby, a large neo-gothic building draped out in Italian colors for the event. Many of the patrons were recognizably Portland old money—couples in their sixties and seventies wearing furs over designer gowns or stiff suits and wielding rubber-tipped canes. They were drinking martinis.

Others were Portland new money—younger men, also in suits, but looser versions, with open collars; the women wore satiny barely-there dresses along with a dozen or more versions of Princess Diana's revenge dress, tight off-the-shoulder black numbers. They drank champagne in flutes or straight whiskey.

After that came the Portland no-money group, people who lucked into tickets or splurged for a fancy event. The majority were dressed either in department store knockoffs of the wealthy patrons or jeans and flannel shirts, but some were having fun with it, going all out in theatrical costumes, with tutus, capes and extravagant makeup that reminded Kassi—in a good way—of Cyndi Lauper. They drank beer or sipped surreptitiously from smuggled-in flasks.

"Great people watching, isn't it?" Nick asked.

She nodded.

"I'll grab drinks. They have a special Negroni for tonight's performance."

Kassi had promised Samantha she would call to say goodnight and wished now she had thought to ask to use Nick's car phone. That would have been fun to tell Sam she was calling her from a car.

"I need to quick call Sam. By intermission she'll be asleep. Do you know if they have pay phones?"

"Second floor. I'll meet you there," Nick said.

She took the stairs, fished a quarter out of her clutch and dialed Barry's number.

A woman answered. "Hello?"

"Uh, hello. Is Barry there?"

"No, sorry, he's out."

"Is Samantha there?"

"Yes. Who's calling?"

"Her mother," Kassi said.

"Oh, of course," the woman said.

"Who are you?"

"Stella. I'm Barry's girlfriend. He's working tonight. Tennis championships."

"Can you put Samantha on, please?"

There was a long silence, then Sam picked up the phone. "Hi, Mommy."

"Hi, baby. How long has Daddy been gone?"

"I don't know. A long time. He dropped me off and went away to work. Stella and I are having fun. We're eating pizza and playing horsies."

Nick walked up with their drinks and smiled at Kassi, then read the tension in her shoulders.

"Was Stella there when your dad brought you to his house earlier?"

"Yes."

"Do you know when your dad will be home?" Kassi asked.

"Um, after bedtime maybe?"

"My plans were canceled at the last minute, so I'm going to come get you and we'll go home."

Nick looked at her, confused.

"See you in a few minutes," she said, and hung up.

She turned to Nick. "I'm sorry. I need to go. Something came up with Sam."

"I can drive you."

"No, stay. Enjoy the opera. Tell me later how the tenor was."

"Soprano."

"Right, soprano."

"Are you sure?" he asked.

"Yes, totally sure. You've been looking forward to this for a long time. I'm sorry I complicated things." She took the drink from his hand and drained it. "Thanks. I needed that. I'll catch a cab and see you at work tomorrow."

She turned before he could answer and made her way down the steps two at a time. He stood there, watching her leave, a drink in one hand, an empty glass in the other.

Kassi hailed a cab and pulled up in front of Barry's place fourteen minutes later.

"Wait here," she said to the cabbie, and then walked up to the door and rang the buzzer. A woman answered. She was a few years younger than Kassi with a quick smile, wearing a PSU tennis team sweatshirt. "Can I help you?"

"I'm Kassi, Sam's mother. Could you please get her ready?"

"Oh, uh, I mean ... are you sure? I got a hold of Barry after you called, and he should be here any minute."

"Stella, is it?"

Stella nodded.

"No offense, because you seem nice, but Barry and I have an agreement and this violates it."

"Whatever," Stella said, walking back inside and leaving the door open. "Sam, your mom's here."

"Mommy, can we stay a little longer?" Sam called from inside. "We're in the middle of a game."

"Sorry, honey, it's time to go," Kassi said.

A few minutes later, Samantha came to the door in her jacket, holding a backpack full of toy horses.

"Hi, Mommy. You look pretty."

"Thanks, baby. Let's go."

"Sorry about all this," Stella said, "but we were fine."

Kassi looked at her but didn't respond. They probably were fine but that wasn't the point. Barry pulled up in his BMW, flashed the lights and honked the horn.

Kassi walked to the cab and put Samantha inside. "Wait here, honey."

She closed the cab door and stood in front of it as Barry rushed up, dressed in his tennis coaching whites and a PSU pullover, a far cry from the suit he had been wearing not more than two hours ago when he picked up Sam.

"What do you think you're doing?" he snarled.

"Taking Samantha home."

"The hell you are. She's with me tonight."

"No, she's with your girlfriend. Our deal is that you are with her on your days, or she's with me. You can't just dump her with a stranger. That is literally in the separation agreement."

The deal existed because she knew Barry would leave Sam with a babysitter just to keep her from being with Kassi, as some sort of warped punishment. He was that angry at Kassi, and his anger had been steadily growing since the first day they were married.

It was as if once he had her, he gave himself permission to be a different person. And then over the years, some sort of transference happened; whoever or whatever childhood trauma had caused this dysfunction in him was now her fault too, because he hated himself when he raged and needed to blame someone. Kassi was that someone. After she left him, no punishment was enough. He convinced himself that Sam would always be better off in his realm, no matter what. That's why there could be no backing down on the babysitter issue. He would push it as far as he could. This had to be her red line.

"She's not a stranger, you psycho."

"Stranger or girlfriend or babysitter, it doesn't matter," Kassi said. "If it's not you, then you have to let me know, and I saw you just two hours ago. You didn't say anything, even though you knew you wouldn't be home. I always get first priority and if I can't be with her, then and only then can you put her with a babysitter or your girlfriend or whoever, as long as it's safe. That's our deal, and you broke it."

"Get out of the way." He grabbed her elbow and gave her a body-shove.

She held tight onto the cab door handle and stood her ground.

"Are you going to push me down?" Kassi whispered. "In front of our daughter, your girlfriend, all your neighbors? Is that what you want? Get ahold of yourself, Barry. You know I'm right."

"You're a fucking psycho and have no right to do this." His voice crackled with anger, but he kept it low enough so only she could hear. "I won't forget this."

"Tell me you understand why, and that you won't do it again. Talk to me like a normal person, Barry. It's the only way we can make this co-parenting work."

"You will never tell me what to do," he said. Then he pivoted and stormed back toward his house.

She got into the cab and tried to stop her hands from shaking. Should she have let Sam stay? Had she overreacted? Everything in this situation was insane, and she hoped she was doing the right thing but was never sure. How could she be?

"Were you and Daddy fighting?" Samantha whispered.

"We just had a little mix-up," Kassi said, pulling her into a hug.

"You got someplace safe to go?" the cabbie asked.

"We'll be fine. Thanks." She gave him her address and after he dropped them off, he waited until she got inside before pulling away.

Still in her fancy dress, Kassi got Samantha ready for bed, read her a story and tucked her in. In the living room, she turned on the TV and found an old movie. *Plan 9 from Outer Space.* She turned it down low for background noise, poured herself a glass of wine, sat down at the kitchen table and began to write.

A love scene.

In the scene, the restaurant was closed and the main characters were alone, drinking beers and flirting. Her character challenged him to an arm-wrestling match as an excuse to hold his hand. He let her win, then didn't let go. Instead, he cupped his other hand around hers and pulled her closer and they kissed slowly, tentatively across the table. The kiss deepened and he pulled her to the floor.

She scratched it out. Too clichéd. Would never happen. Plus, the floors in a restaurant are gross. Who would ever kiss around all that gunk and germs?

Kassi took another sip of wine and suddenly, without warning or reason, all the stress and uncertainty of the night, of her life since moving to Portland, of the years living with Barry, slipped past the walls she kept up, the walls she needed to survive, to protect Sam.

She felt tears running down her cheeks. Was it possible to feel any more alone?

Nearly as fast as the walls slipped down, they went back up. Kassi pushed the sadness away and re-read the scene. Maybe they should do it on top of the bar. Cleaner and better angles. She jotted the idea down, then got up and checked on Sam. Her little girl was sleeping peacefully. Kassi slipped into the bathroom to brush her teeth.

16

INT. ROSE AND THORN KITCHEN – DAY

CLAY works the breakfast shift. The line
is chaotic. KASSI slices lemons. She's
bad with a knife. There's blood. Call a
MEDIC!

The next day, Kassi had put the incident with Barry mostly
out of her mind, but she was fighting an emotional
hangover. It wasn't a good day to be distracted because the
restaurant was unexpectedly packed.

"Did everyone in fucking Portland decide to fucking eat
breakfast at this restaurant today?" Clay asked, flipping a
pair of omelets in sequence.

She wasn't the only one unhappy about being at work
this morning, Kassi thought, as she frantically sliced a
lemon on the salad prep counter.

Clay wasn't supposed to be on shift today. He rarely
worked breakfast, but everyone knew Ione had called Clay
for the early shift after the new guy poured too much oil
on the grill, then pushed the brick too hard and too fast
and sizzling oil splashed up from the back and rained down
on his arms. They ran cold water over his forearms, but it
was too late. The skin sloughed off in sheets. Kassi was so
glad she missed that. Molly had to drive him to the hospital.

"Anybody seen Kassi?" Clay yelled. "Her food's getting

cold." He pointed at the pancakes with a side of scrambled eggs wilting under the heat lamp.

"I keep ringing her," Rob said, slamming the bell again. "Kassi, order up!"

"I'm right fucking here," she yelled back. "I have to get some lemon wedges to a table full of fucking pissed-off iced tea drinkers before they lose their shit."

Clay smiled. "That's the first time I think I've heard you curse like you mean it."

He stooped down to look at her as he slid the omelets onto plates. "Be careful though. The way you're holding that knife you could easily—"

"Shit!" The blade slipped off the thick fruit rind and sliced deep into her finger.

The knife clattered to the floor as she clamped her hand around her wounded finger.

"Rob, take over for me," Clay said, dropping the pans on the sideboard by the grill. "Roz run those pancakes to table six."

"But I—" Roz started to say.

"Just do it," Clay snapped. "Dave-two, slice a lemon, put it in a boat and take it out to the iced-tea drinkers."

"Which table?" Dave-two asked.

"The one with all the fucking iced-tea drinkers looking longingly at the guy with the lemons."

He came around to the counter and stood in front of Kassi. "How bad is it?"

"I don't know," she said, opening her fist. Blood welled up between her fingers and pooled onto her open palm. "Pretty bad, it seems."

"Let's go back to the first aid kit and take a closer look. I don't think you'll need stitches, but if so, I can run you to the emergency room. You can say hi to the new guy."

"What about my tables?"

"Someone will cover. Tell Ione," he barked at Rob.

She let him guide her toward a storage area in the back of the kitchen. He was holding her hands lightly with one hand, the other on her shoulder leading her away from the cutting board and lemon halves now splattered with blood.

"I'll be fine," she said, but she felt wobbly, like her brain was weaving drunkenly between extremes. "I can manage this."

"I know you can," Clay said, "but is it okay if I help a little?"

"I guess so," she whispered. "I think it's pretty deep." She looked back at the trail of blood droplets behind her.

Clay pointed at the chair next to the employee lockers. She sat down. "Don't worry. I was a medic in Vietnam. I'll get you patched up."

She nodded and then looked at him curiously. "Wait, what? You're too young to have been in Vietnam."

"Just trying to calm you down a little," he said with a smile.

"By lying about serving in a war?"

"We're talking about that instead of your finger, right?"

He pulled a couple of paper towels loose from the dispenser by the sink and held his hand under hers. "Let's take a quick look." He squeezed her shoulder with his other hand. "I'm not a medic, but I have been around a lot of kitchen cuts, so I'm pretty good at this. Trust me?"

"Yes," she said.

"Good, but maybe don't look directly at it. Sometimes the sight of your own blood can mess up your head."

"I did give birth." She opened her fist and they saw the cut gaping deep into the side of her finger and blood oozing out of it. "Shit, is that bone?"

"No," he said, pressing the paper towels around her finger, "but it's a bleeder, this one. How about you focus on something else while I take a closer look."

"Like what?"

"I don't know. Anything really."

"Your face?" she asked.

"If that works, sure," he said.

He moved her hand over to the sink and ran the water until it was warm. She stared intently at his face while he focused on the wound. He had a very strong jawline. His skin was soft-looking, even with his day-old stubble. He had unusually long eyelashes for a man.

"I'm going to just get a little soap in there. It will burn a bit. You okay?"

She nodded as Clay let warm water stream into the cut, and then lathered up the soap, using his fingertip to gently work it into the cut. She felt a flash of burning pain but it was mostly offset by the strangely sensual intimacy of the moment. She continued staring at his face. She wondered what it would be like to kiss him.

He rinsed her finger with cold water and blotted it dry with a clean paper towel.

"Hold that a second," he said, wrapping the paper around her finger.

He opened the first aid kit and left the hinged lid extended to use as a shelf as he located the gauze, first aid tape and antibacterial cream. "When I say go, you move the paper and I'll put some ointment on the cut so it won't get infected. Then I'll put some gauze on it, a little tape and you'll be all fixed up," he said.

"I'm ready," she said.

"Go."

She moved the bloody paper towel, and he trailed some ointment into the cut—the bleeding had mostly stopped— then wrapped her finger in clean, white gauze and secured it with tape.

"Too tight?" he asked, still holding her hand.

She shook her head no. "You're good at this. Maybe you should have been a medic. It's not too late to get out of the restaurant business."

"I'm working on a different escape plan."

"Really? What?"

"A mobile food truck."

"A mobile food what?"

"Truck. I'll tell you about it some other time. I should be getting back to the line."

"I'm getting a divorce," Kassi blurted out.

"I ... okay," he said.

"I don't know why I told you that," she said. "I just, I want you to know I'm getting a divorce. We've been separated more than a year. Sam's dad is, well, he's not easy. And my life will probably get worse, and I ... but I didn't want you to think ... I don't know. When you saw him last night, he was picking up Sam. Nothing else."

"Okay," he repeated.

"I don't want you to get the wrong idea. Because I like you. As a friend, I mean," she said, then winced. *A friend?*

He was still holding her hand and looking into her eyes so deeply that to Kassi it felt like he was searching for something important in the depths of them. The energy between them was almost unbearable.

"I'm divorced, you know that, I think, but Crystal is coming around again," he said. "She hurt me pretty bad. I was, maybe still am, a train wreck. I was blindsided. I shouldn't have been. She was always out of my league."

"Trust me, you aren't out of any league, you are in a league of your own," Kassi said. She laid her free hand on his forearm and squeezed.

"It messed me up. I'm not sure I have it in me to trust again." His voice was thick with emotion.

She felt dizzy and winded. "I get that. I really get that," Kassi said. "I guess we're both card-carrying members of the walking wounded. But we're going to be okay. Both of us. We're going to heal. We're going to have better lives someday." She squeezed his arm again. "Maybe even find love again."

"You sound like you know what you're talking about," he whispered.

"I do," Kassi said. "I'm a psychiatrist and I trained under Sigmund Freud."

He laughed.

Roz poked her head around the corner. "If you two are done holding hands, we need Kassi back on the floor."

Kassi moved her hand from his arm and Clay let go of her other hand.

"Also, your rich guy is asking for you," Roz said. "He won't sit in any other section. He's obviously into you. Good chance for a single mom." Roz turned back into the kitchen.

Clay and Kassi stood, and looked at each other awkwardly, embarrassed by the intensity of the last few minutes.

"Thanks for patching me up, doc," she said at last, raising her bandaged finger into a quick salute. "I better get back to the front lines. The sliced finger may force me to take more trips than usual between table and kitchen, but I'll manage."

Clay nodded and reached for his chef's coat. "Next time the restaurant is slow, I'll show you how to use a knife without putting any more fingers at risk."

"You wouldn't mind?"

"Not at all," he said as she turned away. "What are friends for?"

17

INT. DANTE'S DANCE CLUB ON BURNSIDE
STREET - NIGHT

The place is packed, the music is loud,
the air is heavy with cigarette smoke
and the throbbing possibility of sex.
CLAY and ROZ talk. And dance. And?

"I can't believe you said yes," Roz said.

They were at Dante's for a show. One of Clay's favorite bands—the Low Budget Bastards, a country rock outfit from Austin—was playing and Roz just *happened* to have two tickets.

"Hard to say no to the Bastards," Clay said.

The place was mobbed, and the house music was cranked, warming up the crowd before the opening act. Clay and Roz were standing near the stage.

"I had no idea you liked them so much," she yelled. "I wanted to make it up to you for the other night, showing up all drunk at your house. This is my peace offering."

Roz wore tight jeans and a flannel shirt tied off high so that it emphasized her pierced belly button, and with enough open buttons up top to reveal a low-cut, silky pink half-camisole underneath. She was turning a lot of heads.

"Whatcha thinking about?" Roz yelled over the music.

Clay was thinking about the interaction with Kassi the

day before, feeling confused. Kassi had plainly told him she was getting a divorce and that he should not give up on love, and that she liked him but only as a friend. Still, that weird and precious moment between them felt like more than friends.

Until that moment yesterday sitting by the sink littered with bloody paper towels and holding her hand, he'd told himself he could never come between a woman trying to save her marriage and family. It gave him the safety of an impermeable barrier between his thoughts and his actions. He could fantasize about Kassi all he wanted, but nothing could ever happen.

Now that barrier was down.

"Hey, you there! What's on your mind?" Roz asked again, poking him gently on the arm.

"Nothing," he said, trying to refocus. "Not thinking about anything. Sorry, I'm a little spaced out tonight."

"Should I get us some drinks?" Roz asked.

"You know the deal. You have to stop."

"I can have one," she said with a mock pout.

"And I can go home," he said.

"Fine. But just because I'm dry doesn't mean you have to be."

He shook his head. "I don't need booze to have fun."

"You need something," she said airily, trying to make a point. She put her arm around his waist and pulled him into her body.

She smelled rich and mysterious, and he caught himself leaning close to breathe in the scent of her hair and look down the front of her shirt at the tops of her breasts straining the camisole.

Roz hooked her finger into the belt loop of his jeans to keep him close.

"This is fun," she said. "We should do more stuff like

this. As friends, I mean."

"Nights are kind of tough for me."

"Clubs stay open late, past the dinner shift," Roz said. "We could go dancing. Or just hang out. Listen to music. Watch movies."

"I like movies," he said loudly over the din. "What's a good one you've seen recently?"

"I rented *Even Cowgirls Get the Blues* last weekend. Keanu Reeves is cool, and Uma Thurman, like wow. Have you seen it?"

"I heard it was shot here in Oregon. The director, Gus Van Sant, lives in Portland, up in the West Hills."

"Really?" Roz seemed surprised by the news of a Hollywood celebrity living in Portland. "Imagine if he came into the restaurant. I would die. And if he brought Keanu with him? I would die twice."

"If he does, you have to tell him Kassi is working on a screenplay. Did you know that?"

"Yes. Everyone knows that. It is an inescapable fact of the Rose and Thorn. You know, I write too. Poetry. Maybe you'd like to read some?" Roz said, the irritation barely suppressed in her voice.

"Okay, sure, but I don't know much about poetry," Clay said.

"Maybe I'll teach you. You didn't answer my question. Have you seen *Even Cowgirls Get the Blues*?"

"No, I tend to watch older movies."

"Like what?"

He thought about it. "I watched *Nightmare Alley* the other night."

"That sounds scary," she said, hugging him closer, returning to flirty mode. "What's it about?"

"A conman, madness, addictions, a traveling freak show, murder. Mostly doomed love."

"I'll pass on that. Hey, the opening band is coming on."

"I'll get us something to drink," he said. He returned shortly with soda and bitters, each with a wedge of lime. A table against the wall opened up and they grabbed it, sipping their drinks as the local band, a grunge-inspired hard-rocking foursome, got the crowd revved up.

They were near the speakers and with the live music, it was too loud to talk, even shout-talk, and he spent most of his time thinking about Kassi and pretending to watch people dance as Roz watched him.

When the Low Budget Bastards finally took the stage more than an hour later, it was late, and he was tired and restless. The band started off with their biggest single to date, a rousing rock anthem called "Not Drunk Enough Yet."

"Come on," Roz said. "Let's dance!"

She grabbed him by the hand and pulled him onto the packed dance floor before he could say no.

It was impossible not to move to the song. The room was hot, the energy was high. He slid his hand around her waist, and they swayed together, slowly grinding. She was flushed and looked happy, a sheen of sweat glistening on her forehead. The lights were flashing, the bass was thumping. Roz slipped her hands around his neck. He had his eyes closed, enjoying the feel of a woman in his arms, lost in the music.

She pulled him in tighter. He was growing hard as their hips pressed together and she leaned up and kissed him softly. He started to kiss back, pressing his lips against hers hungrily as instinct took over. He grabbed her bottom and pulled her into him, lost in the pleasurable feeling of blind sexual contact.

"I want you," Roz whispered. "I want this so bad."

In his head, it was Kassi he was kissing and when he

heard Roz's voice the fantasy crumbled. His eyes flew open and he pulled back.

"Roz, I'm sorry. I don't know what came over me."

"What?" she said, confused. "Sorry? Why sorry? I want this. I want you. I've always wanted you."

"This isn't happening. I told you, I'm not interested in a relationship."

"Let's just fuck then," she said, unwilling to let him go. "It doesn't have to be a big deal. Just hot sex between friends. If it's great, even if it's just okay, maybe we do it again. It's not like we're getting married or anything."

He shook his head. "I can't."

"Clay, I felt your hard cock pressing into me, you want this. Let yourself have some fun. Let yourself come. You won't regret it, I promise."

He turned away. "I need to go. Let me give you a ride."

Roz shook her head, frustration turning to anger. "No, I want to stay."

Clay caught her by the shoulders. "Listen to me. Don't do anything stupid. You're beautiful, smart and kind, but I can't do this with you. I can't do this with anybody."

"Pretty sure that's a lie," she said.

"What the hell does that mean?" He steered her toward the back of the club, away from the crowd.

"Nothing, forget it," she said, but then the sting of his rejection got the better of her. "Seriously, you can't let your past ruin your future. We all go through shit. Crystal fucked you over, so what? Frank fucked me over. And then I did the same to him. I'm still trying. I haven't given up, I haven't given in. I haven't let myself become nothing more than a walking heartache. You should try it. You're a good guy, you deserve love. Or at least you deserve sex. And silly me, I want to be the one to give it to you."

He hugged her, then stepped back.

"Roz, we're friends, and because of that, I need to be honest with you. You're gorgeous and if this was about sex, we never would have left my place tonight. But I need more than sex, and I can't be disappointed again. It would destroy me."

"You can't possibly be serious about her," Roz said.

"Who?"

"Okay, if we're talking like friends, let me tell you something honest. How can you get involved with someone who has a kid and is going through a divorce? If, by some miracle, you're more to her than a rebound relationship, do you know how hard it is to raise someone else's kid? You're worried about being disappointed? That situation has disappointment written all over it in big blinking neon lights."

"I never said I was interested in Kassi."

"You don't have to say it. It's visible from outer space."

"Please, let me drive you home," Clay said, feeling as if the walls were closing in. "I don't want to leave you here by yourself."

Roz looked at him for a good ten seconds, at his pathetic hang-dog expression, and then being the pragmatist she was, made her peace with the inevitable. She stood on tiptoes to kiss his cheek. "You go ahead. I want to stay."

He felt bad about leaving her there, but not bad enough to stay. He headed for the exit as Roz pushed up to the bar.

His emotions inflamed, Clay slammed the door behind him when he got home fifteen minutes later. He poured a double whiskey and sat down in the dark. He turned on the TV and searched for an old movie. He found one he'd seen before. *Gun Crazy*. About a gun freak who falls for a carnival trick shooter and their violent, dysfunctional relationship.

"Perfect," he muttered, thinking about holding Kassi's hand as her blood dripped onto his open palm.

***

Across town, Kassi had the same movie on in the background. She was staring at the blank page in her notebook. She was distracted by thoughts of Clay and reliving the first aid incident too.

I don't want you to get the wrong idea. Because I like you. As a friend, I mean.

She smacked her forehead. "Friend? Why the hell did I say that?" she asked out loud. "I'm such an idiot."

She knew he was out with Roz tonight. Roz made that abundantly clear to everyone at work. Kassi knew she had practically pushed Clay into Roz's arms. He had been keeping Roz at arm's length for weeks, even when she showed up at his house, and then in fifteen seconds, Kassi basically gave him the green light. There was no way Roz would let a hot, sweaty concert slip by without pressing herself all over him. Clay was only human and Roz was attractive. Not, Crystal-level attractive, but not far off.

As a friend? Every cell in her body wanted more from him, his arms around her, his lips on hers, his skin against hers, his hard cock inside her. Shit. She was getting steamed up thinking about him, about him holding her hand and taking care of her.

"Vietnam medic," she said quietly. "What was that all about? That's for sure going in the script."

She shook her head. It didn't matter anyway. Best to be realistic. Her life was way too complicated. Clay deserved better, and even Roz was probably better than what she could offer. Kassi needed to focus on Sam and on the divorce. Her only job now was to be a good mom.

And to finish the screenplay.

And to pay the bills.

She poured herself another glass of cheap chardonnay and dropped her pen, reaching over to turn up the television slightly.

"We go together, Annie," the lead actor said. "I don't know why …"

"… maybe like guns and ammunition go together," Kassi whispered.

18

INT. ROSE AND THORN KITCHEN - DAY

CLAY and GILROY are talking. Sexual
secrets are revealed. The dining room is
besieged by a jovial death cult.

"How was the date last night?" Gilroy asked. He was chopping garlic. It seemed like he was always chopping garlic. Angel made him shower and scrub the second he stepped into her place, and it was still never enough.

Clay saw Kassi look up from slicing lemons, her finger still bandaged and the knife now held safely.

"It wasn't a date," Clay said.

"Sorry," Gilroy said. "Then, how was the show?"

"I didn't, uh …" He didn't want to admit he left Roz there.

Just then, Roz walked in from the dining room. "The show was great but I am so tired. We danced all night. Didn't get to sleep until like four this morning. I mean, I guess we weren't really sleeping," she added, with her characteristic giggle. "I even wrote a poem about it."

Clay watched as Kassi quietly set the knife down, picked up the dish of lemons and walked out front.

"We did not do any of those things," Clay said.

"I didn't mean with you." Roz turned to Gilroy. "Clay left me there, but luckily, I met someone nice. His name is

139

Marble. He's in a band."

"His name is Marble?" Gilroy asked.

"He's the lead singer for the Marble Coffins."

Gilroy stroked his straggly mustache with one hand. "Coffins aren't made from marble. Headstones, maybe. Coffins are usually wood."

"Ironic, right? He's cute and fun and into me. I'm going to see them play tonight. Clay, can we chat someplace private for a second?"

Clay nodded toward the walk-in cooler, the only private place in the kitchen. She followed him in.

"Listen," he said, once the door closed, "I'm sorry about last night."

"Don't be." The cold air was making her nipples stiffen under the thin fabric of her T-shirt and she zipped up her sweatshirt. "I want to tell you something. I'm crazy about you. Always have been. I've tried everything, including getting undressed in front of you, but last night I got the message, loud and clear. You don't feel the same way. Maybe someday you will."

He shifted uncomfortably.

"Until then, I'm going to have some fun. This guy, Marble, it won't last. I'll leave him in a second if you want to give us a go. But he's fun and he doesn't drink, at least not much, and he's got a big ..." She let her voice trail off and smiled. "He's good in bed."

"I'm happy for you."

The door opened and Dave-two took a faltering step inside, then stopped.

"What?" Clay asked, glaring at him.

"I need some zukes?"

Clay handed him a bag of zucchinis. "Close the door."

When he was gone, Roz continued. "You have a thing for Kassi. I get why. She's cute and damaged, birds of a feather. Like I said last night, she has a kid. Do you want to saddle yourself with that kind of responsibility? Do you have any idea how complicated that's gonna get? She has a baby with someone else. That's forever."

"I don't have a thing for her, not like that."

"I know you're scared to try again, and maybe that's why you're falling for someone so ludicrously unattainable. Anything with her is doomed to fail. But who knows, maybe you need a practice run. No matter what, I'll always be right here when you're ready."

She leaned up and kissed him on the cheek just as the door opened.

It was Kassi, searching for more lemons. She shut the door and stepped back.

Inside, Roz laughed and pushed the door open. "Don't worry," she said to Kassi. "It's not what you think."

"I don't think anything," Kassi said.

"Good, because I was just telling Clay it's over. I met someone last night, after Clay abandoned me at the club. Someone who isn't all twisted up on the inside."

She brushed past Kassi. Clay stood there awkwardly, his breath coming out in frosty clouds.

"Would you mind handing me a lemon?" Kassi took the lemon from his hand and thanked him. "Sounds like you had a complicated night."

Clay brushed his hand through his hair, feeling self-conscious, and uncertain what to say. Kassi dropped the lemon in the pocket of her apron and returned to the dining room before he could figure out a response.

"Was that as awkward as I imagine?" Gilroy asked as Clay left the walk-in and picked up his knife to continue prep work.

Gilroy had moved on from garlic to mincing parsley.

"You're an asshole," Clay said.

"You wound me," Gilroy said. "You didn't even get to hear the Bastards play?"

"Their first song," Clay said. He began to julienne red peppers.

They heard whistling from the back. Rob was clocking in.

"Hey guys," Rob said, tying his white chef's apron on as he walked in. "How's it going?" Before they could answer, he kept talking. "Me? Glad you asked. Turns out my girlfriend, the love of my life, is using me for research on her thesis about deviant sexual behavior." He paused. There was an awkward silence as they stared back at him.

"Girlfriend?" Clay asked.

"Yeah, girlfriend. Meredith," Rob said. "Didn't you hear what I said?"

"I'm shocked."

"Thank you," Rob said, pulling a knife off the magnetic rack.

"I thought you were the one who said relationships were for suckers or whatever?"

"Yeah," Gilroy said. "Mister 'I could never limit myself to one girl' says he has a girlfriend? A girlfriend. Truly shocking."

"I meant the sexual deviant part," Rob said.

"Oh, that? No, that lines up for me," Clay said.

"Totally," Gilroy said. "She seems normal. We all kind of wondered why Meredith would be into you at all, but as a research subject that makes sense."

"I feel humiliated by it," Rob said, looking at the prep list on the whiteboard.

"Don't you, kind of, you know, get off on humiliation?" Gilroy asked.

"Under carefully controlled sexual situations, sure. Guys, it's like you don't even know me at all. This isn't sexual, this is … clinical. She's treating me like a guinea pig or something."

"I don't think most scientists get intimate with their lab rats," Clay said.

"We should ask her," Gilroy said. "Is Meredith working today?"

"I hope not, because I am not talking to her." Rob began to chop onions for a red enchilada sauce.

Roz came in and read off a ticket—a pastrami, a grilled cheese and a kid's alfredo—then hung it.

"Hey, Rob," she said. "Or should I say, Patient X?"

Rob's shoulders slumped. "Great, everybody knows," he muttered.

"There are no secrets in a restaurant," Gilroy said. "Plenty of innuendoes and gossip and half lies and full lies, of course, but no secrets."

Kassi came in with a pair of tickets. "Hi, Rob," she said. "I think it's so brave of you to be part of a research study. I hope Meredith finds a cure."

"I do not need this," he said, putting on his Walkman headphones and blasting the music.

***

An hour later, the lunch rush ended with a thud before it ever got rolling. It was gloomy and raining outside. There was one customer left in the dining room, an elderly woman by herself, and the wait staff was wandering around cleaning things or hanging out in the kitchen. Meredith was staying mostly out front in the dining room to avoid Rob. Clay was staying in the kitchen to avoid Roz.

Ione came on, took one look around and then gathered up the servers. "Listen up. It's slow. I'm sending two of you home. One of you can cover until the night shift arrives. I'll help out if needed. Any volunteers?"

"I'd love to get out early," Meredith said. "I've got some work to do on my thesis."

"Fine. How about you two?"

"I'm fine either way," Kassi said, cognizant of her table-hog reputation.

"You can stay," Roz said. "I know single moms are always scraping by. And I have a date tonight."

"Thanks, I guess," Kassi said, ignoring the passive-aggressive swipe.

"I'll be in the office if you need me," Ione said.

The lone remaining customer stood and using a cane walked slowly to the register to pay her bill. She was wearing threadbare clothes that were out of style thirty years ago and carrying a battered leather satchel stuffed with newspapers and clippings and tattered papers.

She started to count out change for a cup of coffee and a cinnamon roll, carefully stacking up pennies and nickels.

"I forgot to mention this when I took your order. We're having a special on rolls today. Free with a cup of coffee," Kassi said to her.

The old woman smiled. "Oh, that's lovely news, dear. I have to get to the office. I have an important account to work on, but I'll come back soon and give you a big tip."

"I look forward to seeing you again after your business deals slow down."

Kassi swept the change into the community tip jar—this week, it was raising money for a dishwasher whose bike was stolen—and then crumpled the ticket and ripped out the duplicate page.

This was shaping up to be a crappy tip day. Kassi was running through her mental expense list, and the numbers were not adding up in her favor. The story of her life.

"I saw that," Clay said. With Roz gone, he was able to

stop hiding out in the kitchen.

"That poor thing," Kassi said. "She tries so hard to look like she's still working. I think she lives in the shelter over on Sandy Boulevard."

"You're nice," he said. "Listen, I'm sorry about all that stuff with Roz. Somehow I gave her the wrong signal."

"Can't blame a girl for trying."

"I think that's probably all over now."

"I doubt that," Kassi said.

"Geez, I hope so," he said. He affected an old-fashioned voice. "I've been kicked around all my life, and from now on ..."

"... I'm gonna start kicking back," Kassi finished. "Did you really watch *Gun Crazy* last night?"

"Most of it. I love that movie."

"Me too!"

"Speaking of old movies, did you see *The Furies* is playing at Cinema 21?"

"The Western with Barbara Stanwyck?"

He nodded.

"I haven't seen it but it's high on my list."

The door swung open and a rain-drenched man peered inside. "Are you open?" he asked.

"You bet," Kassi called from the back of the dining room.

"For a quite large party? We're obnoxious, but we're big tippers."

She looked around the empty restaurant, then at Clay, who shrugged his shoulders. "Sure, we can handle it."

Ten minutes later, thirty-two undertakers in town for a convention were racking up a huge bill on food, drinks and desserts. Kassi and Ione were running nonstop, keeping wine and beer glasses full and laughing at the raucous fun, including ricocheting undertaker jokes.

"Nothing lasts forever," one said.

"Unless you're assisted by an excellent embalmer," another finished.

Peals of laughter filled the restaurant.

"Why didn't the funeral director go to the funeral?" another shouted.

"He wasn't a mourning person!" someone yelled.

When they finally headed out, they left Kassi a three-hundred-dollar tip and a half-dozen business cards from funeral parlors with hand-written phone numbers scribbled on the back.

Feeling high from the rush of adrenaline and the wad of cash in her pocket, she walked through the kitchen to grab her coat. Clay was standing by the time clock looking at the schedule.

"I just hauled in some serious cash. Want to go see a movie?" Kassi asked.

19

EXT. MOVIE THEATER – NIGHT

The marquee lights flash but seem dim in comparison to the joy lighting up CLAY and KASSI'S faces.

The air was cool outside Cinema 21 in Northwest Portland as the sun drifted toward the horizon. The smell of a recent rain hung on the breeze swirling down from the West Hills. A small crowd milled around the theater entrance, trying—like Kassi and Clay—to choose which film to see.

"Sorry *The Furies* isn't showing anymore, not sure how I messed that up," Clay said.

"Doesn't matter," Kassi said. "I'm excited to be out and seeing any movie."

With you, she added in her head.

Sam was with Barry for the night. It wasn't the normal schedule but it was his birthday, so it only felt fair. Not that he would return the favor.

"Do we go for doomed love and beautiful scenery in Montana or dysfunctional obsession and blood-sucking monsters?" Clay asked, moving his hands like a scale weighing the choices. "I'm leaning toward—"

"Vampires?" Kassi said. "Definitely."

"*Interview with the Vampire*? Really? I never would have figured you as a vampire fan."

"Correction. I'm a Brad Pitt fan. The question is, do I want to see him as a cowboy in *Legends of the Fall* or as a seductive, undead lover?" she asked.

"You're telling me the real draw here is Mr. Pitt?"

"Obviously." She squinched up her eyes and a furrow appeared between her brows as she examined his face. "Has anyone ever told you that you look like Brad Pitt?"

"Sure, all the time. My face is made for the movies," he said, striking a pose, hands on hips, chin jutting out. "It's just that I love cooking way too much to move to Hollywood."

She laughed. "Given that my financial windfall is due to a bunch of over-tipping drunk undertakers, vampires seem like the way to go."

"Might be gory."

"But it's not real, not real blood, it's all fake."

"We're in luck. Starts in ten minutes."

"Come on," she said, grabbing him by the sleeve. "We don't want to miss the previews. That's the best part."

At the window, she paid for two tickets. Clay tried to give her money, but she insisted it was her treat, reminding him that the undertakers tipped her three hundred bucks, and while she certainly did provide great service—*"don't I always?"*—it was only fair she make it up to him for getting all those orders cooked and plated so quickly.

She felt one flicker of regret when she got the change from her purchase, knowing she should be saving every single penny for the daycare bill due next week. Just this one time, she told herself, no guilt. She made a solemn vow to go right back to being a frugal, stressed-out mom first thing in the morning.

"Fine," Clay said. "But you got the tickets, so I get the popcorn."

"Extra butter and a Dr. Pepper."

"Deal."

A leathery faced man with a plastic flower tucked behind his ear panhandled for change as he played doorman, waving them inside the classic old theater with a deep bow. "Blessings unto you," he said when Clay dropped a quarter in his paper cup.

After loading up on goodies, they walked into the dimly lit theater and Kassi made a beeline to the front row. "Is this okay with you? I can't stand having anyone in front of me at the movies. You're tall, so you don't notice, but for me, it's hard to see around people's heads."

"Works for me," he said.

"Do you like the front row?"

"Not really. But I'm willing to sustain a minor neck injury for a free movie with a friend."

"Right, a friend," she repeated.

They sat in the plush velvet seats, the arms unevenly worn down to the wood, and when the theater darkened, the curtain swooshed opened and the first preview came on, they simultaneously tilted their heads back. He held the popcorn bucket, she held the Dr. Pepper, and they switched back and forth, their heads following the action on the screen like synchronized swimmers.

"Did you just sigh?" he whispered when Brad Pitt made an appearance on the *Legends of the Fall* preview. "Like a sigh of longing?"

"I did not sigh," she said, elbowing him. A few kernels popped out of his hand and rolled onto the floor. "I was thinking of the casting for my own screenplay, and he could seriously play the main lead."

The hot chef character based on you, she thought.

Finally, the titles scrolled for *Interview with a Vampire*. Kassi snuggled down into her seat. She wanted to hold his hand and lay her head on his shoulder but didn't dare after she had set the ground rules of them being just friends.

"How's your finger?" he whispered.

She grinned in the darkness, the lights of the film flickering across her face like starlight. He was thinking about her hand too.

"Healing quickly, due to the excellent emergency care I received from my personal medic," she whispered back.

Two hours later, the theater lights flared back to life.

"Wow," Kassi said. "That was something."

"Yeah, no shit, that was a crazy film," he said.

"I'm a little stunned, to be honest. What a story."

They moved along with the crowd until they were outside the theater, now being shooed away by the pretend doorman to make room for the next showing. "I need to talk about that movie, dissect it and stuff," she said. "What did that all mean? Did the reporter become a vampire at the end? Why do I feel so sad about Claudia's death? Wasn't she already dead? Do you want to grab a drink somewhere?"

"Absolutely. I know a place a couple of blocks away. A real dive, but in a good way."

"I love dive bars."

They chatted about the film on the short walk to Nob Hill Tavern, retracing the plot, discussing what worked and what didn't, both agreeing that to their surprise, Tom Cruise was unexpectedly believable as a vampire, and deciding which parts of the plot seemed implausible.

"Implausible," Kassi said with a laugh. "It's an amazing feat of writing and acting that we're critiquing a vampire film for being implausible, as if vampires themselves are plausible. They don't exist."

"Pretty sure they do," Clay said. "That movie has me convinced. Brad Pitt should play a cowboy-vampire next time. *Legends of the Vampire*."

He opened the door to the bar. The place was mostly empty. A Johnny Cash song spilled out of a battered jukebox, beer signs and country music memorabilia covered the walls. Cigarette smoke hung in a translucent blue layer just below the ceiling.

They grabbed a corner booth. Clay went to the bar and brought back two draft beers and two shots of whiskey. He wouldn't let her pay for the drinks and, after a few attempts, Kassi relented. They sipped for a bit without talking, the mix of nervousness and joy keeping them on edge.

"A film like that is daunting," Kassi said, breaking the silence.

"How so?"

"How can I write something like that?"

"You can't," he said. "You won't."

She looked at him curiously. "Thanks for the vote of confidence," she said with a laugh.

He shook his head. "I mean, you won't write something like *that*. You'll come up with your own story and put your own stamp on it, your own experiences."

"I heard Anne Rice wrote the novel because she was grieving the death of her young daughter, and the little vampire girl in the story was her way of letting her daughter live forever."

"Or finally letting her go," Clay said, sipping his whiskey. "As sad as that is, it illustrates my point. You'll write something that reflects your life."

"Like at the restaurant," she said.

"Is your script about the restaurant?"

She paused before answering, not wanting to make things awkward, to seem like she was observing everything just to write about it.

"It's a love story set in a restaurant," she finally said.

"Our restaurant?"

"More or less."

"Main characters?"

"A waitress and a chef."

He leaned back, grinning slyly. "I can't wait to see how it turns out."

"I'm not very far along. I'm still working out the big picture parts, building the three-act structure. I haven't done too much else yet, at least not much that I like."

"Three-act structure?"

"Girl meets boy, girl loses boy, girl gets boy back."

"Oh, got it. Are they always in three acts like that?"

"Most of them. There are variations, of course, could be boy meets girl, or boy meets boy, but it still usually falls into three definable sections."

"The boy meets girl part means boy falls for girl?" Clay asked. "You said your script is a love story, after all."

"Exactly. Oh, I forgot one part. The false ending."

"What's that?"

"Somewhere in the third act it seems like the bad stuff, like the boy losing girl, will be resolved, but it's fake. The viewer gets all happy and then, bam, they're crushed when it all goes to hell." She drained her beer.

"A bait and switch, so to speak," he said. "Every good movie has one."

"Yep."

"The last part of the third act is about resolving the false ending?"

"Right."

He nodded at the bartender for another round. "Does there always have to be a false ending?" he asked. "Sounds painful."

"Not if there's some other way to introduce tension to the plot at that point. Because you have to have tension."

"Which act are you working on now?"

"Still the first one," she said, "and I'm running out of time."

"Does the boy get the girl in the end?" he asked.

"Or maybe the girl gets the boy. It is the nineties after all."

"Of course. My bad. I meant is it a happy ending, this restaurant romance?"

Kassi wondered if there was a deeper level of meaning hinted at in his question.

"I haven't figured out the ending," she said. She could feel her neck getting hot and it wouldn't be long before it would spread to her cheeks.

"I hope they can make it work. I like happy endings."

Before she could respond, the bartender interrupted them with the second round of beers and whiskeys. She was rail-thin with red hair braided tight and wearing what Kassi was now convinced was some sort of Portland uniform—a plaid flannel shirt over jeans.

"Hillary, thanks for bringing them to the table. This is Kassi," he said, tilting his head in her direction. "We work together."

"Dammit," Hillary said. "I was hoping you were on an actual date. I worry about you, Clay."

There was a crash as someone by the door stumbled over a chair on the way outside to smoke. "Settle down, Roy," Hillary yelled and hurried off.

"Here's to friends," Clay said, and they clinked shot glasses and downed the whiskey in one go.

The booze was going to her head, and she knew her face must be hot pink by now.

He pushed his beer away. "I'd better switch to water since I'm driving."

"Lucky me, I don't have to drive," she said, reaching for

his beer. "Tell me your favorite thing about cooking."

"Is this for the script?"

"It's for me."

"I like the creativity, the artistry. I love how every ingredient has a part to play."

"Like parts in a movie," she said.

"Exactly, and the parts come in all shapes and sizes, also like in the movies. Recipes have a few starring roles, usually the proteins, and then vegetables or grains are the supporting actors, and the spices, they're sort of like the light and shadow of the cinematography."

"No wonder we get along."

"It's cool that my form of art nourishes people, like it literally helps them live."

"I love talking to you," she whispered. "You're so, I don't know, smart and uncomplicated. It's like you live closer to the cosmic consciousness than the rest of us."

"The cosmic what?"

"You know, universal wisdom and stuff."

He smiled. "I'll take that as a compliment."

"You should. Also, I might be officially tipsy."

She put her hand near his on the table so their fingertips were brushing ever so slightly. He moved his hand on top of hers and she pulled hers back quickly, as if burned by his touch.

"Oh, I'm sorry," he said. "I misread the moment ..."

Kassi looked at him feeling a mixture of wonder and lust. "There were sparks," she said. "Actual sparks."

She put both hands back on the table and he reached out and covered them with his own. Her breath quickened and she could feel her heart rate getting faster. She spread her fingers and entwined them with his.

"I should drive you home," he said, his voice cracking. "We both have early shifts."

She nodded, but then half stood and leaned across the table to kiss him. At first, it was light and tender, their lips barely touching. Their eyes closed simultaneously, trying to freeze the moment and focus only on the sensations—the taste, the warmth, the feel of their lips pressed together. Then he raised one hand and brushed his fingertips through her hair and then held the back of her neck as he kissed her harder. Her mouth opened, yielding to his, and she felt her pulse thudding in her ears.

"Oh, Clay," she whispered, pulling away. "That was, I don't know what that was …"

"Just work together, huh?" Hillary was standing next to their table, smiling. "You want something else to drink or the check so you can get a room?"

"We'll pay up," he said, handing Hilary a twenty.

"I don't know why I did that," Kassi said.

"Was it bad?"

She shook her head. "I didn't want to stop."

He looked at her for a long heartbeat. "Does it have to?" Then he seemed to catch himself. "Kassi, sorry, that was too much, I'm not trying to pressure you."

"You're sorry you let me kiss you?" she asked, his awkwardness spreading to her.

"No. No way. No. I'm sorry I kissed you back so, you know, so enthusiastically. This wasn't supposed to be a date. We're supposed to be friends. I feel terrible."

"Do you really?"

"No," he said, smiling. "I feel fucking amazing. You?"

She nodded again.

"What's your schedule like the next few days?"

"I have the long lunch shift tomorrow and then the employee appreciation event."

He groaned. "Do we have to go to that?"

"I think so, yeah. I mean, aren't you kind of in charge

of cooking for it?"

"What about the next night after that?"

"Sam won't be with her dad for another four nights."

"Okay, let's get together then, four nights from now."

"You won't have to work?"

"I'll get it off. LuRon will cover."

"You sure?" she asked.

"One hundred percent."

As they walked out into the night, she slipped her arm through his and leaned her head on his shoulder, marveling at how natural and comfortable it felt.

20

INT. ROSE AND THORN RESTAURANT - DAY

KASSI'S wealthy customer, WALTER, makes
his case. Do charades and cheesecake
count as foreplay?

Walter was finishing a late lunch and watching the staff set
up the restaurant, a mixture of curiosity and envy on his
face.

"Why are you closing early?" he asked.

"An employee appreciation event," Kassi said. It was
slow, and she was leaning over the back of the chair across
from Walter to chat and he was having his own employee
appreciation event looking down the gap in her loose
blouse.

"That sounds nice," he said.

"I hear it is," Kassi said, straightening up when she
realized the depth of the show she was inadvertently
putting on. "Molly does this twice a year. Free food and
drinks, and the pooled value of the tokens she gives us for
games and contests all goes to an employee assistance fund.
A former employee is going through medical bankruptcy,
so we're trying to raise cash for her."

"What employers do that?" he asked. "I sure don't."

"She's pretty great," Kassi said. "I mean, she's kind of
an odd-ball, but in a good way. Yells a lot and pulls her hair

out sometimes, staples whole zucchinis to people's paychecks and believes computers will usher in the apocalypse."

He arched an eyebrow.

"I know, weird, but she's got a good heart and this whole restaurant exists to build community and create a safe space for people facing real hardships in the world."

"You've got a good heart, too," he said. "I like that about you."

"Gosh, I rambled on there."

"Not at all." He fished out his wallet and handed her two one-hundred-dollar bills. "One's for lunch, and keep the change. The other is to help with the medical bankruptcy."

"Walter, let me ask you something," Kassi said, as he stood. "Why do you tip so much?"

"I thought it was obvious," he said with a smile. "Because I can and because I like you."

"Like, *like* me?"

He put a hand on the back of his chair. "I'd be lying if I said I didn't find you attractive, and kind and smart, but I'm in no rush. I'm fine with things the way they are if that's how it goes. But I'd be fine if it went in a different direction too."

"You're sweet. I like you too."

She hated to say what else needed to be said out loud, knowing the tips might dry up, but the evolving situation with Clay required it. She was still replaying the kiss from last night in her mind, and she could not lead this man on, nor could she do that to Clay.

"I'm not looking for anything romantic, I want to be clear on that," she said.

"I'm patient. Maybe someday we'll think about doing something outside the restaurant, you'll let me spoil you a little. Or not. I just like having a connection with someone like you." He smiled again. "I hope you have fun tonight." He left with a little wave.

Tess was sitting by herself at a booth working on the schedule and Kassi sat down across from her. "Okay to join you?"

Tess nodded. "You seem to have hit it off with Walter," she said.

"Yeah, he's nice. And quiet. And rich." Kassi slid one of the hundreds across the table. "He left this for tonight."

Tess took a sip of herbal tea. "I heard what you said about Molly. That was kind. You get it. Not everybody does."

"What do you mean?"

"Some of the people who work here are pretty ... damaged, I guess is the right word."

"You mean like me?" Kassi asked.

"No, not you. I don't think so, anyway. There's a difference between bent and broken. You'll snap back, but that's not the case for some of our colleagues. They're past the point of return. They're so used to being victimized, or scared, they don't recognize it when someone is in their corner."

"Like Molly."

"Yeah. Did you know she's a lawyer and a damn good one?"

Kassi shook her head.

"That's her real job. She's won some major cases about sexual discrimination and gay rights, and takes on clients big and small, doesn't care if they can pay. Right now, she's working with a group of undocumented immigrants, going with them to hearings, giving them jobs here so they can get work permits," Tess said.

"I had no idea," Kassi said.

"To be blunt, doesn't need this restaurant. She keeps it going because she wants a safe place for women and others who are regularly, casually victimized by society. And she wants to do something positive for the community. What's better than giving people good, healthy and reasonably priced food, jobs and a safe space?"

"I'm not sure that Hungarian mushroom soup counts as healthy," Kassi said. "I've seen them make it."

Tess laughed. "Fair enough, but mostly."

"How do you know so much about her?"

"She represented me when I was going through my own tough time, when I needed to be emancipated from my father. Long, ugly story. She helped turn my life around. I've been here ever since," Tess said. "She's trying to help Roz now too."

"Roz?"

"Her sister was convicted on a charge of eco-terrorism, it was all over the news a while ago, before you moved to Portland."

"Eco-terrorism?"

"Yeah, she firebombed an SUV dealership. Well, somebody did. She denies it. Molly told Roz she'd look into it, see if there was enough evidence to call for a new trial. Just between us, I think this sister stuff is what caused Roz to fall off the wagon."

"Wow, I had no idea. She never talks about it," Kassi said, suddenly realizing she didn't know Roz at all.

"That's just for your knowledge. I probably should have kept it to myself," Tess said. "If Roz wants to talk about it with you, she will."

"My lips are sealed."

"On another topic, I wanted to let you know that Nick quit," Tess said.

"Why?"

"Because he would have been fired. Turns out he was overly interested in our female employees and their body parts. Did some really inappropriate stuff."

"It was just a date to see the opera," Kassi said. "Nothing happened."

"You too?" Tess asked, shaking her head. "Geez, that makes seven waitresses. We're running a help-wanted ad this week in the newspaper for his replacement. This time, Molly wants to include the staff in the decision. Are you willing to help with that?"

"Sure, absolutely."

Tess returned her attention to the schedule. Kassi stood and drifted into the kitchen.

She was surprised to hear that Nick had asked out so many servers in the restaurant, but she was more surprised to learn what Roz was going through. Kassi didn't have any siblings but she could still imagine how worried she would be if one was in prison. She wasn't sure it excused Roz's mean-spirited behavior, but maybe it made it a little more understandable.

It was Clay's day off and the kitchen was much less interesting without him, but he would be getting here soon. He was cooking for the employee event. Kassi wandered past the grill, ignoring the chatter and noise, to the back area near the lockers by the first aid kit. Sitting quietly, she again replayed their kiss from the bar last night, savoring every sensation, his taste, his lips, the tender strength of his hand cradling her neck. Then she pulled out her notebook and began to write.

An hour later, at four o'clock, she helped Tess usher out the rest of the lagging customers and flipped the cardboard sign to *closed*. Tess scribbled a note and taped it to the door: "Closed for employee appreciation event."

As Tess pushed together a bunch of tables, Kassi and

Meredith moved the rest out of the way so there was just one long conjoined table in the middle of the dining room. Clay showed up shortly after. He pushed through the swinging door and smiled at Kassi, raising his hand in a shy, hopeful wave. She returned the wave, then looked down to keep from blushing.

He backed into the kitchen, almost knocking over Dave-two who was bringing out plastic containers of dressing for the salad bar.

Clay started making pizzas. There were three kinds: cheese, sausage and vegan, the latter drizzled with a tofu cream sauce that approximated cheese. Dave-one was putting together a family-style bowl of tossed salad and Gilroy was making pasta with tomato sauce and parmesan.

Counting a few guests, twenty-eight people showed up. Molly kicked things off with a little speech.

"I want to thank you all for being part of the Rose and Thorn," Molly said, reading from carefully printed notecards. "This is a special community, and we couldn't do what we do without you. I'm thankful you work here. All of you. Except Russell, who seriously needs to stop drinking."

Russell laughed. "It's iced tea," he said, pointing to his glass.

"Don't lie, Russell. I see you," Molly said. "Get help." She refocused her attention. "As for our guest of honor, Lynne, we're here for you. I'm sorry I can't provide health care benefits to everyone, but it's too expensive. I don't know why this country makes it so hard to get health care. I am hopeful our elected officials will change that soon, but in the meantime, here's hoping the money we raise tonight can make a difference in your life."

Lynne, who was pale and weak, smiled and nodded. The staff raised their glasses and whooped and hollered.

"After you eat, there will be dessert. I had real New York cheesecakes flown in," Molly said.

That brought more cheers. Clay, Gilroy and Dave-two started bringing out the food, eliciting another round of cheers.

"It gets better," Molly said. "I'm leaving. You don't need your boss sitting around while you have fun. Ione, lock up when you're done and put whatever we raise in the safe."

Ione nodded and Molly left to more good-hearted cheering.

After the family-style meal and a few rounds of beer and wine, it was time for games. Charades was the first order of business and people started teaming up.

"I insist you two pair up," Kristoph said, putting his arms around Kassi and Clay. "For charades, I mean."

"The rules are easy," Ione said. "To play, you have to donate ten tokens each. Then, each team has a minute to guess as many answers as they can and the pair with the most correct answers wins a cheesecake. All tokens go into the fund. The game topic is movies."

Roz and Dave-two were up first, and they got three right. Rob and Meredith got two. One of them was *Psycho* but Rob kept answering *Caligula* to everything else. Luckily, one correct answer was in fact *Caligula*. Four other pairs took their turns before LuRon and Gilroy got zero and almost came to blows.

Clay and Kassi were up last. Clay drew first and read the clue, then pinched his fingers together and pretended to take a drag and hold it.

"Joint," Kassi said.

He nodded and tipped his hand like he was drinking.

"Gin joint. *Casablanca.*"

He nodded and handed the bag over. She reached in for

her clue, smiled and clicked her heels together.

"*Wizard of Oz?*"

"That's right." She passed the bag back to him.

He read the card, thought for a second, then signaled four letters. He sneered and punched at the air.

"Uh, the singer, Billy Idol?"

He motioned for her to keep going. "Eyes Without a Face. Rebel Yell."

He nodded.

"Wait, *Rebel Without a Cause.*"

"Yes," he said, pumping his fist.

There was widespread groaning, Roz loudest of all. "You two are cheating," Roz said, realizing they were about to pass what she and Dave-two had scored.

"We are not," Kassi said.

"They just make a good pair," Kristoph said.

Kassi pulled a title from the bag and bent low and began snapping her fingers close to her waist.

"The, uh, Jets and Sharks," Clay said. "*West Side Story.*"

"This is quickly becoming not-fun," Roz said.

Clay read his next title and then pretended to pull on a hat with a visor, operate an adding machine and count out money.

"Bank, accountant," she said.

He pushed his collar up like he was cold and looked heavenward.

"*It's a Wonderful Life,*" Kassi said.

Her turn. She read the clue and grimaced.

She started pantomiming walking up a lot of steps.

"I don't know," Clay said.

"Ten seconds," Kristoph said.

She pretended to lean on a rail and look down, then wobbled unsteadily.

"*Vertigo,*" he said.

She shook her head.

"Five seconds."

She looked longingly into his eyes and held her hands over her heart.

"*An Affair to Remember*," he said.

"It sure will be," Kristoph said. "And we have our winners. Congratulations on your new cheesecake!"

The party transitioned to open mic night and Clay pulled on his jacket. "I'm heading out," he said to Kassi. "You should take that cheesecake home to Sam."

"She doesn't need that much sugar. You take it."

"Doesn't fit my exercise goals. I hate to see it go to waste though. Are you in a rush to get home?"

"No," she said. "I've got a babysitter until seven, courtesy of Molly. All the Rose and Thorn kiddos are at a Chuck E. Cheese party."

"I've got an idea. Why don't I drive you home with a stop along the way?"

"Sure," she said.

"I need to grab something from the back. You bring the cheesecake and meet me at my truck?"

Turns out, he was grabbing a bottle of Madeira, two paper cups and a pair of forks. He drove them to Overlook Park and they sat on a bench looking down at the river and the lights twinkling in the industrial section.

"This is lovely," she said.

"One of my favorite views in Portland," he said.

He opened the bottle, poured a splash into each cup and handed one to her, then opened the cheesecake box between them on the bench and handed her a fork. She took a bite of the cheesecake. A line of cars streamed across the arch of the Fremont Bridge. A container ship loaded with new cars moved slowly downriver.

"Thanks for sharing it with me," she said.

"You won it too."

"I meant the view."

She took a sip of the Madeira. "Yum. I didn't know I liked Madeira."

"This is a nice bottle. One of the perks of the job. I get to order nice bottles for myself from our wholesaler."

She looked into his eyes for a long moment.

"I can't believe you got *An Affair to Remember.*"

"You looked like Deborah Kerr with that wistful longing in your eyes. I could feel it. Maybe you should be an actress instead of a screenwriter."

"Not sure I was acting," she said softly.

He stopped mid-bite to look at her.

"We still on for Monday?" he asked.

"Oh yeah." She checked her watch. "Dammit, but we'd better go. Times up on my Molly-sponsored babysitter."

He nodded and stood, feeling elated and unsteady.

A man was sleeping in the shelter near the restroom and Clay put the cheesecake and a fork next to him, then handed the bottle to Kassi. "Think of me when you drink this," he said.

"I might be drinking all the time," she said.

He opened the truck door for her, and she climbed inside. As he walked around to the driver's side, Kassi sighed and watched him, wondering what good thing she had done in her life to deserve this moment of bliss, and also feeling like there was no way it could last.

21

INT. KASSI'S APARTMENT - NIGHT

Date night! Is *it* finally happening? The stars appear aligned.

For their first date, Clay spent a lot of time agonizing over what to do, what Kassi would like and how to make it special. Finally, after much deliberation, he settled on a drive along the Columbia River to catch the sunset in the gorge, and then dinner at Multnomah Falls Lodge. He hoped she might enjoy seeing these famous Oregon sights. After that, they'd decide what to do next together.

He parked his truck, jumped out and then trotted to the door. Slow down, he thought. You are acting like a kid with a crush. Don't embarrass yourself.

When she opened the door, she looked more beautiful than ever. Sam was perched on her hip, clutching a blanket and sucking her thumb, her head nestled onto Kassi's shoulder. Sam brightened at the sight of Clay but remained silent and then snuggled in more tightly.

"Come on in, I'll be just a few minutes," Kassi said. "Just up from a nap."

"You or Sam?"

Sam giggled.

"Just Sam, silly. Moms don't sleep. Ever."

He pulled out two sunflower stems from behind his back. "I brought you these."

"Oh, that's sweet, thank you. I love sunflowers, they're my favorite, so joyful. Mind putting them in a vase while I get this little sweetie cleaned up?"

"Is Daddy coming?" Sam asked, her voice muffled into the side of Kassi's neck.

"Yes, honey, he'll be here soon, so let's get you dressed and ready, okay?"

Mother and daughter slipped into the bedroom. As Clay looked around for a vase, he listened to them talking softly—Kassi cajoling Sam into her clothes, insisting she brush her teeth, then tickling her. The sound of Sam's laughter was sweet and exhilarating, and Clay had a momentary feeling that nothing in the world could ever go wrong and at the same time that he had to make absolutely sure nothing could ever go wrong again.

Finding no vase, he pulled a spaghetti sauce jar from the trash, ripped off the label, rinsed it out, filled it with water, cut the stems down and then stuck the flowers inside.

Sam burst out from the bedroom, now fully awake, clean and wearing a dress with ruffles. She ran toward Clay like a rocket and threw her arms around his knees. "Hi, Cooker!"

He patted the top of her head. "You woke up! How do you like the flowers?"

"I love them! They're my favorite too."

Kassi followed, a hairbrush in her hand. "Come on, Sam, we need to get your hair finished." Sam ran around the small apartment, hiding and ducking whenever her mother came near.

At first, Kassi played as if she couldn't catch her, but Clay could see Kassi's patience was wearing thin. A minute later, when Sam's tiny sprints brought her in range, he reached down and caught her, then swung her up high. She squealed with delight, as he brought her down gently and placed her squarely in front of Kassi.

"Do it again, Cooker, do it again!" she pleaded, holding out her little arms.

"After you finish your hair, but only if your mom says it's okay."

Kassi smiled, but he couldn't read her expression. Had he stepped over a line?

"Come on, Samantha, be still." Kassi's voice was stern now. She brushed her hair and then pulled it into two pigtails on either side of her head.

"Ouch! That hurts," Sam said, squirming, trying to get free. Kassi finally let go and Sam ran to the front door, crouching down in front of it. "Mommy, will Daddy bring his friend? The one I like? I forget her name."

The phone rang and Kassi got to it by the second ring.

"Hello?" she said with a smile. Her smile faded. "Is everything okay?"

She waved reassuringly at Sam. She turned toward the wall, lowering her voice to a near-whisper. "She's counting on you. She's got her best dress on." There was a long pause. "Yes, I do have plans but that is not the point."

Sam took a few steps toward Clay. She stretched up her hand to reach his. Clay squatted down to Sam's level. "What's your favorite color?"

"I like the rainbow," Sam said, "but purple is my best favorite."

"I like purple too."

"Do not talk to me like that," Kassi angry-whispered. "This is not normal behavior."

Clay picked up Sam and she wrapped her arms around his neck.

"Let's go count the purples in your fairy window."

They could still hear Kassi, but not as distinctly. After a few more minutes, Clay heard her say "Arghh!" as she slammed the phone back into its cradle.

Clay walked back in with Sam, who looked at her mom nervously.

"Daddy's not coming?"

"I'm sorry, honey."

"Why?"

"Something super important came up," she said, unable to keep an edge of bitterness from her voice. "An important tennis thing. One of his athletes needed him."

Kassi slumped down onto the threadbare couch, looked up at the ceiling and then back over at Clay.

"Samantha, why don't you go get some of your books and then we can read together?"

"Okay, Mommy." Sam hopped into her room. "I'm a kangaroo!"

"Looks like our date is canceled," Kassi said. "I'm sorry. You took off work for nothing."

"Why is it canceled?" he asked.

"Because he's an asshole. I didn't understand his excuse, to be honest, and then he hung up on me and it's too late to call a sitter, if I even had anyone to call."

"No, I mean, can't we have an at-home date?" He sat down next to her on the couch. "All three of us. I'll make dinner."

She was quiet, and Clay realized she was trying to find the words for something hard to say.

"Go on," Clay said.

"I can't let Sam get attached to you," she said, then shook her head. "I know that sounds presumptuous because I'm assuming you'll be around long enough for her to get attached. But that kiss, our kiss ..." She took his hand. "I don't know where this is going, but until we are sure, really, really sure, I have to protect her. She's got a lot going on, the breakup with her dad, the cross-country move, the new daycare, and well, other stuff. I can't add this to her hurts."

He squeezed her hand. "We can be friends for however long it takes for you to feel comfortable."

"You sure?"

"Of course."

"I'm sorry. My life is pretty messed up right now, and honestly, I'm not sure how I got here. Working in a restaurant again, barely making ends meet, hoping against all odds I win some random screenwriting competition."

"We're right where we both belong."

"Not exactly sure how to take that," she said, but when she looked into his eyes, she saw truth and certainty there.

"Take it as a commitment to something bigger," he said.

"I suppose we could be more than friends when Sam's not around," she said.

"I'll take what I can get of you," Clay whispered and leaned close to kiss her, pressing his lips to hers and drinking in her heat and taste. He pulled back quickly so they wouldn't get caught and they both sat there, hearts hammering, as Sam walked into the room.

"Is this enough, Mommy?" Sam asked, carrying a precarious stack of books. Clay stood up quickly, moving into the kitchen. Sam dumped the pile of books onto the floor in front of her mother.

"I think that will be plenty."

"I'm hungry," Sam announced as she started flipping through them. "What's for dinner, Mommy?"

"You know, it so happens I am a professional cooker," Clay said from the kitchen. "How about I make my two new friends dinner and then I'll head home?"

Kassi looked up at him and it seemed by her expression

she was deciding what to do, deciding if she could trust him in these perilous circumstances. She was right of course, right to be cautious, and he admired her for it, for the sacrifice it meant.

"Sure," she said finally. "That would be nice but there isn't much here. Maybe a few chicken breasts in the freezer and some potatoes under the sink?"

Clay looked in the fridge and pulled out an onion, two carrots and half a jar of miso. "Any spices?"

"Salt."

"That's technically not a spice," he said, opening one cabinet and then another. "Bingo. This will do nicely." He grabbed a new jar of Dijon mustard, a can of corn and two boxes of mac and cheese. He opened the freezer. The walls were so thick with ice that hardly anything other than the bag of chicken breasts could fit inside. "Holy shit! Oops sorry. Where's the swear jar? But seriously, holy Batman!"

"It was like that when I moved in," Kassi said, pulling Sam onto her lap. "I don't know how to defrost a freezer."

"What's a swear jar, Mommy?"

"Sometimes when people say bad words, they put money in the swear jar to show they're sorry," Kassi said, opening *Harold and the Purple Crayon*.

"Seriously, you just unplug the damn thing and wait," Clay said. "I'll bring a hatchet next time."

Kassi looked up. "A hatchet?"

"This freezer is a cry for help. Desperate times call for desperate measures," he said. He put the chicken breasts into a plastic bag and then into a bowl of cold water to thaw. "Okay, you two keep reading. Dinner will be ready in … hmm, let's see, about five books. Maybe six."

"Yay!" Sam said, clapping her hands twice. "Thanks, Cooker!"

Clay looked at Kassi and saw the lingering concern in

her eyes, but there was something else too. Maybe gratitude or hope. Or whatever existed in the border between the two.

"Mommy, when's Daddy coming next?"

"He said he'd be here in three days, and he's taking you to the beach overnight," Kassi said while looking at Clay.

A full night, he thought, that happened to coincide with his next shift off. Was it possible that next week he would finally get a night alone with Kassi?

She nodded a yes to his silent question and he smiled wide and started cooking.

22

INT. ROSE AND THORN KITCHEN – DAY

The COOKS focus on prep work for the night, marinating in the weird banter unique to restaurant kitchens. Temperatures go way up in the walk-in cooler.

"Someday that dude is going to kill us all," LuRon said.

No one bothered to ask who he was talking about. They all knew it was Bill.

Bill was a busboy who'd worked at the restaurant for three years. He was another one of Molly's rescue projects. In his mid-forties, Bill was older than traditional busboys. A busman, really. He was handsome in a quirky way, with a sun-beat face, clear and curious eyes, and shoulder-length gray hair cut in a mullet that looked good on him. He was a poet and philosopher, partial to Sartre, and was convinced his right leg spoke to him.

It was alarming for people when they first met him to see an otherwise normal adult pause mid-conversation to argue with his leg. True to the general welcoming nature of the Rose and Thorn, once people got used to it, they accepted it. That didn't prevent rampant speculation.

Meredith thought he had schizophrenia. Roz thought he had taken too much acid. Clay was certain he'd suffered a brain injury. LuRon didn't care about the cause, only the outcome.

"His leg is going to tell him we're not his friends, that we're lizard people or something, and then he's going to come in with an axe. I swear, it's every man for himself," LuRon said.

"What about the women?" Kassi asked.

"I'm sorry. That was sexist of me." LuRon rolled his eyes. "Every person for themselves."

"He's exactly the reason I keep a loaded .38 in my backpack," Rob said.

Kassi froze, a look of disbelief on her face. Clay paused mid-chop, squares of diced onions clinging to the edge of his knife. "Rob, you cannot keep a gun in here," he said. "That's a huge liability. It's a shared locker."

"Yeah, but I share my locker with Gilroy, and he's super trustworthy."

"It's true," Gilroy said. "I am trustworthy. I saw it the other day. Your bag was open. It's cute, with a pearl handle like cowboys used to carry."

"I guarantee you, no cowboy carried a pearl-handled pea shooter like that," LuRon said.

"Certainly not a .38," Jon said, poking his head around from the dishpit. "The .38 special round wasn't introduced until 1898, replacing the underperforming .38 Long Colt. The Colt revolver chambered in .45 was considered the quintessential cowboy gun."

"This is by far the weirdest conversation we've ever had in this kitchen," Clay said, "and that's saying a lot. New rule. Don't bring guns to work. No matter what caliber. It's a liability issue, and a stupidity issue."

Rob nodded and winked. "Got it. No gun."

"I'm serious, you dumb ass. I'm going to be checking and if I see it in there, you're fired that second. No, worse, you're getting busted down to dishwasher. In fact, go unload it right now."

"The dish rack?"

"Unload the gun and give me the bullets."

"Fine," Rob mumbled, "but if Bill ever kills us all because we're unarmed, I'm gonna laugh my ass off."

Bill came in from the front carrying a tub of dishes. He took a quick scan of the room, cataloging the awkward silence and the averted looks. "Leg doesn't like it when you talk about him," Bill said, his voice even.

"Fair enough. But let me ask you something," LuRon said. "Does your leg have like, you know, its own little brain and everything?"

"Please," Clay said. "Stop it."

"You're going to thank me for bringing pearly today," Rob mumbled as he came back in, stuffing five bullets into Clay's hand.

Bill paused and looked at LuRon for what felt like an eternity, then smiled. "Nah, man, that would be crazy. It's more like a metaphysical energy thing. Thanks for asking. Makes me feel less weird to talk about it." He stopped. "What's that? Oh, right. Leg says he appreciates it too."

Bill moved past and started unloading the bus tub. One of Bill's regular activities was debating philosophy with Jon, a scientologist and neo-Kantian who believed in a universal imperative that provided a moral framework, even if that imperative was alien in origin. Bill was an existentialist, firmly in the existence-precedes-essence camp. Leg was a metaphysical spiritualist. When the conversation got heated, it wasn't unusual for Bill to interrupt Jon only to interrupt himself to restate and rebut a statement from Leg.

They were gearing up for another clash as Kassi hung a ticket.

She was glad things felt so weird and hectic in the kitchen. It kept her mind off the one thing occupying her thoughts, consuming her really. Tomorrow night she would finally be alone with Clay.

No Samantha, as long as Barry didn't fuck everything up again. No ambiguity. No more awkward emotional fumbling. And hopefully much more kissing. And other stuff.

The thought of it made her feel a little woozy and stoned. It had been a long time since she'd been with a man. As she thought back, the numbers were depressing.

She and Barry got married because she was pregnant. She was twenty-four at the time and they had already been dating almost a year. Before him was Donnie, the shy, handsome guy in her freshmen English class. Donnie was such a good kisser. Clay was better though. Big and strong and confident, but gentle and slow.

She shook her head to dislodge the vision of Clay holding her close and pressing his lips against hers. Back to the sexual reckoning. If she was thinking it through correctly, she hadn't had sex at all in well over a year and hadn't had sex with anyone other than Barry in five years, and their interactions were infrequent and unfulfilling for at least the last two years. Angry, even.

She suddenly had a flash of fear. What if she'd forgotten how to do it, how to enjoy sex, and how to make it enjoyable for Clay?

Her breathing was shallow and rushed. The pressure was too much. Wait, she thought, are we for sure going to have sex? Am I reading too much into this? Maybe he'll just want to take it slow. Sounds like Crystal messed him up.

She realized she was staring at Clay's back, his broad shoulders, his muscular legs in those damn running tights he sometimes wore under the chef coat that so perfectly outlined his thighs. She also realized Gilroy was saying something. She focused her attention.

"Are you?" Gilroy asked. He was looking at her looking at Clay.

"What's that?" she asked.

"Are you okay? Do you need something?"

She shook her head and hurried out front.

"What the hell is up with her today?" Gilroy asked.

***

Clay was lost in his own thoughts, also about sex.

He hadn't been with a woman since the day he caught Crystal in bed with that jerk. It was a pathetic day all-around. He slipped on some dried penne noodles spilled on the floor and twisted his ankle. When Molly saw him hobbling around, she sent him home early. It was the first shift he'd missed since he started working at the Rose and Thorn. He didn't call home to let Crystal know he was coming. Why would he?

He could hear them right away, but his mind couldn't make sense of the sounds. At first, he thought it was the neighbor's cat trying to throw up or that there was something wrong with the washing machine. He walked into the bedroom completely unprepared for the image that was now forever burned into his brain.

Crystal was on top of the car salesman, leaning over him and holding the bedframe with both hands, her long hair trailing down onto his chest. She was slowly grinding her hips into him as he thrust inside her. He had his hands on her breasts, cupping and caressing them vigorously, and moaning. He couldn't see Clay from his vantage, but from the doorway, Clay could see her face reflected in the mirror over the dresser. Crystal looked flushed and satisfied, beautiful. Then she saw Clay.

She didn't stop, didn't even slow down. She looked startled for a split second, but that was quickly replaced by something between curiosity and sadness. Curiosity about what he would do and sadness about what was going to happen to them. He didn't say a word, just turned and walked to The Hideout Bar where Mel was serving and drank a great deal of whiskey. When he came home hours later, she was gone along with her clothes and the expensive bottle of champagne he'd been saving for a special occasion.

That was two years ago. He was simultaneously nervous about the date tomorrow night, plunging into the unknown with Kassi, yet yearning for it more than anything before in his life. The thought of seeing her even partially undressed, of feeling her skin and kissing those lips ...

Shit, he was getting hard. You better work like this tomorrow tonight, he told his cock. Christ, he thought. I'm turning into Bill. I'm serious though, dick.

Dick answered him. Wait, nope, that was Gilroy talking.

"What is up with everyone today?" Gilroy asked LuRon.

"I don't always understand white people but it seems like those two have a serious case of the yearnings, if you know what I mean."

"Saint Clay the Perpetually Celibate? Get out."

"Everybody needs to stop talking now," Clay said.

They didn't.

"Love can wreck you," Rob said. "For I too once loved a woman only to have my emotions twisted as if by a faulty nipple clamp."

"Nope, too much. No sex-toy metaphors, no matter how heartbroken you are," Gilroy said.

Clay put down his knife and went to the walk-in. He needed to cool down.

***

Kassi was out front talking to Meredith as they filled saltshakers. It was slow and they were trying to look busy while also prolonging the work so Ione wouldn't make them do something else, like clean the toilets.

"How are things with Rob?" Kassi asked.

Meredith shook her head. "Terrible."

"Really?

"I like him."

"Why is that terrible?" Kassi asked.

"He's such a freak and a loser."

"Then why were you interested in him?"

Meredith stopped and looked at Kassi like she was a child. "It was supposed to be for my research on sexual extremes. I needed a way to get into that community. I mean, look at me." She flipped her long hair and smoothed it into place. "I'm on the fast track for my doctorate in psychology. I have a clinic interested in hiring me after I get my degree. A prestigious clinic. In Switzerland. Do I look like someone who would fall for a pervert with pierced nipples and a do-it-yourself sex dungeon in his spare bedroom?"

"A sex dungeon??"

"Barely a sex dungeon. There's a swing, and a kind of a rack thing. But it's made from PVC. Pretty sure I broke it last time."

"I'm having a hard time keeping track of everything," Kassi said, pouring herself a cup of coffee. "Is weird sex really that good?"

"Oh, it's amazing," Meredith said, with a sly grin, "and

so naughty. But that's not the reason."

"What then?"

Meredith sighed. "Under all the weird sex stuff, he's a nice guy. Funny and shy and insecure and attentive and kind." She shook her head.

"And that's bad?"

"Terrible. My paper is wrecked. I can't move forward with any of the profile work I was doing. When he found out I was collecting data on him, he got so pissed off that we're barely talking. He thinks I was using him."

"Were you?" Kassi asked.

"Only at first. It's complicated."

"Ladies, seriously," Ione said, passing through the dining room. "Time to lean, time to clean."

"Love is the worst," Meredith said, grabbing a rag and swiping at the counter half-heartedly. "I wish I'd never let him blindfold me and handcuff me to the bed and leave me on the edge of an orgasm for an hour before giving me the best two orgasms of my life."

"Yeah, that sounds terrible," Kassi said, starting to feel a little warm. "Why don't you just tell him you like him and find some other, you know, less perfect deviant to research. I'm sure he knows plenty of them."

"Love is not a rational thing. I thought you knew that by now."

"If you're good together, you should give it a try," Kassi said, patting her arm. "I have to grab some half-and-half for my coffee."

"But there's some in the pitcher," Meredith said, but it was too late, Kassi disappeared through the swinging door into the kitchen.

She didn't need any creamer. She wanted to stand in the walk-in for a minute or two. Carrying her coffee, she pulled open the walk-in door and stepped inside, startled to see

Clay there. He was sitting on a case of five-pound sour cream tubs with his chef jacket open, flapping the edges to create a breeze.

He looked up in surprise as she pulled the door slowly shut behind her. "Sorry," she said. "I was looking for some half and half ..."

Clay stood, took her coffee cup and set it on the shelf. He slid one hand behind her head and the other into the small of her back and pulled her in close. The feel of his lips pressing against hers made her knees weak and she gave into the feeling, slipping her hands under his coat and around his back, pulling him closer and holding the kiss, tasting him, melting under the pleasure.

With their bodies so close, she could feel him growing instantly hard, his erection pressing into her. She let one hand drop down to caress him through the thin fabric of his running pants. They both moaned as she traced the length of his rigid shaft and then he cupped her bottom and pulled her tightly into him.

"God, you feel so good," he whispered, then kissed her again.

The tip of her tongue darted into his mouth and that, along with her gentle touch, had him immediately on the brink of an unexpected orgasm.

Then the walk-in door opened. It was Bill. He looked at them for a long second as they pushed apart, flustered.

"I'll be damned," Bill said. "Leg told me you two were getting close, but I wouldn't have believed it if I hadn't seen it myself." He pointed at the fruit and vegetable shelf. "Hand me a pomegranate. LuRon has a special order."

23

INT. CLAY'S HOUSE - NIGHT

A cute bungalow in east Portland. Date
night, second try. Will *it* finally
happen for KASSI and CLAY? Will it be as
hot as all the buildup? (Yes, and then
some.)

For the second try at a date with Kassi, Clay was totally and uncontrollably nervous. It was an unholy mixture of anticipation, insecurity and straight-up fear. He didn't want to be the kind of guy who expected sex, but he was certainly expecting something more than holding hands after what happened in the walk-in.

He brushed his teeth for the second time and rinsed. He tried to comb his long hair into submission for the third time, a useless exercise. He ran his fingers across his cheek and chin. Smooth. He'd shaved a few hours earlier so he wouldn't chafe her delicate skin if, when, they kissed again.

Walking into the bedroom, he looked at his unmade bed. When was the last time he changed the sheets? A month? A year? If he changed the sheets now, right before Kassi got here, did that make him the asshole who makes assumptions about sex? But if he didn't change the sheets, Kassi might be too repulsed to get into his bed.

He rifled through the closet until he found the spare set

of sheets. They were mismatched and the pillowcases were too snug, but they were clean. He threw the white down comforter over the bed, the only nice blanket he owned.

Opening the drawer on the nightstand next to the bed, he checked for the hundredth time for the two condoms. He bought them on his way home, feeling embarrassed and nervous that he was assuming too much. But deep down, he was pretty sure something special was going to happen tonight.

Wait, he wondered, would two be enough? Too late now. He'd run out for more if needed.

In the kitchen, he checked to make sure the wine was cold and then plated the few appetizer-type things he had prepared. It wasn't much. If she was hungry, they could always walk down to the Greek place on the corner for falafel and feta salad.

***

On the other side of town, Kassi was getting ready, and was also nervous. Barry had come by two hours ago to pick up Samantha and by now they were well on their way to the Oregon coast. The handoff had been mostly silent, which was okay because silent was better than angry. That was progress, of a sort. Better for Sam.

Kassi took one final look in the mirror. She always looked tired these days but on the upside, she was having a good-hair day. Her mother said her hair was her crowning glory. Today the curls were spiraling ideally, not corkscrew tight, which happened sometimes in the rain, just a little past wavy.

She moved dramatically around the small bathroom, swaying and swiveling, pretending to be on a fashion catwalk to see the effects of a good-hair day. She stopped and readjusted the lacy bra, the one sexy undergarment she owned, pushing her left boob back into place—all the bouncing around was more than the flimsy bra could handle.

The cut of the black T-shirt she picked for tonight was deep enough to show cleavage, something she rarely did, because she found her breasts clumsily annoying most of the time, always getting in the way and drawing too much attention. After giving birth and breastfeeding, now they were soft and droopy. She sighed, thinking of the stretch marks across her belly. They had faded some since the pregnancy but not all the way.

She hoped Clay would find her body attractive. She considered keeping the lights off when she undressed. If she undressed. Then she thought about how hard he got in the walk-in and how fast. He liked her body just fine then, but he hadn't seen it without clothes.

She checked herself one more time in the bathroom mirror, standing on tiptoe to get a better sense of her outfit, the tight jeans and sexy bra peeking out of the T-shirt. I'd sleep with me, she thought. That was certainly her intent with Clay. She had no illusions. Barring any unexpected objections or issues, tonight was the night.

Two honks from the cab waiting outside. She swooshed Vaseline across her lips, checked for the hundredth time her diaphragm was in her purse, along with the jelly, then pulled on her favorite pink fleece and ran out the door.

The cab was a splurge. She probably should have taken the bus, but she was already late. Clay had offered to come to her place, but she wanted to get out of her apartment. Plus, it would be good to see his home, get a sense of his tastes, make sure he wasn't into something weird, like sex dungeons or taxidermy, and find out if he went to the trouble of changing his sheets for her.

***

"Hi," she said.

"Hi."

He stood there staring. She could feel him taking her in, and she hoped he liked what he saw. She watched his eyes drop to her neckline, then lower to the tops of her breasts cupped in the lace of her bra.

"Are you going to invite me in?" She grinned as he struggled to bring his eyes back to her face.

"I ... shit. Yes. Please, come in," he said, standing to the side. "It's just, you look so beautiful. Like even more beautiful."

"You don't look half bad yourself. I like the shirt."

What she really liked was the man underneath the shirt. How the fabric hugged his shoulders and swelling biceps and tucked in around his narrow waist and angular hips. Out of his chef whites, out of his ratty concert T-shirts, his hair out of the usual ponytail, he looked like a Hollywood leading man. Gentle brown eyes, long hair framing his face, tall, strong.

She could still remember the first time she saw him, how she had been stunned by his good looks. And yet, he walked through the world without the slightest concern, or even awareness, of how women, and sometimes men, responded to him.

They were wearing basically the same thing—black tees and jeans—and she wondered if they would start to look more and more alike as they got serious? If. If they got serious. They should not get serious. She wasn't up for that. It would be much easier all around to keep this thing, whatever it was, on the casual level.

Stop, brain, she thought. Stop over-thinking. Just be present. Don't make this harder than it needs to be.

Kassi walked inside from the porch and gave his place a quick once-over. It was clean and tidy, more so than her apartment where Sam's toys were scattered everywhere, along with baskets half-full of perpetually unfolded laundry. There was a dining room table with three folding chairs, two mismatched side tables next to a comfy looking recliner in the middle of the main room, a lumpy couch and a tiny kitchen off to the side, with a peninsula-style counter separating it from the living area.

"I'm surprised your kitchen is so small," she said. "I mean, given your job and everything."

"I don't cook much on my own."

She turned to him and smiled. "Your place is cute. I love the little yard out front."

"Thanks, but that's a kind lie. I'm hardly ever here and seems weird to drop more money on a house I won't be in for too long."

"You won't be here long?"

He shrugged. "Probably not."

"In Portland or in this house?"

"Either one, I guess. Or both. Want some wine?"

It was odd that he left that hanging, Kassi thought, but honestly, she didn't know how long she would be in Portland either, so why should she expect anything else from him? At least he was being straight.

He crossed the room in three long strides, pulled the wine from the fridge and then stuck the end of a corkscrew in the top. Kassi joined him and took the bottle from him, their hands touching briefly. "Let me," she said. "This is part of my job, after all. I'm pretty good at it."

Effortlessly, she twisted the corkscrew, her other hand firmly grasping the bottleneck. They each watched silently as she turned it, and turned it again, pulling out the cork with a pop.

"Expensive?" she asked.

"Expensive enough. Like the Madeira, I get a deal."

"You spend money on booze but not furniture."

"I've got my priorities straight," he said, pouring the wine.

She took a sip. "You do have good taste."

"I do." They locked eyes. "I know exactly what I like."

She felt butterflies in her stomach. Big ones. Big happy ones. He was more forthright tonight, more confident, and it was seriously turning her on. They continued sipping, standing close to each other but not touching. It wasn't awkward. Being next to him felt natural, like their bodies already understood each other.

"What kind of music do you listen to?" he asked. Kassi glanced around and noticed the stereo on the card table against the far wall.

"I don't often admit this to people, but I don't listen to music."

"What?" He seemed genuinely shocked.

"I may have some sort of neurological impairment or something."

"No music at all?"

"It just doesn't do much for me. I mean, I like Michael Jackson and Roy Orbison. And sometimes Sam and I listen to Raffi, that kid's singer. But I don't go out of my way to listen. Most of the time I forget music is even a thing."

He looked at her with tempered amazement, as if he'd just discovered an alien life form.

"I like songs when someone else plays them or I hear it on the radio. So please, go right ahead."

"I pretty much always have music on, but I need to get some Michael Jackson and Roy Orbison CDs. And Raffi."

"You'll never be able to get *Baby Beluga* out of your head," she said. "Shit, now it's in mine."

"Sing it?" He smiled, drained his wine and refilled it, topping hers off too.

"No way. I have a terrible voice."

"I doubt that. Are you hungry?"

"You have food?"

"Some little things, but we could go out if you want, if you're hungry I mean."

"I'm okay staying here."

The wine was going to her head fast, and she was glad because it was softening the edge of all the crackling energy passing between them. She was hyper-aware of every word, every movement—it all felt amplified and crystalline and infinite.

"Is there somewhere I can put this?" she asked, shrugging out of her jacket.

"Like a closet?"

"Yeah," she said, grinning a crooked smile, "like a closet."

"Right by the door."

"Back in a flash."

She could feel his eyes on her as she walked toward the closet.

"Oh, wait," he said. "Don't go in there yet."

It was too late. "What is this?" she asked, holding the closet door open.

"A typewriter."

"The one from Goodwill?"

"I know you said not to, but I …" His voice trailed off.

"You went back and got it?"

"Yes."

"How long have you had it?"

"I went back the same day."

She put her hands on her hips, looking at him intensely.

"Is it for me?"

Clay nodded cautiously, with a pained expression that made clear he was worried he had gone too far, that she might feel he went behind her back, against her wishes.

"When were you planning on giving it to me?"

He shook his head. "I hadn't thought it through. When the time was right, I guess. Is the time right now?"

"Is it ever," Kassi said.

24

INT. CLAY'S HOUSE - LATER THE SAME NIGHT

Typing lessons heat up.

They were on their second bottle of wine, sitting side by side on the floor leaning into each other, their backs against the couch.

They were taking turns banging away on the typewriter, which was on the coffee table in front of them, a candle on either side, the only light in the small room. Kassi had her head tilted onto his shoulder, enjoying the warmth and strength of his body.

"I remember this from high school." He typed: *The quick brown fox jumped over the lazy dog.* "It has all the letters in the alphabet."

"Yours doesn't," she said with a laugh.

He'd actually typed *the quick brong dong jump voer the lasy box.*

"Mrs. Keepers would be disappointed," he said.

"My turn."

She leaned forward and advanced the paper by a few turns, then let her fingers fly across the keys, typing quickly and confidently. *Clay, please kiss me now.* Then she rolled up the sheet of paper so it was visible and turned to look at him.

He reached out and touched the side of her cheek,

turning her head slightly and tilting it up, then leaned in for a long, deep kiss. Their lips met, their eyes closed, and they kissed until they both had to sit back from the heat and intensity of it.

"I'd like us to do more," he whispered, his voice ragged. "Is that okay?"

She nodded and he stood, helped her up onto the couch, then tugged her shirt off over her head. He pulled his off too and sat beside her and she slid her hands across his thick chest and broad shoulders. He mirrored her moves, his hands shaking slightly as he felt her smooth skin and then gently cupped her breasts and slowly circled his thumbs on her nipples, faintly visible through her bra.

"Oh god," she breathed out with a long, slow sigh, closing her eyes.

He kissed the side of her neck softly, then reached down and unbuttoned her pants. She raised her hips slightly and wiggled to help him carefully pull them down her legs and then off, flinging them across the room.

She was nervous and felt vulnerable as he studied her, now just in her bra and panties, worried still that her body was so different than before the pregnancy, softer and fuller, less tight. She pressed her knees together in the half-light. He moved his hands up her thighs so slowly and so carefully that she relaxed into his touch and forgot any worries.

He rained kisses on her lips, then down her neck to the tops of her breasts, then to her nipples through the fabric of her bra and she moaned again and swirled her hands through his hair.

Clay pulled back slightly and slid his hands behind her back to fumble with her bra clasp. It came loose and she shouldered out of it, watching his face as he saw her breasts for the first time. He leaned forward to carefully cup then kiss each breast in turn, taking the nipples carefully between his lips.

"You are so beautiful," he said, his voice cracking.

He stood and dropped his jeans, kicking out of them.

He wasn't wearing underwear and his hard cock sprang free and bobbed with each breath and motion. She felt a sense of awe mixed with lustful expectation at the sight of it and reached out to touch the crown, then circled her hand lightly around the shaft and pulled carefully, gently. She used her other hand to cup his balls, weighing the feel of them in her palm and tugging softly. Her lips parted and she leaned forward, her intention clear.

Clay, delirious with pleasure, whispered, "Not yet. I'm already too close. It's been too long."

He knelt before her on the couch and reached for her panties, pulling them down her legs and off, then tossing them aside.

He ran his palms up her thighs and cautiously spread her legs and scooted her closer to the edge of the couch, then began kissing the inside of her thighs tenderly, nuzzling his way closer. He used his fingertips to hold her gently open and kissed, then darted his tongue inside, and around, again and again.

"Oh god. It's been so long for me too," she whispered.

Within seconds, the first tremor of an orgasm rippled through her, and she held her breath, tensed her body and began to tremble. He pressed his tongue against her and licked in quick circles until the pleasure became too much and she froze as the orgasm blossomed, enveloping her. He held his tongue at the epicenter of pleasure as wave after wave of bliss rolled through her.

When the ecstasy slowly subsided, she leaned back and stretched out on the couch, parting her legs. "I need you inside me."

"I'll get a condom," Clay said, cursing himself now for not planning ahead.

"You don't need it," she said, grabbing him by the wrist and pulling him on top of her. "I'm protected." Kassi had slipped in her diaphragm in the bathroom earlier.

He was painfully hard. She reached between them to guide him into her, sighing with pleasure as he slowly pushed inside. He was long and thick, and she felt full and electric as he entered.

They locked eyes, and she watched his face as he rested for a second, now fully inside her, as if trying to memorize the feeling of pure, enveloping pleasure. Their hip bones were touching, and the heat between them was intoxicating. She circled her hips slowly, lost in the feeling of being filled so completely.

Clay pulled out slowly, deliciously slowly, until he was only barely inside her, then pushed back again with a groan. She had her arms wrapped around him, fingernails raking his back, legs curved around with her ankles against the back of his legs, pulling him deeper with each thrust, trying to hold him inside.

He began to pick up speed and she anticipated his rhythm, clenching each time he started to pull out to intensify their pleasure. The friction was too perfect to endure.

"I'm so close," he said.

"Let yourself go," she whispered.

His pace increased, frantic now, driving in and out as the pleasure radiated out from the bliss of their connection.

With a moan, he gave one last mighty thrust and held himself at the bottom of it as his orgasm unwound. She felt him throb and spill himself into her. Another wave of ecstasy carried her away, a long, slow delicious wave, and she held him so tightly her arms hurt.

For a few minutes, neither of them spoke. He shifted slightly to slip out and then rolled onto his side, sitting on the floor, to take his weight off her. He looked up at her on the couch.

"Kassi, I ..." he didn't know what to say. "That was ..."

She leaned forward and kissed him, regarding him with wide, serious eyes. "I don't think I've ever felt so good in my life."

"It was as if our bodies were made for each other, like we've done this before."

He slid up to sit beside her, and they held each other tightly, side by side on the couch, in silence, skin on skin, in a state of physical wonder, for several minutes, until a gurgling growl brought them back to reality.

"Was that your stomach?" he asked.

"I didn't eat much today."

He disentangled himself from her, pulled on his jeans, found her wine glass and poured out the last of the bottle. "Let me see what I can whip up. You relax and have some more wine."

Kassi tracked down her panties, made a quick trip to the bathroom to wash up, and then slipped into her shirt as she sat back down on the couch.

She watched him banging around in the kitchen, occasionally swearing. Soon, good smells began to fill the air. Kassi tucked her feet under her and looked out into the night through the living room window. A light rain was falling, again. She knew Portland had a reputation, but never thought the rain would be this relentless. Tonight, it looked magical against the streetlights.

There was a notebook on the coffee table, and she opened it and began flipping through the pages. It had crudely drawn logos, blueprints of trucks and kitchens, and recipes.

"What's this notebook?" she called.

"Nothing worth talking about," he said from the kitchen.

"Oh geez, I don't know what came over me, I'm sorry. I was being nosy." She pushed it away, embarrassed.

"No, it's fine. I'm trying to come up with a mobile restaurant design. And a name, a business plan and a menu. It's boring, but I'm not hiding anything. Including how boring I am. I use that notebook to jot down ideas. Go on, keep reading. I don't mind."

She opened it again and leafed through. "It's not at all boring. But I think Meals on Wheels is taken."

"Yeah, those kind, helpful bastards."

"Is this why you may not be in Portland much longer?"

"Yeah."

"I'd like to know more."

"I'll tell you everything, but first, let's eat." He walked to the couch with a tray of food.

"Oh my," she said, putting the notebook down. "What's all this?"

"I turned some of the ingredients I had for appetizers into grilled cheese sandwiches and heated up some cream of tomato soup."

He pushed the typewriter out of the way and set the tray on the coffee table. The soup was steaming in two bowls, and three sandwiches grilled golden brown on crusty bread and sliced in half were piled up on a plate.

"That's a balsamic glaze drizzled on the soup," he said, "and the grilled cheese is chevre and gruyere with a little fig jam."

She took half of a sandwich and long strings of cheese dripped onto her arm, dangerously close to her shirt.

"Oh, dammit," he said. "Hold on."

He grabbed one of his sweatshirts from the closet and

she pulled it on, swimming in it but warm and happy.

She took a bite of the sandwich and rolled her eyes. "This is even better than the sex," she said, then reddened. "Sorry, that was … I was trying to be funny and maybe we don't know each other well enough for that yet."

"I think we know each other pretty well," he said, reaching for the other half of the sandwich. "I hope we get to know each other even better." Then he stammered, "I don't mean we should have sex though. Or we should not have sex, either, I mean, I absolutely would like to, but only if you want to. I just, I meant getting to know each other."

He stopped and took a big gulp of wine. "Sorry, I'm not used to being around someone I like," he said. "And I'm blowing it."

"You're not blowing anything." She took his hand. "This night has been perfect so far, and it doesn't have to be over. We both have the day off tomorrow …"

He looked at her curiously.

"Yes, I checked your schedule, and Sam isn't due back from her beach trip with her dad until late afternoon. You'll probably be praying for me to leave by then."

"I don't think I could ever get tired of seeing you."

"You say that now."

After they finished the soup and sandwiches, he brought out dessert—a strawberry and peach trifle made by a friend who was a pastry chef at The Heathman Hotel. Layers of fruit, custard, whipped cream and sponge cake. He spooned out two bowls and on her first bite, a piece of cake rolled off her fork and dotted whipped cream on her chin.

"Dammit," she said.

"You're super messy with food," Clay said, then fished out a chunk of cake and tossed it at her, leaving a blob of cream on his sweatshirt.

"Hey!" She dipped her fingers into the dessert and painted a sweet stripe across his lips. Laughing, he kissed her fingers and pulled her close.

"How about we save dessert for later?" he asked.

She nodded. He scooped her into his arms. She giggled. "You're carrying me?"

"Is it okay?"

"No one has ever carried me before. And yes, definitely okay." She snuggled into his body, wrapped one arm around his neck and with the other she grabbed her bowl of trifle. "I bet we can come up with a good use for all this custard and whipped cream."

25

INT. CLAY'S BEDROOM – THE NEXT MORNING

New feelings. Different positions.

Kassi sighed as the early morning sun swept across her face. She couldn't remember ever feeling so fulfilled and content.

"Why the sigh?" Clay whispered into her neck with a kiss.

"I'm so happy."

"Me too. It's kind of weird, to be honest."

Kassi turned over and sat up, shyly pulling the sheet over her breasts, whisking away some cake crumbs and dried smudges of whipped cream. "I know, right?" she whispered. "I'm not sure how to process it. It's such a foreign feeling."

"What about before, you know, when you were with …" he let the thought trail into silence.

"Barry," she said. "It's okay to say their names. I wondered the same thing about you and Crystal."

"If we were ever this happy?"

"If you were ever this happy. I'm sure she was. How could she not be happy with someone like you?"

Clay pulled her in tight again, and they slipped back into the spoon position. She relaxed into his strong chest pressing against her back and shivered when he curled his arm around her and cupped her breast. They were quiet, reveling in the newness of the blissful feelings, like tasting something sweet for the first time, curiously examining the novelty of the exquisite flavor.

"I can honestly say I have never been happier in my life than this second," he said at last.

"I almost feel guilty," she said. "As if I don't deserve to feel this good."

He squeezed tighter. "You do. We both do. I'd like to stay this way forever."

"We'd starve."

"We can live on love," he joked, then stiffened. "Well, what I mean is, I'm not saying—"

"I don't know if we can live only on love," she said. She knew it was a slip of the tongue, not an official *I love you* and she didn't want him to worry about anything, so she kept up the joking tone. "But I'm willing to try until four forty-five this afternoon."

His body relaxed. He laughed and kissed the back of her neck. "It's a little strange how right this feels."

She rolled over to look into his eyes. "To me too."

"What can I do to stay close to you, to keep this going, to support you?"

"Just what you're doing now, the only thing I want is to be here with you this second."

"Beyond that though. I know you don't leave things to chance. Not with Sam in the picture."

"You mean besides chancing into the one restaurant in Portland where the hottest chef in the world works?"

"Yeah, besides that."

He was right of course, she thought. She left little to chance. Even now, she had given Clay's phone number to her mom in case Barry suddenly decided he was too busy to keep Sam. He would be enraged not to reach her and would eventually call her mom.

"You're right. Sam comes first. I want to be a good parent and get her to adulthood in one piece, physically and emotionally."

"A worthy goal," Clay said. "What about for you?"

"There isn't much left for me after that. It's pretty consuming. That's my reality for the next fifteen years. Or it was until I met you."

He stroked her hair, letting his hand drift down to her shoulders.

"What about the screenplay contest?"

She nodded. "I want to live a creative life, one where I find meaning in creating things. I want to feel sustained by that, the way you feel sustained by cooking. But I've got to pay the bills. That's where the contest comes in. It's a long shot, an impossible shot really, but there's prize money and it could open some doors, maybe allow me to get a job writing for television or something."

"A reasonable plan."

"No, it's not, not really. It's out and out fantasy. When I don't win, I'll try something else. And then try again. That's the thing about having a kid. It forces you to get clear-eyed about reality."

"She's a great kid, your best creation so far."

"We have to be careful with her," she said. "She can't get hurt."

"I understand."

"What about you? Tell me about the food truck thingy."

"My plan is to build a fully functional kitchen in the back of a truck, like a step van. When I get that done, I'll quit the restaurant and sell gourmet food from the truck. Like a small mobile restaurant."

"Are you close?" She rested her hand on his hip.

"I'm getting there. It's a big chunk of cash."

"Where would you park it?"

"Anywhere, that's the beauty of it. I could travel, see the country or stick around and see all of Oregon. Or follow Phish around—that's a band, by the way."

"I know who Phish is," she said, lightly punching his arm.

"I could sell food to stoned hippies at a concert or park near a beautiful beach and offer a nightly seafood special. Maybe I'll follow the seasons, go south in the winter, north in the summer, stopping at farms to get the freshest local food available."

"It sounds exciting." She felt a little wistful that she couldn't just pick up and travel.

"To be honest, my dream is evolving now," he said, as if reading her mind. "After last night."

"You can't give up your dreams because of me."

"I said evolving, not giving up."

A blue jay landed on the windowsill and peeked in, startling them both. They watched the bird watching them, cocking its little head back and forth until it abruptly flew off.

"Is that what happened between you and Crystal, she didn't support your dreams?"

"In a way, I guess. She wanted me to open a fancy gourmet place where she and other celebrities could hang out."

"She's a celebrity?"

"She's been on TV. I guess that makes her a Portland celebrity, at least. She wants to be a movie star and hated the idea of a food truck. Our dreams never fit."

"I love imagining you running a food truck, with a long line of stoned hippies waiting to chow down."

"That wasn't why we broke up." She could feel his hesitancy to talk about his past, and she didn't want him to feel forced.

"I figured, what with all the razzing you take about it in the kitchen."

"She cheated on me, I caught her in the act, in our house, in our bed, well, not this bed. I threw it out and bought a new one."

"It's super-comfy." She patted the mattress lightly. "I'm sorry. That sounds like a terrible situation. We don't have to talk about it."

"You deserve to know. And yeah, I admit, it was a bad time, and not because I loved her so much. In hindsight, I can say I didn't really, but because I totally trusted her."

"Were you good at communicating?"

"Not so much. We got married young and never figured out that part."

"I suppose infidelity is a form of communication when you can't say things any other way," Kassi said.

"Promise me you'll never communicate like that."

She laughed. "Never, not in a million years."

The blue jay flew back onto the sill, took another look at them and then flew away.

"I think that bird is a spy," Kassi said. "It's taking information about us to someone."

Clay laughed. "Okay, your turn. Why did you and Barry break up?"

"That's an easy one. He spent most of our time together raging at me for stupid things. Sometimes all I had to do was say 'pass the salt' the wrong way. The real question I've struggled with is why I ever fell in love with him in the first place."

"Do you have an answer?"

She sighed. "When I first met him, I thought he was smart and confident and interesting. And he was, still is, all of those things. He engaged a part of me that no man ever bothered with before, my brain. The other side of him came out when we got serious. But I'm an optimist, you know? I thought he would change. I suppose it's something we all do, or maybe just me. We think if people love us enough they'll change, but he was either unwilling or unable to change. Either way, it ended in flames."

"Did you ever consider not marrying him?"

"That would have been a hard choice because I was pregnant. Up until and shortly after Sam was born, I endured it all because I believed he would *want* to change. That even if it wasn't for me, having a daughter would cause him to get help, to come to terms with his anger and figure out its source. Turns out I was the one who changed. Samantha needed something more from her mother than naively hoping her dad would stop screaming at me. I realized the best thing I could do for Sam was to be an example of strength, of independence."

He held her tighter. "I'm sorry you had to go through that."

"And I'm sorry you had to go through your shit with Crystal."

"We've got each other now. Let's leave all that in the past."

She sighed again because she understood what he meant, even if it seemed absurd that they could feel this way, so certain, after one night.

Kassi felt his growing erection pressing against her belly. She wiggled out of his embrace so she could slip her hand between them and wrap it around him. He moaned, a sound that seemed to pass through the air to vibrate between her thighs. She kissed his chest and then moved down his body, biting and nipping gently as she made her way to his cock. She spread his legs, then licked and sucked him while stroking his stiff erection. Gently, she took his head in her mouth and he shivered as she sucked and pulled and swirled her tongue around the crown.

He was a good size for her, big enough but not so big that she couldn't take all of him. She leaned forward bringing him all the way into her mouth. He moaned again, closing his eyes, whispering her name, and sinking into the vast pleasure of it all.

26

EXT. NEIGHBORHOOD PARK – LATER THAT SAME
DAY

KASSI and CLAY go for a personal best.

When they finally emerged from Clay's house, it was early afternoon. The sun was shining brightly in a cloudless sky. They both squinted and laughed at the painful and awkward transition from their little cocoon of bliss into the outside world.

"It's so bright," Kassi said, putting on her sunglasses.

Clay nodded. "Let's get some coffee and something to eat. I'm feeling a little wobbly."

"Coffee sounds great," she said, taking his hand in hers. She paused. "Wait, is this okay? In public, I mean."

"More than okay," Clay said, relishing the warmth of her touch.

They walked slowly toward the coffee shop, which was on the other side of the neighborhood park. The world looked new and happy, like it was perpetually frozen in the golden hour when everything—every tree, every blade of grass, every street sign, every car—looked its absolute shiny best.

"That was the best night of my life," he said. "The best morning. The best now."

"For me too. I don't think I've ever ..." Her voice

trailed off. "I mean, how many times did we, you know, do it, or make love, or whatever?"

Clay shook his head. "I lost count. Maybe five?"

She concentrated and replayed the night, furrowing her brow and raising fingers to keep score. "There was the first time on the couch, which was so good. Amazing. Then we had some wine and moved to the bed, on top of the covers, with a little whipped cream action. Then more wine ..."

"Whiskey, actually," he said.

"Right, whiskey. Then we decided to clean up. And we took a shower."

"That was nice," he said.

She recalled the memory of them showering together, Clay slowly soaping her body, her wet hair plastered down as they kissed under the steamy jets, how he held her in his arms with her back against the tiles, to make love standing up.

"Then we had some trifle for real, and we did it on the couch again. After that, we got into bed under the covers and talked for a while until ..." She had four fingers up now.

"We were both getting pretty sleepy by then."

"But that made it so nice," she said. "Like drifting off together in such a lovely way, like we were half dreaming and half awake. A lovely sex dream that was also real."

"This morning when we first woke up. Don't forget that time."

"You kind of woke up ready."

"That was really only about me. Not sure it counts."

She smiled at the memory of him in her mouth, moaning with pleasure as she brought him off, the taste of him. "It counts," she said. "It definitely counts."

He nodded. "Six times in less than twenty-four hours. That's just ..." He shrugged, at a loss for words. "Epic, I guess. Probably a world record."

Kassi slid her arm around his waist and leaned into him. "This has been pure magic," she said. "It's been so long for me, and not just the sex. I mean, that too, but it's been so long since I've been able to let my guard down for just half a second and feel such joy, feel so … cared for."

Clay put his arm around her shoulder. "I feel the same way. Truthfully, my brain wasn't sure my heart was ready to feel like this, but my heart is all, 'fuck you, brain, we're doing this.'"

They paused at the edge of the park to kiss, not caring who was watching.

"Let's swing for a minute," she said, pointing at the empty swing set near the basketball court.

Hand in hand, they walked to the swings and he sat down.

"Think it will hold both of us?" she asked.

"Only one way to find out."

She straddled him and sat facing him and they began to kiss again. She had both hands at the back of his neck, holding his head in place as they kissed slowly, deeply, sensuously. Clay used his legs to swing them gently, the rocking motion and the passion making them both feel like they were slowly flying.

"I feel like a high school kid," Kassi said breathlessly between kisses. "Making out with my boyfriend and the whole world all narrowed down to just us."

"The world *is* just us."

"That's not exactly true," Kassi said. "I have a child. It complicates things."

"I didn't mean to leave her out. I totally get that you're a package deal and I want to be part of that package. I want to do it right, not confuse her, or you. I know you and Barry are going through stuff. I'll do whatever it takes, on whatever timeline you tell me, to keep you in my life. To keep you both in my life."

Kassi rested her chin on his shoulder and put her arms around him, hugging him tight. "This is all new territory for me too, but I know we can figure it out. Samantha does seem to like you."

"What's not to like?"

"Absolutely nothing." She moved her head back to look into his eyes. "I could stay here all day, just swinging and making out."

"I'm not sure the after-school moms would like that."

"We could put on a little show for them. Help spice things up for them later in the bedroom," she said.

She wiggled in his lap, grinding into his crotch, and could feel him growing hard. He slipped his hands under her jacket, then she nuzzled into his neck. The fire between them was fast rekindling.

"How committed are you to coffee?" he asked hoarsely.

"I could skip it," she said, moving her hips against him, unable not to. "I'm so charged up. I'm practically ... I'm close just from this."

"Me too. Let's go."

She slipped off his lap and then he stood, awkwardly, adjusting the bulge in his jeans. She looked at her watch. "I have to be home for Sam in two hours."

"That gives us plenty of time for number seven. And possibly number eight," he said.

They hurried back to his place. He fumbled the key into the lock, threw the door open and they stumbled inside, laughing.

By the time they crossed the living room, they both had their shirts off. By the time they made it down the hall, their pants were gone. By the time she lay across the bed, he had slipped her panties off and was softly, gently fingering her and she was pressing her lips to his, arms outstretched and gripping the comforter in each hand. The both moaned as he entered her, lost again in the heat of the moment.

Later, when he drove her home, they barely talked—overwhelmed by the power and intensity of this thing between them. They just sat in the truck quietly, smiling.

"What happens next?" he asked at last.

She squeezed his thigh. "We'll figure it out. For now, let me out a block away. Barry is unpredictable and I don't want him to know about us quite yet."

He nodded. "I can't wait to formally meet this asshole."

She kissed him and then hopped out. "Thanks for a wonderful night and day."

She slammed the door, and then high-tailed it to the driver's side and leaned in through the window to kiss Clay one last time. Lost in the feeling, neither of them noticed the BMW driving past. It was Barry dropping off Sam.

Kassi walked the block to her apartment, where Samantha and Barry were sitting on the front stoop.

"You're late," he said.

"Hey, cutie," Kassi said, ignoring him. "How are you?"

"Don't be late again. I don't like to be kept waiting," Barry said. "We have an agreement, remember?"

Kassi continued ignoring him, refusing to let him drain her bliss.

"Mom, can we have mac and cheese for dinner? The kind that Cooker makes?"

Barry kissed Sam on the forehead, stood and walked to his car, without another word.

Kassi scooped up Sam. "We can have anything you want for dinner, my darling, even ice cream and jellybeans. Mommy is in a very good mood!"

"Oh yay!" Sam squealed.

27

EXT. PUTT-PUTT GOLF COURSE - DAY

KASSI and CLAY try to behave in front of
SAMANTHA. A writing 'emergency' is
declared.

"I never knew the Eiffel Tower leaned quite so much," Clay said, looking at the weathered miniature version. "Or at all, actually."

"Stop trying to distract me," Kassi said, concentrating and putting her ball through its tattered base onto the ragged green on the other side, stopping near the cup. It would be a two-stroke hole for sure. She handed the club to Clay. "You'll never beat that. You can't get past me."

"Who knew you were so competitive? I'm learning so much about you."

He lined up the ball carefully, then hit it through the miniature tower so that banged into Kassi's ball, knocking it two feet away from the hole.

Her face fell. "You are a mean player. I'm learning so much about you."

He grinned. "Sam, you ready?"

They were playing putt-putt golf at a course near a strip mall in Hillsdale, a suburb of Portland. This was their first official date with Sam. While Kassi and Clay were seeing each other as much as possible, they decided to stay 'friends' around Sam, moving gradually to introduce her to their relationship. Today was the first step.

Sam walked up to the tee holding the child's size club, which was still too long. Kassi watched as Clay leaned down behind Sam, showing her how to grip the club and together they swung at the ball and missed. They tried again. The third time they hit it, but it dribbled off the tee onto the pathway and out of sight.

Sam looked distressed.

Clay slapped his forehead. "I just remembered an important rule for putt-putt golf."

"Let's hear it," Kassi said.

"Players over three feet tall are required to use clubs at all times, but players under three feet can throw, kick, roll or otherwise propel the ball however they see fit."

"Is that truly a rule?" Sam asked.

"Absolutely," Clay said.

"Am I above or below three feet?"

"Below."

She clapped her hands.

"You could do it like this." He rolled the ball toward the Eiffel Tower, then scampered to retrieve it. "Now you try," he said. She rolled the ball but it only traveled a foot or so.

"Silly me, I forgot the most important part of the rule," he said. "Players who roll the ball can do it from the place of their choosing."

Sam looked at him, confused, then at Kassi.

"That means you can move closer and then roll it under the Eiffel Tower," Kassi said.

"What's an Eiffel Tower?" Sam asked as she stepped up to the base of the battered replica.

"A French word for a lot to see," Clay said. "Like, the tower is an eye-ful."

"That is not true, you crazy man," Kassi said with a laugh, and Sam laughed because their joy in each other's presence made her happy, even if she didn't know exactly why.

Sam bent down, a look of concentration on her face, and rolled the ball under the tower. It smacked into Clay's ball, sending it to the far reaches of the putting green.

"That's my girl!" Kassi said. Sam laughed again and took Kassi's hand. They skipped around the wooden French tower to finish the hole.

One hour and seven fake miniature world icons later, including a Dutch windmill with spinning rotors that Sam tried to crawl through, and a Venice canal bridge that she ran over holding her ball and then dropped it directly into the cup, they declared Sam the winner of the game. Clay rewarded everyone with snow-cones.

As they strolled back to his truck, orange syrup leaked through Sam's snow-cone cup, staining her favorite white ruffle blouse. When Sam looked down and saw the neon stain, it was too much for her tired brain to bear and she squatted down on the sidewalk, chin quivering.

"Oh, poor thing, she's reached her limit," Kassi said as Sam started to cry and then wail.

"Happens to the best of us," Clay said.

Sam looked up at them both, tears staining her dusty face, the snow-cone now a melting mess next to her foot. She reached out her arms to be picked up and when Kassi leaned down she pulled away and said, "I want Cooker."

Kassi turned to Clay who looked at her questioningly. She nodded, so he handed her his snow-cone to hold. "My pleasure," he said, leaning down to pick up Sam and swinging her gently into his embrace. She snuggled her face in his neck and Kassi, walking behind them, saw her daughter smiling. She felt a twin sense of simple happiness at Sam's contented expression and a terrible sense of dread.

Later, back at her apartment, Kassi tucked Sam in for an afternoon nap before dinner. "I won't let her sleep too long otherwise she'll be up all night." She and Clay were on the couch and she had her feet on his lap.

"Were you okay with how that went?" he asked.

"It was a fun day."

"I mean with how Sam and I were together? I know this makes you nervous, and it was the first official time the three of us hung out like that."

"I don't think it could have gone much better," Kassi said. "Except for the meltdown at the end, but you know, that's life."

He began massaging her feet and she sighed in pleasure.

"Speaking of life, how is your screenplay coming along?"

"It's stalled," she said. "I've had better things to do with my time."

He pinched her big toe. "That's no excuse. When's the deadline?"

"A little more than three weeks."

He moved her feet off his lap. "Maybe you should be writing now?"

"Instead of getting a foot massage? I don't think so. Plus, a lot of writing is thinking and planning, and this is definitely helping me think and plan."

"Come on now, three weeks is not much time."

"I know, but Sam will be up soon, and then there's dinner, and story-reading time, and … well, you get it."

"How about this? For the next three weeks, I'll help out whenever I can. I have some time off accrued at work I can burn. You write nonstop, at least whenever you aren't at work, and I'll watch Sam and do the cooking. Starting this second. Get going now and when she wakes up, I'll read some stories, then she and I will go for a walk, I'll make dinner and read some more stories or play with the horses. That should give you three solid hours."

"Really?"

"Yes, let me help. I know this is important to you."

She was thinking of her agreement with Barry about baby-sitting girlfriends, but she wouldn't be gone, just writing, so it wasn't like leaving Sam with a stranger when he wasn't home. She would never get the screenplay done without Clay's help, and maybe not even with his help.

He could see the hesitation in her expression.

"Seriously. It's just three weeks, then everything goes back to normal. This is a genuine writing emergency."

"A writing emergency? I'm not sure that's a thing. What will it cost me?"

"Sexual favors, of course."

"That hardly seems fair since I benefit as well." She moved her feet to the floor and leaned over to kiss him, letting her hand snuggle in between his legs. Their kiss was taking on a heated urgency. Abruptly she pulled back.

"Sam's awake," Kassi said.

"I don't hear anything," Clay said, slightly panting.

Kassi tossed a pillow over his crotch as Sam called from the bedroom. "Mommy?"

"Out here, baby."

"Okay, that's spooky," Clay whispered. "Are you like psychically connected or something?"

She nodded. "Yes, we are."

Kassi went into the bedroom and carried Sam out in her arms wrapped in a blanket. Clay was rifling through the pile of books on the floor. "Samantha, your mom needs to get a little writing done. She's asked her buddy Clay to help out. How about I read you some stories?"

Sam nodded vigorously, and after getting her a juice

box, Kassi placed her on the sofa next to Clay.

"Do you like *The Very Hungry Caterpillar*?" Clay asked.

"It's my favorite," Sam said.

Kassi sat down at the kitchen table, threaded the typewriter with a new sheet of paper and began to write. *He sat on the couch reading the little girl her bedtime stories while she pounded away on the typewriter.*

"Hey, are you writing something about us, right this second?" Clay asked from the sofa.

"Of course not," she said.

28

Nothing is ever easy.

"This isn't the kind of message I want to leave, especially to a single mom but the rent is overdue now by two weeks and—"

Kassi clicked off the message. Today's lunch shift had been great after Walter left her another hundred-dollar cash tip. She should have shared it with the rest of the wait staff, as well as the kitchen crew, but instead she slipped it into her front pocket. She would make it up to them somehow another time.

The hundred meant she could make rent now, barely.

Her precarious financial situation was becoming harder and harder to justify. If Barry knew the desperate straits she was in, she was sure he'd use it against her somehow, maybe even try for full custody. That was probably why he wasn't paying the child support he owed.

She would never let Barry get custody. Even though he was mostly fine with Samantha for the moment, she couldn't count on that lasting. When the sweet, adoring, pliant child grew into an independent, self-sufficient and occasionally sullen teenager, one ready to talk back to her father, the real Barry would come out. The blind rages and expletives and insults. When that day came, she vowed to

217

be there for Sam, to protect her, to be her rock.

On top of all that, it was starting to feel weird that Walter was basically supporting her. She would have to figure out something different to make more money soon, but not yet, not until after she finished the screenplay. She stuffed the hundred-dollar bill in an envelope, wrote a check for the balance of the rent, scribbled the address and licked a stamp. That would go in the mail in the morning. She looked at her watch. An hour to work on the script.

For the past week, Clay had been true to his word, taking over most responsibilities for Sam's entertainment and cooking for them both. As promised, he took vacation days as needed, much to Ione's irritation. Kassi kept up her end of the bargain, using every free minute to write.

She was almost done with the first draft and feeling pretty good about how it was turning out. At least that's what she told Clay. If she was honest with herself, it was more than pretty good. She was certain she had created something amazing. So much so that while she wanted to win the contest, she almost didn't care because she knew it was that good. She had proven to herself not only that she could write, but also that she could finish something big, something potentially sellable.

She sat down at the dining room table and threaded a fresh sheet of paper into the typewriter. The dialogue in this scene was critically important, and Kassi wanted to get the tone perfect. She had decided there would be no third-act false ending in her screenplay. That was what would make it unique, unexpected. After she finished this scene, she'd be racing through to the end.

The door to the apartment swung open. Barry stood there with Sam next to him. "Hi, Mommy," Sam said.

"Hi, sweetie. Welcome home," Kassi said. She looked at Barry with questioning eyes. Clay was supposed to pick up Sam today. Was something wrong with Clay? If so, why would he call Barry? Wait, that wasn't possible. He didn't even know Barry's phone number.

"How dare you let that hippie pick up my daughter from daycare," he said, his voice crackling with anger.

"Sam, honey, please go to your room and put away your school things, okay?" Kassi said.

Sam looked up at them both and Kassi could see the first seeds of fear sprouting in her eyes. She was getting old enough to recognize his anger, even if she didn't yet understand its origins. "It's okay, darling, everything is fine." She looked hard at Barry, sending him the message with her eyes to back down.

He waited until Sam went into her room then looked Kassi up and down. "You're letting yourself go, aren't you?"

Kassi had so much experience with Barry's bouts of rage that she had developed a survivor's instinct to gauge intensity. This looked like a big one, a full-on fury fest. Shit. She needed to defuse it and keep Sam out of earshot.

"Let's go outside to talk," she said.

He glowered and started to yell but then held himself back. When they walked through the door, Clay was standing there on the stoop. Barry must have known Clay followed him to her apartment.

"Kassi, you okay?" Clay asked.

"I am," she said. "Barry, if you have an issue, let's please talk about it like adults. We can't co-parent if—"

"You have no right to have your boyfriend pick up my daughter," Barry said.

"First, as far as Samantha knows, Clay is just a friend," she said, willing her voice to stay calm.

"You lost your shit when Stella was watching Sam at my house. You're a hypocrite."

"I told you in advance that these three weeks would be a grind for me," she said. "I gave you the chance to pick her up yourself. You never returned my phone calls."

"Why would I help you?" Barry yelled. "And why the hell would you possibly need help? You work at a god-damned restaurant for tips, no better than when you were a student. You were a loser then, and you're a loser now."

"Okay, that's enough," Clay said. He took two steps forward, putting himself between Barry and Kassi. Part of her wanted nothing more than to see Clay knock him out. Clay was taller, stronger and younger and knew how to throw a punch. But that was the irrational part of her, not the mother part, it wasn't the part that knew what seeing Clay hit her father would do to Sam.

"Don't tell me how to talk to my wife," Barry said.

"I am not your wife," Kassi said.

Barry glared at her for a few seconds, then spun around and stormed off to his car. Kassi and Clay watched him drive off.

Clay took her hand and pulled her in close for a hug, feeling the tension in her arms and back.

"Well, you've met him now. I imagine you wish you hadn't," Kassi said, whispering into his neck. "Sorry to put you through that."

"Did I tell you when I'm not at the restaurant I'm an undercover agent for her majesty's secret service. I don't have a license to kill, but I do have a license to rough people up a little."

"And you're a Vietnam medic?"

"I'm a busy man."

She laughed, but only a little, and then pulled back from their embrace.

"This tantrum wasn't even that bad, truth be told. Probably because you were here," she said.

"Let's get inside and settle things down," Clay said. "You've still got a night of writing ahead of you but first, a little happy hour." He pulled a bottle of red from his knapsack. "It's the good stuff, a pinot noir from one of the best wineries in Oregon."

They turned to go back into the apartment. Sam was watching from the doorway of her room.

"Hi, Sam," he said, trying to be nonchalant. "Sorry I missed you at school today, but it's nice that your dad picked you up."

She nodded, carefully examining their expressions to see if everything was okay.

"Hey, isn't it time for Sesame Street?" he asked.

"Elmo!" she shouted. He opened the bottle of pinot and poured Kassi a glass. Sam was already parked in front of the television, watching her show.

"Let me wash my hands and then I'll get dinner going," he said.

"Mac and cheese!" Sam yelled from the front room.

"That would make three nights in a row," he said. "I've got something else in mind for you tonight, little cutie. Something better."

Kassi sipped on the wine—it was delicious. She angled her body so Sam couldn't see her face. She was having a tough time shaking off her upset and was afraid if Sam said anything, she might burst into tears.

She replayed the situation. Why had Barry gone off? Was he jealous? That seemed impossible given he'd been involved with at least three women she knew about since their split, and probably one before. But this was the first time she'd been involved with someone since their break-up. Was that making Barry insecure? Or was he genuinely concerned about Clay's potential role in Samantha's life? If so, he had a funny way of acting paternal, picking fights.

No, she thought, don't do this, stop now. Trying to rationalize abusive behavior is a symptom of abuse. He is just a mean person. But she had really believed all this would be over when she left, that Barry would simply tire himself out or distract himself with a new woman.

Even as these disjointed thoughts were flying through Kassi's mind, a bigger question was percolating up beneath them.

"Cooker, hurry up," Sam yelled. "You're taking too long."

"Sam, don't be rude," Kassi said.

But he was taking a long time in the bathroom and he could have washed his hands in the kitchen. Kassi bent forward to get a different angle and could see him through the half-open door, his hands gripping the sink, looking in the mirror, trying to slow his breathing.

Why in the world would someone as wonderful as Clay ever stay with her?

She realized now she should never have gotten involved with him, never should have let her guard down. Too late now, but it was time to start mentally preparing herself, and Sam, for the inevitable breakup. People like Clay don't stay in dysfunctional situations like hers. Kassi turned more sharply toward the wall as tears welled up. She took another swallow of the wine.

"Boy, that's good," Clay said, back in the room now, taking a long sip of the wine he poured for himself.

Kassi quickly wiped away the traces of tears but not before Clay saw. He didn't say anything, just took a deep breath and forced a smile.

"Okay, little cutie, if Sesame Street is over, are you ready to help in the kitchen?"

"Yes, Cooker! Do you have my step-up stool?"

"I do." He turned to Kassi. "Hey big cutie, why don't

you spend the next half hour writing? If there's a murder in your plot, I've got a couple ideas of which character should, you know, go kaput." He dragged his thumb across his throat dramatically.

29

EXT. USED CAR LOT - DAY

CLAY shares his dream and butterscotch milkshakes. BARRY ups the ante on his bad behavior.

"Are you sure you want to do this?" Clay asked. "You should be writing."

"I need a break and it sounds fascinating," Kassi said.

"It's a broken-down food truck on a used car lot. It's not remotely fascinating."

"Well, it's *your* broken-down food truck, and you did say something about butterscotch milkshakes afterward. So, I think it's fair to say we're both quite interested, right Sam?"

Sam nodded seriously. "I like milkshakes very much. I've never tasted butterscotch before."

"I think you'll like it," Clay said.

"I don't like a lot of things."

"Isn't that the truth," Kassi said.

Three days had passed since Barry's flare-up, and neither of them mentioned it again. But the incident still weighed heavily on Clay's mind. He felt terrible that Kassi had been through so much with Barry and was still going through it now. He had considered confronting Barry himself. While personally satisfying, he knew that would only make things worse for Kassi and Sam. Rather, where he felt he could make an impact was to try to make her life better, to offset the Barry shit, and Clay decided he would commit himself to that goal.

Part of that, he concluded, was giving her space to live without having to think about him, which wasn't too difficult given they couldn't keep their hands off each other. When Sam was at daycare and they weren't on shift and Kassi wasn't writing, they split their time between making love, showering together, making love again, and laughing, always laughing.

When Sam was around, they had to fight the urge to snuggle together, hold hands or kiss, but they were still taking it slowly and carefully so Sam didn't get confused or anxious, to give her time to get used to having Clay as a significant presence in her life. They agreed to more outings, as friends, in addition to the time Clay spent watching Sam while Kassi wrote.

For this second outing, they loaded up into Clay's truck and drove across town to Townsend Motors, a used car lot run by one of his friends from high school. Clay drove past rows of faded sedans, hatchbacks, battered pickups and the occasional Trans Am. At the very back of the lot, he parked in front of a dented step van set up on blocks, with a cracked windshield, peeling beige paint and a missing front bumper.

"What do you think?" Clay asked, unmistakable pride in his voice.

"This is it? It's, I guess … I mean, it has so much potential."

"She sure does."

Samantha peered over the dashboard. "Was it in a wreck?"

"No. Just abandoned for a little while."

"Like, since the sixties?" Kassi teased.

"Tough crowd. She's a little rough on the outside, but she's got great bones. Come on, let me show you inside."

"Is it safe. It won't fall of the blocks, right?"

"It's safe. Sometimes I climb in and pretend to serve up meals just to get used to the space."

Clay led them to the truck and opened the door. Kassi and Sam peered into the darkened interior suspiciously. He hopped in and then reached back to pull Samantha up, then Kassi after her, holding her hand a few seconds too long. She gave him a fleeting smile of longing in response that made him go a little weak in the knees.

He turned on a battery-powered lantern near the door. The inside flashed into bright view. Some of the cabinets were missing doors, others hung open crookedly and a makeshift prep counter slanted dangerously. The stove was partially melted, and there was a gaping, blackened hole where a deep fryer used to be. Clay opened the service window and swept dust off the chipped surface with his hand.

"It smells funny in here," Sam said. "Like the alley behind our apartment."

"Do not play back there without me," Kassi said. "Promise me."

Sam nodded.

"It's seems already partially built out," Kassi said. "I don't understand. Did someone have this idea for a food truck before you?"

"It's not a secret concept, but they aren't widely used, so I think I'm getting in on something big on the ground floor. The real differentiator is that my food will be on the gourmet side, not hot dogs and burgers and chips. I lucked out finding this one. For whatever reason, it didn't work out for whoever did this initial retrofitting."

Clay opened an old fridge with gray-green mold on the

inside, then quickly closed it. "A little fresh paint and some elbow grease and she'll be good as new."

Sam turned to Kassi. "Mommy …"

"No, honey, there's no such thing as elbow grease. It's just another way of saying hard work." She turned to Clay. "I love it. We can help you get it ready, right Sam?"

Sam did not look convinced. "I don't know if I have enough elbow grease in me."

They both laughed.

"Don't worry about it," Clay said. "Sam has school, and you need to stay focused on mom-stuff, plus celebrating when you win that script competition. I will serve you the very first meal though."

"Deal," Kassi said. "When can you take it home?"

"Not for a while. I put two thousand dollars down so my buddy will hold it for me until I raise the full ten thousand."

"Ten thousand! Are you sure he's your friend?"

Clay smiled. "These trucks are expensive. I've got most of the rest saved. I just need to build a little more cushion so I can pay to finish the retrofit and get it all up and running."

"Will you quit the Rose and Thorn then?"

"A topic to discuss over our butterscotch milkshakes."

Sam brightened at the prospect. He helped them down and then took them to a diner hidden in the West Hills.

"They have the best milkshakes here," he said, ordering at the counter.

They took a table by the window while they waited.

"Seriously, does this mean you'll quit your job?" Kassi asked.

Clay shook his head. "I'll keep working for a while and run the truck on weekends or days off. Like at festivals and events, until I see how it goes and work out all the bugs."

"Any new ideas for the name or the menu?"

"I'm still figuring that out. You saw the notebook."

"When did you see the notebook, Mommy?" Sam was coloring one of the placemats with crayons but listening to every word.

"Oh, uh, when Clay had it at work."

"He carries a notebook around like you?" Sam asked, not looking up from her artwork.

"I sure do. It's how I keep track of all my ideas. Right now, I'm thinking about soup and gourmet grilled cheese sandwiches for the menu."

Kassi smiled, and he hoped she was thinking back to their first night together and the post-sex grilled cheese.

"That sounds delicious. With fig jam?" she asked.

He nodded, silently sharing the heat of the memory with her. "Yes, but I'm never, ever cooking that goddamn Hungarian mushroom soup again."

"Mommy, he swore," Sam said.

"He's rough around the edges," Kassi said.

"Sorry," Clay said. "I'm not used to being around such delicate flowers. What do you think should I call my truck?"

"How about … Thrilled Cheese?" Kassi asked.

"That's not bad." He pulled out his notebook and a click-pen and wrote it down.

"The Lunch Wagon? Clay's Cart, which is alliterative. Clay's Mobile Café? I could go on forever."

He wrote them down too. "No bad ideas."

"Samantha, what do you think he should call his food truck?" Kassi asked.

She thought about it for a long minute, then giggled. "How about Elbow Grease?"

"I'm writing that down in big letters," Clay said. "In fact, I'm probably going to call it that now, so your mom can just stop. You're way better at this than she is."

Sam stopped coloring. "The Cooker Truck?" She was really giggling now, but it stopped the second the server arrived with their milkshakes on a tray.

Clay and Sam had butterscotch. Kassi got chocolate just in case. All three were topped with whipped cream and sprinkles.

"My gosh," Kassi said. "They're huge."

Sam tried to pull a sip through her straw but it was too thick, so she gave up and used the long-handled spoon and took a bite along with a little dab of whipped cream. Her eyes widened at the taste, and she took another, then another.

"Butterscotch is my favorite," she said.

Clay nodded happily and started on his own milkshake. They left the diner full and jittery from the sugar. Back at Kassi's place, Clay came inside and they agreed she would write for the rest of the day and evening, but first, she said, a cup of tea.

He watched her moving around the kitchen to clean teacups and boil water and was filled with an overwhelming sense of contentment and a pleasant longing for her. Even with the Barry shit, he could not remember a time before when he felt like life was just as it was meant to be.

When she returned with the cups, he scooted some of the letters on the table out of the way, revealing a past-due electric bill. He saw it, and she saw him see it.

"Daycare comes first," she said, tucking it out of sight. "Sorry, not sure how old this tea is. The last tenants left it behind."

He let it steep, then pulled the bag out and took a sip. "It's great, thanks."

She took a sip and grimaced. "Oh no, it's not. It's awful." She put her cup down. "My drink budget is pretty small, and most of it goes to wine. Cheap wine. That's how I fuel the script writing."

"How about—"

There was a knock at the door. "Hold that thought," she said.

It was Barry, returning art homework Sam left at his house. Sam was excited to see him and ran to the door. He picked her up and kissed her on the cheek. "Here's your project for your teacher," he said.

"I wish you'd called," Kassi said.

"Do I need to schedule time to see my daughter?"

"Our daughter, and when she's at my house, yes, you do need to schedule time. That's literally the way it works."

Barry peered past her at Clay, who had turned his chair around to watch the interaction. "You've got a lot of nerve to lecture me about anything when you're tumbling into bed with the first hippie you meet."

"Hey, hold on," Clay said, standing. He couldn't believe that this man was going to start things all over again. If he kept this up, there would come a time he would have to confront Barry himself. Men like him didn't back down unless they were forced to.

But Kassi shot him a look and shook her head slightly and he sat back down, jaw clenched. She spun to face Barry again. "Clay is my friend. We work together. I would never confuse Sam like that. Ever."

Samantha was looking up at them, eyes wide and her face pale and pinched.

"Don't come here unannounced anymore," Kassi said. "And you're three months late on support. Fix that, or I will take action."

Barry stood in the doorway. "All I ever was to you was a paycheck. I see nothing has changed."

"Come on, man," Clay said, standing and, instinctively,

curling his fist.

Barry glared him. "What, hippie, you've got something to say? Or do?"

Clay saw the anger and embarrassment in Kassi's eyes. He took a deep breath, and unfurled his first. "Yeah, I got something to say," Clay said. "You have an awesome daughter. Some guys are lucky like that."

"Fuck off," Barry said, stomping away. They heard the car door slam, the engine rev and tires squealing as he sped away.

"I'm sorry about that," Kassi said. She sat down on the floor and hugged Sam. "Daddy should never use curse words like that around you," she said. "Or anyone. Please don't ever repeat it."

"Mom," Samantha said quietly, burrowing into her arms. "What's a hippie?"

30

EXT. KASSI'S APARTMENT - DAY

KASSI and CLAY research how to write a
sex scene. Again, and again.

Three days passed and they hadn't heard anything more
from Barry since what they now jokingly referred to as the
great homework incident.

But this time, they had openly discussed it. Kassi was
convinced, ever the optimist, that Barry would eventually
adjust to the situation and accept Clay in Kassi and Sam's
life. And then, she argued, he would lapse into a tolerable
general belligerence, rather than continued pointed jabs at
Clay.

Clay didn't share Kassi's optimism but he kept that
opinion to himself as part of his commitment to helping
her have a life without Barry always in the forefront of her
thoughts.

And Kassi had, for the most part, let go of her fear that
Clay would leave because Barry's behavior didn't make a
dent in their happiness or their still white-hot sexual
attraction.

They were naked and spooned together, his arm over
her shoulder, luxuriating in the scent and heat of each
other, feeling mildly drugged from the chain of orgasms
linking back to ten minutes after Clay first stepped in the

door two hours ago, in the few hours between lunch and dinner shift when they were both off.

"Clay, I need to tell you something," Kassi said, dragging her finger along his shoulder.

"What's up?" he asked drowsily.

"I'm done."

His breath caught in his throat.

"What?"

"I'm through. Finished."

He slowly disentangled his arm and sat up. "Where is this coming from?"

"What? Oh, no, sorry, that came out wrong. I meant with the script, and you're ridiculous."

He sank back into the mattress. "You almost caused my heart to stop."

She rolled over. "I finished it last night. Now I have a huge favor to ask. Would you read it before I send it in? I'd love to know if it sounds real to a chef, and if the story resonates with you as a movie-goer."

"It's our story, right?"

"It's loosely based on our story, super loosely. Lots of other stuff happens, stuff that never happened to us. Don't get all big-headed about your character. It's not really you, but some of the broad strokes might seem familiar."

"Like how he is handsome and funny and smart and a good lover and great cook …"

"Exactly. So, will you read it or will that be weird?"

"For sure I'll read it," he said. "I'm honored to give it the Cooker's seal of approval." He pulled back so he could hold her hands, lacing their fingers together. "I'm happy for you. This is huge."

"I'm sure nothing will come of it," Kassi said. "Other than using up too much of my life."

"Stop it," he said, stroking a strand of hair back behind

her ear so he could look directly into her eyes. "I know you're going to be a success. Why didn't you call when you finished?"

"It was late. Very late, and I didn't want to wake you. Or Sam."

"Fair enough, but now we have to celebrate."

"I don't have anything to celebrate with," she said, watching the muscles ripple across his back as he stood and tugged on his shorts.

"I brought a few things over. If I'm going to spend more time here, I need better drinking options. I have some decent wine, tea from this century, coffee and a bottle of bubbly that I put in the fridge earlier. Perfect timing."

"You're sweet." She sat up, pulling the sheets to mostly cover her naked body. The side of one leg was exposed though, and higher up, the edge of her breast peeked past the folds of fabric. "But I don't need you to take care of me."

"I'm actually taking care of myself. You just get the benefit. Be right back."

She settled back into the pillows while Clay banged around in the kitchen. He came back in with two coffee cups and a bottle of champagne dripping foam down the neck.

He filled the cups until they bubbled over, then handed one to her. "Cheers, to an amazing woman and an amazing accomplishment."

She clinked her cup against his. "Thank you," she said, and took a sip. "Yum."

"I can't wait to read it."

She reached under the bed and pulled out the script.

"You want me to read it right now while we're naked and drinking champagne in bed?"

She glanced at the ceiling, then looked at her nails, feigning disinterest.

"The first few pages, maybe. Seems like you could use a break from all the sex."

Clay laughed and turned the bedside lamp on. "Said no one ever. But okay. I'll start." He flipped to the title page. "Scene one, Interior. The Rose and Thorn Restaurant. Day."

"Not out loud!" Kassi said, covering her ears with her hands and causing the sheet to slip down to her waist. "I cannot hear my words out loud."

"And I cannot read this if you're going to distract me like that," he said, tugging the sheet back up to cover her.

He bent his head to continue reading. "You actually call it the Rose and Thorn."

"I'm sure that will get changed if it ever gets made. That was just to keep me connected while I was writing."

He flipped to the next page, then the next. She watched his face closely.

"Huh," he said, and she stiffened.

"What?"

"I like the way you described the kitchen."

"It's not too much?"

"Not too much at all. It's good, authentic."

"You're not just saying that?"

"Kassi, you're an amazing writer." He kept reading, licking his finger to turn the page.

"That was fast. Are you just skimming it?"

"Have some more champagne," he said.

She nodded and refilled her cup. "You're smiling. Is it funny? Good funny or cringe-funny?"

He looked up at her. "I'm smiling because the chef sounds cool and handsome. I bet Richard Gere will play him."

"He's not that handsome," she said, looking away.

"Brad Pitt, then."

"Of course, I'll make that call tomorrow."

He returned his attention to the manuscript, then paused, narrowing his eyes. "Interesting."

"What? What?" she asked, agitated.

"The new waitress sounds sexy."

"Shit, I can't take this," she said, pressing the heels of her hands over her eyes.

"No, you can't," Clay said, closing the manuscript. "Listen, I can tell it's going to be great, but I can't read it with you watching me and freaking out every time I breathe. How about I take it home with me and read it before my shift tomorrow?"

She nodded. "Fine. That's a good idea. Thank you."

He put it on the nightstand and reached for his champagne. "I could go home early if you want me to focus on that."

She pushed down the sheet and grabbed his arms to pull him closer. "I have a better idea."

"You know I'll be thinking about that new waitress the whole time."

"I'll be thinking of Richard Gere," she said with a laugh as he slipped his hands around her waist.

"Or Brad Pitt," he said.

"Or both," she said.

"Well now, that sounds interesting. Tell me more."

***

The next afternoon, Clay was in the kitchen starting to prep for dinner when Kassi finished the side work from her late lunch shift.

"Hi, Kassi," he said, continuing to julienne carrots for

236

an Asian-themed pasta special.

"Hey, Clay," she said, smiling at him through the orders window.

"You two lovebirds want some privacy?" LuRon asked. "Now that you gave into the inevitable and whatnot."

"Wait," Gilroy said. "What are you talking about? What's going on?"

LuRon had just finished cleaning a mound of shrimp and was pulling off his plastic gloves. He tossed them in a nearby trash can. "How can you be the only person in the restaurant who doesn't know they finally got together?"

Gilroy looked at Clay. "Is this true?" he asked, clearly hurt. "Are you two a thing?"

Clay sighed. "I remember the olden days when private business stayed private."

"Was that before you worked in a restaurant?" LuRon asked. "Because I know you know there are no secrets in a restaurant."

"It's like the opposite of the CIA," Rob said. "Everyone is a double agent. I heard about you two from Meredith who heard it from Ione who heard it from—"

"Me," Jon the dishwasher said. "Ione heard it from me, and I heard it from Roz."

"Is this true, Clay?" Gilroy asked again. "I thought we were friends. Like, close friends. You've been to my house, man."

"We are friends. Friends who don't tell each other every little thing."

"Ending two years of celibacy is not some little thing," Gilroy said.

"Oh, you think you're upset?" Kristoph said, coming into the kitchen from the dining room. "My dream man is off the market and you're upset."

"I mean, I'm happy for you," Gilroy said. "I just wish

you'd share more. Why do you keep so much bottled up?"

"I'm sorry, Gilroy. You'll be the first to know any news from now on," Clay said. "Really."

"And I'm sorry I've come between you and your friend," Kassi said, patting Gilroy on the arm. "Can you give me a second? I need to ask Clay something?"

"I guess so," Gilroy said. "But I'm not happy about it this. I mean, I am happy, really happy for you two, but also a little shaken up." He sighed. "You think you know people."

Clay smiled and gently slapped Gilroy on the shoulder as he and Kassi walked to the back hallway in front of the first aid kit where it all started.

"So?" she asked.

"What?"

"What did you think?"

"About what?" Clay asked.

She pushed him in the chest. "The script, you asshole. Don't joke. I'm very insecure."

"You are the least insecure person I've ever met."

"About life things, not creative things. That's when I am practically paralyzed by insecurity."

He put his hands on her shoulders. "Kassi, it's great. In every sense. I could see it all on screen. I could see myself paying to watch it and enjoying the hell out of it. It's funny, it's dramatic, it's romantic. The way you captured working in a restaurant, you nailed it."

"You mean that?"

He nodded. "It's so good. I got a little teared up at the ending."

She sighed in relief. "I was so nervous that you would hate it."

"The opposite. I think you're going to be famous."

"Don't even let me dream about that. I'm just happy I

finished it, that I set a goal and finished, all while working a new job, raising a kid and falling in love."

Her eyes widened and she clapped her hand over her mouth.

"Oh shit," she mumbled through her hand. "Please say you didn't hear that."

"I did hear it."

"I'm sorry, it slipped out. I wasn't … I don't want to, I don't want to put any pressure on you, on us. I take it back."

"Don't take it back. I feel the same way. I just didn't want to scare you."

He pulled her in close and they kissed. It was a simple almost-chaste kiss that somehow meant more and said more than anything that had happened between them so far.

"I love you, Kassi."

"I love you, Clay."

Did that just happen, Kassi thought, as they stood smiling at each other. She grazed his hand. He knew what that touch meant. It was official. They were in love.

"Now listen, I know tomorrow is the mailing deadline," he said. "I caught a few things that need to be fixed. Some typos and a couple of culinary terms you got wrong. I marked them up and you need to fix them tonight."

She nodded. "Great, thank you."

"I don't want to overstep, but can I be there when you put it in the mail tomorrow?"

"I would love that," she said, squeezing his hand. "Thank you for everything, for being there for me. I'm not sure I would have finished without your support."

He put his arms around her waist and pulled her close.

"Break it up, you two," Ione said as she walked past. "It's like you're in heat. You start humping, I will throw a bucket of cold water on you."

"Sorry," Clay said, stepping back.

"If I have to take HR training on acceptable workplace relationships because of you horn dogs, I'm going to make your lives a living hell," Ione said, walking into the manager's office.

"We're breaking up immediately," Clay called after her.

31

INT. ROSE AND THORN RESTAURANT – DAY

Today's the day. The screenplay must be
postmarked before KASSI can begin
obsessing. Everything is on the line.

Clay was sitting in a booth in the back dining room
working on the specials menu when Kassi came in. Her
shirt was mis-buttoned and her hair was matted down on
the right side.

"What are you doing here?" he asked, standing. "What's
wrong with you?"

"I was up all night, but it's done. White-out is my new
best friend."

She waved the mailer in her hand triumphantly. "I was
putting your edits in, and then I got obsessed by the first
page, and kept writing and rewriting the opening." She sat
down across from him. "Then that messed up my first page
spacing, so I had to re-type some pages and get a little
creative with line spacing and then I messed it up a few
more times …"

"How many is a 'few?'" Clay asked.

She shrugged. "I don't know. I lost count."

"What time did you go to sleep?"

She looked dazed. "I don't think I did. I mean … I was
typing, then my head was on the table and then the alarm

rang, and I had to get Sam ready for school." She was on the verge of tears. "Oh no. I may have given her an onion for a snack."

"Sit tight. I'll get you some coffee."

When he returned, she had her head down on her arm, sprawled across the table.

"Here, drink this." He handed her a cup with extra sugar and cream.

She dragged her head up and took a sip. "That's good."

"I can't believe you pulled an all-nighter," he said.

"No choice. Today's it. Postmarked today, with a fifty-dollar entry fee that I definitely can't afford but have managed to scrape together. Those are the rules."

Roz walked by. "What's wrong with her?"

"She was up all night working on her script," Clay said.

"Oh, working on the script," Roz said, making quotes in the air. "Is that what you're calling it these days?"

"No, seriously, I wasn't even there. She has to send it out today."

Roz sat down next to Clay facing Kassi. "I hope my character isn't too mean."

Kassi took another sip of coffee. "The character loosely based on you is very sympathetic and kind, and is dealing with a lot of shit that she keeps to herself."

Roz smiled. "I don't quite understand that and probably don't deserve it, but thanks."

"You're a good person, Roz," Kassi said.

"You are delirious from sleep deprivation," Roz said.

"What about my character?" Kristoph asked, stopping on his way to the front with window spray and a clean rag. "Please tell me I'm not that stereotypical gay best friend to women everywhere who is fabulous and offers all kinds of great advice but never finds love."

"It's not like that," Kassi said.

He mock-gasped. "Did you make me straight, you witch?"

"No, no. I just … the characters aren't exact duplicates. No carbon copies. They're inspired by you all."

"The only thing that matters is whether I'm Black," LuRon said, leaning over the back of the booth.

"Of course, yes," Kassi said. She seemed puzzled by the question.

"Why is everyone talking about this?" Clay asked.

"I heard she finished," LuRon said. "I feel invested. We all do."

"She's been talking about it almost since day one," Roz said. "How could we not be?"

Ione poked her head out of the office. "Is there a staff meeting I'm not aware of? Because I have some items we could discuss."

Everyone scattered, except Clay and Kassi.

"Clay, do you have something for me?" Ione asked. "Like tonight's specials?"

He nodded. "Give me five minutes."

"Great. Kassi, you know the post office closes in an hour, right?" She looked at her watch. "Less than an hour."

Kassi looked stunned. "I have to postmark it today."

Ione nodded. "I know. Clay, go with her. After you give me the specials."

He quickly finished writing down descriptions for the specials, handed them to Ione, then took Kassi by the hand. "Come on, I was planning to hit the bank before five. We'll go to the post office first."

It was a beautiful afternoon, warm and sunny with uniform rows of fluffy clouds overhead. Sunset was still hours away, but the light was changing, and the tops of the clouds were tinged with rose gold.

When they got to the post office, there was a long line

and Kassi was distraught. "I waited too long."

"They'll move through it quickly," Clay said.

"Is that your typical experience in a post office?" Her exhaustion and emotions were teaming up to bring tears to her eyes and a quiver to her voice. "If this was all for nothing, I will feel like such an idiot."

"It's going to be fine. There's no reason to worry yet. They'll get through the line before they close."

"Who am I kidding? I'm not a scriptwriter. Let's go."

The man in front of them turned. He was older, tall and thin, with bushy salt and pepper eyebrows, white hair and a thick stubble that matched his eyebrows covering his chin. He reminded Clay of an undernourished Santa Claus.

"You kids give up easily these days. You've been here what, a whole minute?"

"She's tired," Clay said. "Cut her some slack."

"She's a writer, right? A movie writer? I heard her say script. You need thick skin to make it in that business. Why are you upset?"

Kassi shrugged, embarrassed.

"She was up all night finishing her script," Clay said. "It's for a contest. It has to be postmarked today."

"Can she not talk for herself?" the man asked.

"Of course, I can," Kassi said. "I … it's hard to make the words right now."

"Is it good?" the man asked. "The script?"

"I don't know. Probably not," she said.

The man sighed and looked at Clay.

"Yeah, it's really good," Clay said.

"You're not saying that because you're sweethearts?"

Clay shook his head. "I'm saying it because it's good."

The man shrugged. "Fine. You go ahead of me."

"No, I couldn't," Kassi said.

"Okay. I tried. Suit yourself."

She looked confused.

"You're making this overly complicated. You worked hard and you have a nice boyfriend. Go ahead. Good luck." He tapped the shoulder of the young man in front of him. "Hey buddy, she needs her script postmarked today. It's for a contest. Let her cut the line."

The young man was a punk rocker with a Statue of Liberty Mohawk haircut, a constellation of piercings on his face and in his ears, a studded belt around tattered jeans and a leather jacket with a picture of The Clash safety-pinned on the back. He looked her up and down. "Yeah, what's it about?"

"Romance and restaurants," she said.

"Does it work out okay in the end?"

She nodded. "More or less."

"I believe in love. Go ahead." He nudged the woman in front of him. "Hey lady, she's trying to win a contest. She needs to get it postmarked today."

On it went for eleven more people. By the time Kassi got to the front of the line, she was happy-crying and the script had changed to a book of poetry about wildfires.

As a window finally opened up, the postal employee put the *Next window please* sign up and everyone groaned in unison. The woman behind the counter stopped. "What is going on out here?"

"Girl needs a postmark so she can win a contest," the man at the front of the line said. He had a rolling mesh cart filled with a dozen packages to mail. "We all let her cut. Give her a break."

"Never seen such a thing," the woman said, taking the sign down. "Come on up, honey."

After Kassi paid and the clerk stamped the mailer, Clay kissed Kassi, then she raised her arms triumphantly, and everyone cheered.

"Thank you," she said. "This is officially one of the best days of my life because you were all so kind to me."

"You'd better win," the skinny Santa Claus man said, and Clay shook his hand on the way out.

"Was that a dream? I mean, literally, am I dreaming?" Kassi asked.

As they passed through the door, the postal clerk walked over and turned the building sign around to *Closed*. Clay overheard the clerk admonishing the crowd. "Okay, you do-gooders. That was sweet, but I bet all of you knew we would be obliged to serve anyone who got in line before closing time."

"We made her day thought, didn't we?" said the old man with the bushy eyebrows.

Clay smiled and didn't let on to Kassi.

Outside, Clay grabbed Kassi's hand. "Come on, we still have time to make the bank if we hurry. I need to deposit my check, and then we're getting you home and into bed."

She snuggled under his arm. "I wish you could be there with me."

"Me too." He kissed the top of her head. "Soon. Saturday night, right?"

"Yes," she mumbled. "It's so far away."

At the bank, they stood in line until a teller motioned them forward. Clay filled out a deposit slip and signed his check. The teller handed him fifty dollars in cash and his receipt with the balance circled. He smiled and nodded happily and showed it to Kassi.

Ten thousand twenty-two dollars and seventeen cents.

"Clay, you broke ten thousand with that deposit! You can afford the food truck now."

"This is a great day for so many reasons," he said. "Your script, my savings account, but the number one reason is because you're in my life."

"I feel the same way, but I'm so tired, Clay."

He led her back into the restaurant and opened the front door. "Meredith, call Kassi a cab home."

"I can catch the bus."

"It's on me," Clay said.

"I don't need you to pay my way."

"I know, you don't need anything from anyone ever. You've made that abundantly clear, again and again, but I'll worry about you on the bus when you're this tired. Do me a favor and take the cab, and call the restaurant when you get home."

When the cab arrived, Clay handed the driver the fare, hugged Kassi and then walked around back and entered the kitchen, aware that he had an annoying and apparently permanent in-love smile on his face.

32

INT. ROSE AND THORN KITCHEN - DAY

The lunch rush builds, the kitchen
banter swells and a handsome (or
dangerous?) NEW COOK is hired. ROZ takes
note.

"Any word on your screenplay?" LuRon asked.

Kassi leaned on the counter and smiled at him through the order window. "Nothing yet, but it's only been three weeks."

"The suspense is killing me, you know?" LuRon said.

"Yeah. I do know a *little* something about that."

The second day after mailing off the screenplay, even though she knew better, Kassi began checking her mail obsessively. She listened for the mail carrier each day when she was home and raced out onto the stoop to sort through the bills and junk mail dropped into the wicker basket that served as a mailbox. Then she checked again thirty minutes later, and an hour later, just in case the carrier forgot something.

Three weeks later and there was no still sign of an acceptance letter. Or an acknowledgment letter. Or the dreaded rejection letter. Nothing. Zero. Zilch.

"I'm not cut out for this kind of waiting," LuRon said.

"Me either," Kassi said. "I swear you will be the second

person I tell when I hear anything. As long as it's good news. Well, third, I guess. I should tell my mom second."

"Respect that. Moms don't get the love they deserve."

"You're sweet."

"I'm hot, is what I am," LuRon said. "It's like a million degrees outside today."

"Supposed to get up to eighty-seven," Rob said. He wore a bandana to absorb his sweat while he practiced making radish roses. It was slow in the restaurant—the sunny weather was keeping people outside. "They said on the news it was one-oh-one in Phoenix. Now that's hot."

"No, that's not hot. That's Phoenix," LuRon said. "It's supposed to be hot there. It's supposed to be cool here in the Pacific Northwest. This is bullshit hot, hellish hot. I hope this is just a freaky late-summer thing and not some whole other thing."

"It's global warming," Meredith said, pushing through the swinging door from the dining room. "They've been talking about it for a while now. Since the seventies."

"That's a hoax," Rob said. "They just want us to stop eating meat and give up our cars and give the government more money."

"That's not how science works," Meredith said. "Scientists, real scientists, don't lie and they don't falsify results to meet bullshit agendas."

"I could come up with a few notable exceptions to that statement from my point of view," LuRon said.

"Exactly, right," Rob said. "Like the Tuskegee study. Anyway, are you going to talk to me about the ethics of science? After ..." He lowered his voice. "After seducing me under false pretenses?" His knife slipped and he sliced through the radish and swore. "I'm so upset, I can't do my job."

Meredith shook her head and walked back out front.

"That girl has turned you inside out," LuRon said. "But I am impressed you know about Tuskegee. Most white people don't bother with that piece of history."

"That's 'cos it's not in most history books," Rob said. "And that's the real problem. Neither were those Sundown laws you talked about. The librarian had to do some digging for me. It's all white-washed, like literally."

"Rob, you surprise me," LuRon said.

"People always underestimate sexual pioneers."

LuRon laughed, as he browned thick slices of rustic sourdough bread on the grill. "You're a pioneer, now?"

"A ground-breaker at least," Rob said.

Clay slid a plate of pasta Florentine dusted with parmesan into the window, followed by a chicken piccata with mashed potatoes and steamed broccoli. LuRon flipped the sandwich special—a grilled veggie with black olives, thickly sliced tomatoes and sharp white cheddar—onto a plate and spread it open to reveal the gooey interior, then put it into the window as well.

"Kassi, please grab Meredith and Roz, if she's out there, and anyone else working tonight. I need to run through the specials," Clay said.

"Can't she just read the menu?" Kassi asked, a fork at the ready to sample the specials, her second favorite part of each shift.

She was working a night shift because Sam wasn't with her tonight and Ione needed someone to fill in. She didn't mind too much. More time with Clay. Now that the script was done she had time to burn.

"I want to do this in person," Clay said.

With Ione keeping an eye on the front while the wait staff gathered in the kitchen, Clay cleared his throat.

"Before I get started on the specials today, LuRon has something to say."

"Yeah, I have a little announcement. As most of you know Dara and I have been trying to get pregnant again."

"Trying a lot," Gilroy said. "It's all you talk about. That and the heat."

LuRon laughed. "Yeah, well, you know I'm a hard worker. Anyway, it happened. She's pregnant and things look good. We're having another baby."

Everyone cheered and Clay shook his hand and pulled him in for a hug that was really only a shoulder bump. Kassi gave him a real hug.

"That's great news," Gilroy said. "Will I be the godfather this time? Or is Saint Clay on tap again?"

"Maybe stick with Uncle Gilroy for now," LuRon said. "See how you do in that role."

Ione stuck her head through the door. "We've got tables filling up fast. Did you share the news?"

LuRon nodded.

"Good. Molly asked me to put you and Dara on the community tip jar up front for baby stuff. She said to leave it for at least two weeks."

"That's nice of you," LuRon said.

"Nice of Molly, not me," Ione said. "My view is that we should pay people not to have babies. Our planet has enough people. But, you know, congratulations and everything." Before LuRon could formulate a response, she turned her attention to Clay. "The new cook is here. Let him watch your kitchen shit show for an hour or so. He'll be working a regular shift tomorrow."

"Remind me of his name?" Clay asked.

"I don't know. Anderson. Or Carlton. Something. He's filling out paperwork in the office. I'll send him back in a minute."

"Great." Clay looked at the servers. "Try some of the specials before you head out."

251

Meredith, Roz and Kassi advanced on the dishes, forks raised.

"I hope for once we get a cute cook," Roz said.

"Hey," Gilroy said. "What are you saying?"

"That other than Clay and LuRon, the kitchen crew here definitely won't win any beauty contests."

"What happened to, uh, the stone guy?" Kassi asked.

"Marble? It didn't work out. The sex was amazing, but he's into the party scene and even though he is mostly sober, it's still too hard and I'm ..." Roz paused, a little embarrassed. "I need to take care of myself right now."

"Good for you," Meredith said. "I know it's not easy. Let us know if we can help."

"You're sweet, thanks. I'm feeling strong. And I've got Tess in my corner." Roz took a bite of the pasta and moaned. "Oh, that is so good."

Meredith tried it too. "Wow," she said, rolling her eyes.

"Kassi, does it bother you that your man can satisfy so many other women?" Roz asked, just as the new cook walked up.

"Uh, hi. I'm Hudson. The new guy."

Hudson had short black hair and a sun-tanned complexion that made his easy smile stand out like a searchlight. He extended his hand to Clay. Serpentine tattoos encircled his right arm.

"I'm Clay, head chef, and that's LuRon, Rob and Gilroy, line cooks," Clay said. "Dave-one is on the salad bar and Jon is back in the dishwashing bay."

"We've got two Daves," Rob said. "You'll meet Dave-two tomorrow."

"Thanks for helping me piece that together," Hudson said.

"He's very cute," Kassi whispered to Roz.

"Yeah, my wish came true," Roz said.

"On the server side of the house, we've got Roz, Meredith and Kassi on shift tonight," Clay said. "You'll meet Kristoph and the rest of the crew over the next few days."

"Nice to meet you all," Hudson said. "Thanks for taking a chance on me. I appreciate it."

"It's just a job, bro," Gilroy said. "Not a life choice. You'll probably regret ever setting foot in the Rose and Thorn."

Roz, Meredith and Kassi left the kitchen to finish setting the dining room for dinner.

***

"Probably be gone in two weeks if you're like most of the new guys," Rob said.

"Great pep talk, gang," Clay said. "Ignore Gilroy. He's fighting with his girlfriend. Welcome to the team."

"We're not fighting," Gilroy said. "It's worse than that. Angel isn't talking to me. I'm getting the silent treatment."

"Out of the blue?" Clay asked, then pointed Hudson toward a rack of jackets and aprons.

"Basically, yeah. I made plans to see my dad in Taos, and she's pissed because I didn't invite her."

"You didn't invite her?" LuRon asked. "To go on a trip with you. Your significant other."

"Yes," Gilroy said, slowly, as if explaining to a child. "I didn't want her to come with me."

"You're an idiot. She should leave your ass."

Roz came in, read off an order and hung the ticket.

"Hudson, are you involved?" Clay asked, watching Roz pause to hear the answer.

"No," Hudson said with a smile. "I've been, uh, out of the game for a little while."

"Whatever you do, don't listen to anything any of us have to say about relationships," Clay said.

"Guys," Kassi said, poking her head through the door. "I think we're about to get slammed."

Clay peeked through the window. He didn't like what he saw. The dining room was nearly full. The worst thing for a kitchen was to have a dining room get full all at once, with a flood of orders coming in at the same time. Hard to ever dig out from under that avalanche.

"You ready to jump into the deep end?" Clay asked Hudson.

"I'm happy to start now."

"Rob, get Hudson a knife and turn him loose on some prep. We're going to need more mashed potatoes and half a case of broccoli florets."

"And sliced tomatoes," LuRon said.

"And spinach for the pasta," Clay said. "Welcome aboard."

As the orders piled up, Hudson finished the prep easily and offered to help on the line. Clay waved him over and they stood shoulder to shoulder, working on pasta and sauces for the chicken orders. Roz spent more time in the kitchen than usual, watching Hudson. By the time things slowed down more than two hours later, he was working—and cursing—like part of the crew.

As the night came to a close around ten o'clock, Clay pulled off his apron. "Hudson, if this shift didn't scare you off, you're going to fit in well here."

"Compared to my last cooking job, this was fun, and you all seem pretty cool."

"Where was your last job?" Rob asked. "Hell?"

"Kind of. I assumed Molly told you. I was a cook at EOCI."

"Not familiar with that restaurant," Clay said.

"It's not a restaurant. It's the kitchen at the Eastern Oregon Correctional Institute."

Everyone looked at him blankly.

"Prison. I was in prison."

There was a long, awkward silence.

"Probably less shanking here," Rob said.

"Jesus, Rob, stop it," Clay said.

Hudson smiled. "I certainly hope so."

"We're going to finish cleaning up and get things ready for the day shift," Clay said. "Takes about twenty minutes. You get a shift meal and drink for helping today, plus I'll see that these hours make it into your first paycheck. If you can hang around, I'll join you for a beer and we can talk through a few things."

"That's kind of you," Hudson said. "But I'm in recovery so I'll pass on the beer."

Roz came in with a half-full bus tub and paused.

"What's your stance on club soda and bitters?" Clay asked.

Hudson smiled. "That sounds pretty good."

"Roz, why don't you show Hudson where he can wait, and maybe fix him one of your non-alcoholic specials?"

Roz nodded, set the bus tub in the dish pit, and then motioned for Hudson to follow her.

The kitchen crew returned their attention to cleaning the grill, prepping and covering the food, leaving the sweeping and mopping to Jon who was still struggling out from under a mountain of dishes in the dishpit. He'd be working at least another hour.

"Can we address the elephant in the room?" Rob asked. "I should bring my gun back, right?"

Clay was running his knife over the steel to smooth out the micro-damage. "Rob, I will send you to prison if I see that gun in here again. No more talk about this. Or about prisons. We're going to make Hudson feel welcome, and we're all going to drink some champagne and help LuRon celebrate his good news."

"Maybe just one glass," LuRon said. "Dara is getting a little touchy about me staying too late, and drinking when she can't."

"See," Rob said. "That's why you should never, ever get married."

Meredith was cleaning the espresso machine and shot him a withering look. "I don't think you will never, ever have to worry about that."

33

INT. KASSI'S APARTMENT AND A PORTLAND
EMERGENCY ROOM - DAY TURNING TO NIGHT

SAMANTHA takes a tumble. A reckoning at
the local emergency room. BARRY makes it
complicated because that's what he does.
Will KASSI give up?

Kassi steeled herself to check the mail when she got home. She pretended it didn't matter, approaching the wicker basket nonchalantly, as if she didn't want the mail itself to know how much she cared. Again, nothing. Just an overdue phone bill and a grocery store sale flyer with next week's coupons.

She went inside and dropped her backpack on the table. Her stomach grumbled but it was too early for dinner. She wondered how Clay was getting on at the restaurant, wishing he were here with her now. She was counting down the two hours until his dinner shift ended and he came to spend the night.

The phone rang. "Hello?"

It was Barry. "Don't freak out. Sam bumped her head and I'm with her at the emergency room."

"Is she okay?" Kassi asked, instantly and instinctively preparing herself to act on whatever information was forthcoming.

"She seems fine to me, but they want to hold her for a few hours to be sure."

"What happened?"

"She fell off the stairs at the top of a slide."

"Which one?"

"The playground near my work."

"Not which slide. Which emergency room?"

"The one down on Twenty-third Avenue. Good Samaritan."

"I'm on my way."

Even though Kassi was worried and had a thousand questions, she pushed everything away to focus on the immediate need. She grabbed her purse and keys, Sam's favorite stuffed octopus, two picture books plus pajamas and slippers, along with two juice boxes and a bag of goldfish crackers. She was out the door in under two minutes. She ran to the bus stop two blocks away, willing it to come. After a long few minutes, as she was about to flag down the next passing car, she spotted an off-duty cab. She stepped in front of it and begged the driver to take her to the hospital.

Ten minutes and ten dollars later, Kassi was rushing into the emergency room. The front desk nurse checked her identification and then directed her to the exam room at the far end of the corridor. The curtain was open and Sam was lying on the exam bed, clutching a blanket, alone and wide-eyed.

"Oh, honey," Kassi said.

"Mommy," Sam said, her voice weak. She reached out her little arms and Kassi hugged her, then stepped back.

"Let me look at you." Kassi examined her daughter's eyes. They seemed clear. She ran her palm gently over her head, pushing aside her bangs, and saw the angry bruise starting to form around a tender bump in the middle of her forehead, the size of a half-dollar. No blood, thankfully.

"Are you okay?" she asked, gingerly touching the bruise.

Sam winced but nodded, and Kassi pulled her finger back. Her forehead looked as if it had been thoroughly cleaned but no stitches.

"You got a bad boo-boo. Does it still hurt?"

"It wasn't my fault. A butterfly tried to land on my nose and then when I went to touch it, it got mad and the butterfly pushed me off the ladder." Tears began to flow. "Mommy, my whole head hurts."

"You can't trust butterflies." Kassi leaned in to hug her again. "Don't cry, baby. You'll feel better soon."

"I want to go home. With you. Can I please, Mommy? Can we go home?"

"Let me see what's going on."

Sam nodded and tried to stop crying. Kassi held a Kleenex to her reddened nose and Sam blew obediently twice, and then Kassi tossed the tissue into the trash.

"Daddy used some bad words before," Sam said. "He was mad at Gloria and said she was acting like a witch."

Kassi was pretty sure Barry had never said witch in his life. Also, who the hell was Gloria, she wondered?

And where was Barry? Why was Sam in here alone? Kassi looked around the room. She was safe enough. The bars were up on the bed, like a crib, so it was impossible to fall out, but still.

A red-haired nurse came into the room. Her kind face was accented with a spray of freckles. "Hello. I understand you're my favorite patient's mother. She's been eager for you to arrive." Sam smiled a little at the sight of the nurse.

"I am indeed this brave angel's mom, lucky me. Can you please tell me if she's okay and what's going on?"

"She's got a nasty bump on the head, and while it was a good idea to bring her in, everything looks okay."

"Any risk of concussion?" Kassi asked.

"Low but we want to keep an eye on her here for a little bit longer. We're on the lookout for any issues with concentration or if her headache gets worse. So far, she seems fine, and with quiet and another icepack for the next hour, she'll be good as new. She'll have a very colorful bruise to show off, and an amazing story about a mean butterfly."

"She also said ice cream might help," Sam said.

"No memory issues here! The doctor did prescribe a big bowl of ice cream."

"Thank you," Kassi said, relieved. "Why is she in here alone?"

"She wasn't alone, I was outside, recording the doctor's notes. We're always doing more than one thing at a time. I assure you that no one could have gotten in or out of this exam room without me seeing them. I watched you go in after the nurse up front called to say you were coming."

"I'm sorry, that came out wrong. I'm grateful to you. What I really meant is where is her father?"

The nurse smiled sympathetically. "To be perfectly honest, the doctor asked him to leave with his ... wife, maybe?" Kassi shrugged and her expression formed the answer. She didn't know who Gloria was. "They were talking rather loudly, to put it plainly. The doctor suggested they take it outside."

Just then, Barry walked into the exam room. He had on his nice face. Kassi was relieved to see his expression, even as she was freshly exhausted by the need to constantly surveil his mood. But at least this boded well for getting Sam home without any incident.

Barry took two quick steps to Sam and pulled his hand from behind his back, handing her a double-dip chocolate ice cream cone. "Medicine for my brave little girl."

Sam's face lit up, and Kassi was about to say the cone was way too big for her when the top scoop plopped onto Sam's lap, and her little lip began to quiver.

Before Sam, or Barry, had time to get upset, Kassi grabbed a paper cup and towel, scooped up the ice cream from Sam's lap and wiped off the sheet. "The ice cream is saved. You work on the first scoop in the cone, and we'll give you the rest after."

"Okay, Mommy," Sam said, taking a lick. "Thank you for saving my ice cream. I love you."

"Hey, where's my thank you?" Barry asked.

Sam froze, and the deer-in-the-headlights expression on her face nearly broke Kassi in two. "Thank you, Daddy."

"Do you love me too?"

"I love you, Daddy. I always love you."

The nurse put her hand on Kassi's shoulder and squeezed softly. She knew. "I'll take that ice cream to our freezer and then finish the discharge papers so you can go. Do you have a health insurance card for me?"

Barry dug in his wallet for the health insurance card. At least he took this aspect of his responsibility to Sam seriously. That was something, because Kassi sure couldn't afford it. Not for Sam or herself.

"Thanks," she said.

"No problem, I'm glad to be able to have her on my health insurance plan. You know I'd do anything for Sam. And for you too, in my own warped way," he said.

Kassi sighed. In the increasingly rare moments like this, she could see glimmers from their past and was reminded of why they came together in the first place, why she had fallen for him. He wasn't all bad but the part of Barry that was bad had filled up all the space between them, suffocating any hope of a loving relationship.

Kassi knew that on some level, Barry understood he

hadn't been the perfect husband, far from it. He had even ventured to a therapist after the initial shock of Kassi leaving wore off, telling her everything that transpired there. The therapist suggested his rage events might be associated with undiagnosed panic attacks, and advised medication.

But Barry refused. He had convinced himself all he needed to do was tone it down, that everything would be fine if Kassi stopped taking things so seriously, begging her to overlook what he called his 'intensity' for the sake of their family.

She knew it was emotional manipulation at a master level, that he was placing the responsibility for his abusive rage on her. And while it didn't work, there was still a tiny part of her that worried maybe he was right. It was that same guilt that drove her to pack Sam up and move across the country when he got the new job. He had been pretty great before and during that whole move, swearing he would go back to a therapist and take the meds.

That was not the case. Turns out, he already had a new girlfriend when she arrived in Portland. And he greeted Kassi with full-on fury. It was then that she finally understood. He didn't want to change. He would never change. She felt utterly foolish.

Even so, despite everything, they shared a daughter now and she would always strive to remember the good in him, the smart and funny man she fell for, the one who loved Sam like crazy. What they needed to do now was find a way to be decent co-parents. She would take any olive branch he offered, even his throw-away comment about health insurance, if that seemed likely to increase those odds.

"I know," she said. "I appreciate that." He smiled and offered her some of his ice cream. She shook her head. "Will you stay here for a few minutes while I make a call?"

"Who to?" he asked.

"Don't leave Sam alone, okay?"

Kassi found a pay phone in the lobby and turned her back to the room for privacy. She knew Clay was deep into the dinner shift so she dialed his home number, knowing he'd go home before coming to her apartment later. He liked to shower first to get the food smells off of him.

At the first beep, she said, "Clay, it's me. Don't worry, but Sam had a fall when she was with Barry and I'm at the emergency room. We'll be home soon, not sure when. Maybe you could come by in the morning for coffee or something instead of after your shift tonight, because she won't be with Barry tonight. I'm taking her home. Don't worry, I repeat, do not worry. I just want you to know what's up. We are fine. Sorry, I'm babbling, I'll leave the door unlocked, so just come in, and of course—."

Second beep. Out of tape. Answering machines always made her feel long-winded. When she returned to Sam's room, Barry was sitting on the chair by the bed and looked at Kassi with an odd expression.

Three hours later, closing in on midnight, they were finally able to leave. Sam was in her yellow daisy pajamas, hugging her stuffed octopus and in Kassi's arms when they left the emergency room.

At first, Barry insisted it was still his night with Sam and that she should come home with him, but Sam clung to Kassi and refused to let go. Kassi saw a flash of anger illuminate his face, but Barry relented and offered to give them a ride. Relieved to have dodged a fight and given how late it was plus the fact she had no cash for a cab, Kassi accepted.

"Can Daddy sleep over tonight?" Sam asked with wide, serious eyes when they arrived at the apartment.

"I don't think Daddy will be comfortable sleeping on

that lumpy old couch," Kassi said.

"I don't mind. Anything I can do to make my daughter feel better." He made a silly face at Sam.

Kassi felt weird having him under her roof and started to say no, but Sam gave her a pleading look. "I still feel scared," she whispered. "What if a butterfly gets in?"

Kassi nodded. She skipped Sam's bath and used a warm washcloth to clean the sticky ice cream residue off her little hands and face. She checked out the forehead bump, now a shade of lavender mixed with light green, then as Sam was practically falling asleep sitting up, Kassi and Barry tucked her into bed together.

"Thank you for staying over, Daddy," Sam said, "and for rescuing me."

"Just like old times," he whispered. "My little princess."

Sam turned onto her side, clutching her stuffed octopus, and was softly snoring in seconds.

In the living room, Kassi handed Barry a pillow and a blanket. "You need to be gone by eight. Clay is coming over for breakfast."

"I'll be gone. Some people are responsible and work for a living. They don't cut up vegetables in clever shapes and call it a career."

"Whatever. Sleep in your clothes."

He smiled and raised an eyebrow. "You sure? You used to like me out of my clothes."

"Stop being weird. And I hate that I have to ask, but can you please give me the child support check? You're three months behind."

Barry pulled out his checkbook and wrote out a check for three hundred and fifty dollars. "I threw in an extra fifty," he said, eyeing the past-due bills on the table.

"Take it off of next month's check." Kassi did not want to be indebted to Barry, even for just fifty dollars. "Please don't wake either one of us in the morning, especially Sam. She needs to rest. Let yourself out."

"Okay, but I'll go to her if she wakes up tonight, she needs to know I stayed." He kicked off his shoes, fluffed up the pillow and stretched out on the couch. "Can a guy get a drink in this house?"

"There's wine in the fridge," she said, then turned and went into her bedroom and pulled the door mostly closed but not all the way. She needed to be able to hear Sam in case something happened during the night. She played the message Clay left. *Thanks for letting me know. I'll be over in the morning. Give Sam a kiss for me. Hope you're doing okay. Love you.*

She could hear Barry poking around in the fridge, pulling out the open bottle of white and rummaging in the cupboard for a glass. He grabbed two and filled both, then nudged open Kassi's open door a bit.

"Sure I can't tempt you?" he asked, holding out a glass. "It's been a long night."

"I'm sure," Kassi said. "Look, whatever you think is happening is not happening. Nothing has changed."

"Fine, good night." Barry took the wine back to the kitchen, where he drank most of both glasses before stretching out on the couch.

Kassi slipped out of her clothes and pulled on her favorite nightgown. She buried her head in the pillow and wished Clay were next to her. She was completely wrung out and it didn't take long for her to drop off into a deep sleep.

***

Clay pulled to a stop in front of Kassi's apartment and then jumped out of his truck. He leaned back in through the open door and grabbed the carrier tray with coffee for

Kassi and hot chocolate for Sam. With his other hand, he pulled on the string attached to an over-sized balloon shaped like a unicorn. He tugged and it popped out of the cab, bouncing above him like a happy cloud as he walked toward the apartment.

Other than Barry's tirades, this was the first time Kassi and Clay had faced something challenging together as a couple. He was eager to help Kassi and Sam get through this. They probably didn't get home until late. He would make breakfast when they were awake and then the three of them could talk about how the day should unfold.

Like a family.

A trash truck in the back alley banged around and Clay quickly shut the door behind him to keep out the noise. The living room curtains were closed and the apartment was hushed and dark. He tiptoed down the corridor, first turning to look into Sam's room. She was asleep, her face burrowed into the pillow. He smiled.

Clay turned to the other side of the hallway and gently pushed Kassi's half-open bedroom door. He froze.

She was in bed with Barry. They were asleep. Barry was spooned into her.

Clay's mind began to wildly spin as he tried to find a reason, any reason, why this wasn't what it seemed to be.

Barry sat up. Clay exhaled. Barry yawned.

Then Barry saw Clay.

"What the hell are you doing here, hippie?" Barry snarled.

His voice jolted Kassi from sleep. She sat up. At first, she seemed disoriented, looking around with sleepy, confused eyes. She saw Clay in the doorway and started to smile but her expression changed abruptly when she looked at Barry. Her eyes widened.

"What are you doing here?" she asked.

"Don't you remember last night?" Barry asked.

Clay let go of the balloon and it floated to the ceiling.

"What the fuck? Get out of here!" Kassi yelled. "Clay, this is not what it looks like."

"Daddy?" Sam called.

Clay spun around, pausing for an instant at Sam's door. "Cooker?"

Clay didn't say a word, he just put the hot drink cups on the dining room table next to two wine glasses and an empty bottle.

Kassi ran up behind him. She grabbed his arm, but he pulled away. She was wearing a worn, ratty nightgown, the outline of her nude body visible though the fabric.

"Clay, let me explain. This is nothing. Please, don't go." She reached for his arm once more and again he brushed her away. "Please, Clay. This is bullshit. He snuck in bed with me."

"I trusted you," Clay said, his hand on the doorknob, his voice cold. He looked over at Barry holding Sam, who was clutching the balloon string in her little fist. Barry was in boxers and no shirt.

"I'm asking you, please," Kassi said. "Clay, don't go. I'm begging you, begging."

Clay wavered, fighting against the echoes of his past pulsating through his entire being. But he could only hear the cracking sounds of his life being destroyed again, and the need for motion won the moment. He opened the door and walked out.

34

INT. KASSI'S APARTMENT AND LATER AT THE
HIDEOUT - DAY

Old heartaches become new again.

Kassi hung up the phone. She'd called a dozen times and left four messages, but still no word from Clay. He couldn't possibly think she slept with Barry, she thought. Could he?

"He seems a little high-strung," Barry said. "Probably just as well."

Kassi shot him a look cold enough to freeze hell. "Don't talk to me," she said. "No, I take that back. Tell me why you just blew up my life."

"Fortune favors the bold."

"Save me your inspirational locker room nonsense. You know that 'us' is never going to happen."

"Not with that muscle-bound dope sniffing around," Barry said. "I'm just lucky you're such a hard sleeper." He grinned.

"You are a self-centered child, an idiot who plays games with people's lives, with my life. That stunt was beyond the pale and—"

Samantha walked in and they stopped talking.

Barry had agreed to take Sam to daycare. Her head bump seemed fine. It hadn't colored up any further and she was begging to go to school. If the world were a fair place, Kassi would insist she and Sam stay home and read and color and take naps, but she needed the money. No shift, no tips. No tips, no food.

Barry made clear he couldn't take the day off. Times like these made Kassi wish she lived closer to her mom. Or any family member, really. Or a good girlfriend.

Kassi reached down to help Sam finish getting dressed.

"Please think about our future," Barry said. "Just consider it."

"Stop talking about it right now. It's confusing."

"To me too," he said.

She glanced over at Sam. "It's not confusing to me."

Kassi would not subject Sam to a discussion between her parents about the nonexistent future of their family unit. It would only get her hopes up. Kassi was done with Barry, especially after this sick little stunt, and had no idea why his interest in her was newly ignited.

It had to be jealousy, in that weird way men think women are the prizes in a chest-thumping primal game, objects to own and control. In Barry's mind, he lost her to Clay, so suddenly he wanted her back. It didn't hurt that his latest girlfriend probably dumped him after whatever weirdness happened at the hospital.

It wouldn't last. His mood would switch or an inevitable disappointment or imagined slight would release the hounds of rage and send him baying into the arms of another woman.

She needed to talk to Clay. The damage Crystal inflicted on him was triggering his response. She understood that. A simple conversation was all they needed to clear up this misunderstanding. Together, they could manage all the other weirdness around them. They loved each other.

"Sam, stop wiggling and let me zipper your dress," Kassi said.

Sam had picked out a dress normally reserved for a birthday party, a pink and black polka-dot number Kassi discovered at Goodwill with a Nordstrom's price tag still attached. Sam wanted to dress up to add flair to her hospital story and Kassi gave in easily. Besides, Sam was growing so fast that there weren't many months left when the dress would fit.

"Now eat," she said, leading Sam to the kitchen table for a bowl of oatmeal. She turned to Barry. "Make yourself useful and pour your daughter some juice."

"Please," Sam said.

"What?" Kassi asked.

"*Please* make yourself useful. You forgot to say please."

Kassi smiled for the first time that morning.

"I think we can be a family again," Barry said. "We should be a family again."

Kassi knew Sam was listening intently even though she acted like she wasn't. She closed her eyes and thought about what to say, choosing her words carefully.

"You, me and Sam will always be a family, but we will never live together under the same roof again."

"I like it better with two homes," Sam said.

Barry stopped pouring apple juice. Kassi stopped cutting the cheddar cheese with ketchup sandwich she had prepared for Sam's lunch and looked at her curiously.

"More ice cream for me."

"Smarty pants," Kassi said.

Barry looked stunned and she could sense the anger starting to spread like black mold across his emotions. He would probably say terrible things to Sam about Kassi once he was alone with her later in the car, how she had destroyed their family. She had no control over that. She needed to get to work. She needed to see Clay.

Kassi slid the sandwich into a plastic bag, slipped in a

surprise package of Oreos along with four apple slices and a juice box, and latched Sam's unicorn lunchbox. Kissing Sam goodbye outside, she told her she'd see her later that afternoon, refused the offer of a ride from Barry to work—what would Clay think if Barry dropped her off—and got to the bus stop just as it was pulling up.

At the restaurant, she was disappointed Clay wasn't waiting for her in the dining room. He wasn't on the schedule today, but she knew he'd come in at some point later, after the rush died down. During set-up for lunch, Ione asked if she was okay, wondering why she was so subdued. Kassi brushed it off.

As she was filling water glasses on a four-top, she spilled water from the pitcher onto the teenage boy in the group. Kassi then took the family's food order, turned too fast and a coffee cup and a water glass slid off her tray onto the floor, shattering. Ione was by her side in seconds, calling for the busboy to sweep up.

"Dessert is on us today," Ione said cheerfully to the mother, after checking to be sure no eyes were punctured by the flying shards. "How about we move you all to a new spot, I've got a great booth right by the window."

"Also, get them a new waitress," Ione hissed into Kassi's ear as she shuffled the four-top out. "Get your act together or clock out and go home."

Throughout the rest of the lunch shift, Kassi kept looking at the door, expecting Clay to come in, to tell her he was sorry for leaving, to let her explain. He had to know she would never do anything to hurt him.

She was not Crystal.

But why wasn't he here?

She wondered if she could have done anything differently in the moment to keep Clay from leaving. Scream at Barry? Tearfully beg Clay to stay? She did that, sort of. Should she have been more emphatic?

Back in the kitchen as she was hauling a bus tub full of bowls swimming in an inch of watered-down pale pink Hungarian mushroom soup, she pulled Roz aside. "I'm on the long shift today. Any chance you can cover for me?"

"No sorry. I'm ..." A shadow of disappointment darkened Kassi's face. "You know what, sure," Roz said.

Kassi hugged her, surprising them both.

"You seem a little off today. Is everything okay?"

"Sam took a tumble yesterday and I'd like to bring her home from daycare early."

"Poor thing, you and Sam. She's okay, right?"

Kassi nodded, fighting back unexpected tears. "And something happened with Clay. I'm all twisted up."

"I'm sorry. He does that. Go fix things."

"Thank you," she whispered.

Kassi cashed in her tips—not a great day, but not awful, almost thirty-five dollars—finished her side work, clocked out, all while avoiding Ione, and caught the bus to Clay's house.

At his door, she knocked, waited, and knocked again. No answer.

"Clay?"

She put her ear to the door. No noise from inside. Maybe he was sleeping. She looked through the window on the porch. Inside, she could make out the couch and coffee table. Maybe he was hiding. Stop being paranoid, she thought. He was simply not home.

It was a long shot, but she decided to head to The Hideout, his favorite bar. Clay typically wasn't a day drinker, but she didn't know what else to do.

It was a short walk to the bar. Clay had taken her there a few times, and she liked the hole-in-the-wall atmosphere almost as much as he did. She had even gone there once on her own. She felt safe there. Melinda made sure she was left alone.

The world would be a happier place if all bartenders were women.

Kassi opened the door and felt a surge of relief. Clay was at the bar.

He didn't see her come in. He had a shot of whiskey and a beer in front of him, along with what looked like an uneaten burrito. Melinda walked by with a tray of drinks for a table in the back. "Oh, thank god," she said to Kassi. "He's had a few, but he doesn't seem too drunk."

"How long has he been here?"

"He was waiting when we opened."

Kassi walked up behind him and wrapped her arms around his back. He flinched and then froze. She unwound her arms and slid onto the bar stool next to him. He kept his eyes forward.

"Clay, I'm so sorry. I can't believe Barry did that."

He didn't answer, just downed his shot and took a sip of beer. Mel brought over a drink for Kassi.

"I seem to remember you like gin and tonics," Mel said. "This is a double and it's on the house. Clay, you'd do well to slow down."

Clay ignored her too. Mel walked over to a new customer on the other end of the bar.

"Why aren't you saying anything?" Kassi asked.

"What exactly do you want me to say?" His voice vibrated with anger.

"Anything," she said, pressing down her instinctive panic reaction to the signs of a coming rage that she associated with Barry, but now was emanating from Clay.

She steadied herself, and put her hand on his thigh. This was Clay. Not Barry. He turned to face her and then pushed her hand away.

"How could you?" he said, his voice now rising to a full-on shout.

"Don't yell at me," she said quietly.

"Oh, I'm sorry," he said, his voice still elevated. "Am I supposed to smile and say I loved seeing you in bed with your ex-husband? He sure didn't seem very ex to me, lying next to you in his goddamn underwear."

"You think I slept with Barry?" She was incredulous. "Like I would do that to you? Or to me?"

"I saw you in bed together."

"Clay, inside voice," Mel said.

If he heard her, he didn't let it show. Kassi watched, horrified, as the repressed anger from the years of pain Crystal inflicted spilled out of him like rain through an overloaded downspout.

"I helped you with your goddamned screenplay, babysat your kid, made you both dinner, and what do you do? You cheat on me with a man who abused you."

Kassi worked hard to keep her voice calm. "I know that must have been a shock, what you saw. It was a shock to me to wake up with him in my bed—"

Clay didn't let her finish. "So, he just tripped and fell, then all his clothes came off and he landed in your bed? You expect me to believe that?"

"Yes, I expect you to believe that because that's what happened. He wanted you to find us, he set it all up. You know Sam hurt her head, and she asked him to spend the night—"

"She did, or you did?" He was calmer now but his tone was cruelly sarcastic.

"You need to be careful here," Kassi said, her heart rate accelerating.

"There were empty wine glasses. Two of them. It was my goddamn wine."

"I did not sleep with him. I would never do that to us."

"I was a fool to think you'd leave him. The first chance you got, you hopped back in the sack with him. You were using me all along. People warned me but I refused to believe them. Fuck this." He spat the last two words out viciously, and loudly.

The hardness in his voice hit her in the face as if he had struck her. She nodded, slowly and then picked up her drink.

"Yeah, fuck this. And fuck you for thinking so poorly of me."

Kassi threw the gin and tonic in his face and left without another word, slamming the door behind her.

35

INT. ROSE AND THORN RESTAURANT – DAY

Could this day get any worse? (Spoiler alert: Yes, and how.)

Kassi tossed a plate of pasta into the window where it landed with a clank and clatter.

"Gilroy, can you please tell Clay that table six who asked for their pasta without onions would actually like it to have no onions in it?"

Gilroy looked at her, then at Clay who hadn't turned around. "I mean, he's right here, but sure. Clay, Kassi said that—"

"I heard her. You can tell Kassi that unless the kitchen knows about special orders, we can't accommodate the needs of our guests."

Gilroy looked at Clay, then at Kassi. "I don't know what's going on with you two."

"Isn't it clear?" Rob asked. "They're role playing. Angry sex is the best sex."

"I can assure you that we are not role playing," Kassi said. "Gilroy, can you let Clay know that the ticket for table six clearly reads no onion."

Clay spun around to face Kassi. "When we're busy, you're supposed to call it out."

"I did call it out."

"She did," Gilroy said. "I heard her."

"Then it wasn't loud enough for me to hear." Clay grabbed the plate and dumped the contents into the trash, then tossed the empty plate onto the counter where it broke in half.

"Maybe, just maybe, you don't listen to me," Kassi whispered.

Clay stopped and looked at her. "Maybe that's because what you say and what you do are so far apart."

"Okay, I'm starting to get uncomfortable," Gilroy said.

"Me too," Rob said.

Ione came in and stood by the line. "I'm getting complaints about Kassi and hearing that things are weird between you two."

Kassi didn't say anything else, but her expression was stricken.

Clay turned his attention to a pasta pan over the flames. He drizzled in some olive oil and threw in a handful of onions. They flashed and sizzled and then he swore, and reached for another pan to start over without onions.

Ione sighed and shook her head. "This is literally why you don't shit where you sleep."

"I'm not great with metaphors," Rob said. "In this case, is shit like falling in love or is it fighting?"

"Learn when to be quiet," Ione said to Rob. "Clay's doing a double today and we can't make it through lunch or dinner without Clay, so Kassi, you're done. Go home. Luckily, after tomorrow we're shut down for a week for the annual deep cleaning. After that, I'll rework the schedule to keep you two idiots apart."

"I don't think that's necessary," Kassi said. She was still expecting this to blow over between her and Clay, that they'd eventually figure it out.

"I do," Ione said

"Me too," Clay said.

Gilroy stood there, looking worried and holding his chef's knife in both hands like a security blanket.

Kassi pulled off her apron and headed for her locker. Heart heavy, she rode the bus home. Even the gentle kindness of Marcus, her favorite bus driver, wasn't enough to lift her spirits or coax a smile.

He gave it his best shot, though, first with a joke.

"What did the bus driver say to the frog?" he asked.

She shook her head.

"Hop on."

She tried to smile but failed.

Next, he asked about her script. "Any word?"

"Not yet," she said, looking out the window.

Finally, he asked directly. "Kassi, is everything okay?"

"No," she said, with a slight shake of her head.

"You'll let me know if there's anything I can do, right?" he asked, pulling over at her stop.

She put her hand on his shoulder. "Your kindness is enough."

Kassi trudged home to a sad and empty apartment. She slumped on the sofa with a glass of wine. She still had three bottles from Clay's expensive stash. She was halfway through her first glass when she realized she hadn't immediately checked her mail for the first time in weeks.

She went outside and pulled out the letters.

Amidst all the bills and junk mail and ads for toilet uncloggers, there it was. A letter from the Screenwriters Guild Inaugural New Voices Script Competition.

Hands trembling, heart racing, she carried it to the kitchen table and sat staring at the envelope. It seemed too small to contain good news. Or bad news, for that matter. She wished Clay were here to open it for her, or to share in the experience. She felt tears creeping up around the edges of her eyes again.

"I'm an idiot," she said in the silence. "Winners don't cry."

She ripped open the envelope and pulled out the letter.

Dear Kassi,

Thank you for submitting your screenplay Kitchen Heat: Restaurantland to the New Voices competition. Unfortunately, it did not advance into the final round of judging…

There were a few more words, but they blurred into meaninglessness. She sat motionless, all hope knocked out of her. No prize money. No representation. Broke. Nothing to show for the months of work other than a form rejection letter and a broken heart.

It left a bitter taste in her mouth, and she washed it out with more wine and stared out the window into the fading light for the next three hours, watching the streetlights slowly come to life. They can all go to hell, she thought. Clay, Barry, the New Voices assholes who wouldn't know a good script if punched them on the nose. She poured herself more wine.

She had Samantha, and her mom of course.

I should call Mom, she thought, and reached for the phone. She dialed the number, realizing at the last second that she'd accidentally called Clay. She slammed the phone back into the cradle. She took a long sip of wine to calm her nerves and then dialed the right number.

I need to stay strong, she thought, can't let Mom know I'm feeling bruised.

"Hello?"

"Hi, Mom," Kassi said, striving for a neutral voice.

"Kassi, what's wrong?"

The worry she heard in her mother's voice was too

much and Kassi burst into tears. "Oh, Mom. I lost. I got the rejection letter and everything is horrible."

"Kassi, darling, I'm sorry, I know you're disappointed but it's only one contest. You'll write many more great screenplays."

"I know." Tears were streaming down her face. "It's not just that. It's everything. Barry is such a dick …"

"You'll get no argument from me there."

"He ruined everything. Clay and I broke up and then getting this rejection, it's too much. Why is everything so bad?"

She was crying so hard her breath was ragged.

"Baby, it's okay. It's going to be fine. Let it out."

"I don't think anything will ever be okay again," Kassi moaned, then tried to catch herself. "I'm sorry. Ignore me. I'm just feeling down and sorry for myself. You don't need to worry. Seriously."

"It's normal, healthy even, to feel down. It's a natural response to hardship, but it will get better. I promise you. I am old enough to know that to be true." Her mom paused. "Kassi, where's Samantha?"

"She's with her dad until tomorrow."

"Good. I mean, not good, but at least you can fall all the way apart tonight. I'll stay on the phone with you, but you'll need to pull yourself mostly together before she gets home."

"I will," Kassi sniffled. "I promise. Thanks for letting me vent."

"Tell me about what happened with Clay. He's an idiot to let you go."

"He is an idiot," Kassi said, then launched into a lurid retelling of the last three days.

By the time she hung up an hour later, Kassi was feeling better and had only one bottle of good wine left.

In the morning, she called in sick and stayed in bed for ten hours straight watching re-runs of *Perry Mason* and *Columbo* and *I Love Lucy* while eating Oreos and potato chips. When Barry dropped Samantha off after daycare late that afternoon, Kassi listened to her little footsteps coming up the steps. She met her at the door in sweats and a baggy T-shirt, her bed-head hair sloping to one side, her eyes red from lack of sleep and crying.

"Mommy, what's wrong with you?" Samantha looked at her suspiciously.

"Mommy doesn't feel well," Kassi said. "I'm going back to bed. I'll make you a bubble cheese sandwich later."

"Can Cooker make it? He makes them better."

"He can't make it for you tonight." Or ever again, she thought. She went back to bed, this time with a glass of her cheap wine, while Sam played with her horses.

It had grown dark when Kassi was roused from her dozing by a knock at the door. Was it Clay? Finally? Kassi patted down her hair, got up and walked eagerly across the living room.

It wasn't Clay. It was her mother.

"Mom?"

"Grammy!" Sam screamed happily, leaping up and launching forward like a tiny, joyful missile.

Kassi's disappointment was so deep her stomach contracted and she was afraid she would burst into tears again. But that feeling was mixed with gratitude and relief. She needed help.

"What are you doing here?"

"I wanted to check on my baby," Gina said, hugging her, then stepping back. "And possibly convince her to take a shower."

36

INT. KASSI'S APARTMENT - DAY

GINA and SAMANTHA bake cookies, the home is filled with restorative Grandma-love. KASSI is bent, and possibly broken.

The restaurant was closed for five days, the one time each year Molly shut the whole thing down for deep cleaning, repair work and a vacation for the staff. She gave full-time kitchen workers a week of paid time off, and the servers each got a bonus equivalent to one hundred dollars per shift worked the past week. It was incredibly generous, far more than Kassi would have made actually working, and definitely not the norm in the food service industry.

For Kassi, the timing could not have been better. She took Sam out of daycare for the week, and at the insistence of Gina, they had a girls' vacation. Her treat.

On the first day, they rented a car and drove to the Oregon coast for a windy beach walk collecting shells and sand dollars, a fudge overindulgence and endless games of Skee-Ball. Next up was a lunch cruise on the Willamette River, where Sam spotted a river otter. The third day, they visited the Children's Museum along with the retired World War II submarine docked in front of the Science Museum.

The next day, they ate breakfast at a French bakery (Sam

had two chocolate croissants) and went to the Portland Zoo. They all loved the aviary exhibit, a huge dome where birds flew almost free, but the elephants constrained in their tiny quarters made them sad.

Today was a stay-at-home day and baking chocolate chip cookies was the priority.

Kassi watched her mom and Sam mix ingredients, thinking about how great these past few days had been, and she was grateful to her mother. Yet, despite the joy of watching Sam with her grandmother, Kassi couldn't shake her funk.

Maybe some fresh air would help. She decided to take a walk. Outside, damp air blew across her face from a summer rain. She buttoned her rain jacket up to her neck and started walking.

Tomorrow the restaurant would open again, and Kassi would go back to work. Her mom offered to stay one more week and watch Sam, giving Kassi time and space to figure out her future.

Barry uncharacteristically agreed to give up his time with Sam during Gina's visit, possibly feeling guilty over what he had done, even though he'd told her more than once this past week that she was better off without the hippie. Mostly, Kassi was just relieved, and not surprised, that whatever impulse Barry had about getting back together seemed to have already evaporated.

The sting of not winning the screenplay competition was lessening. She always knew it was a long shot but still, the childish part of her that believed in happy endings wanted a different outcome, even though happy endings seemed completely out of reach these days.

What made it worse was that she couldn't share the experience with Clay. Even though she wrote it, the screenplay had really been a mutual creative project, fueled by sex and closeness, capturing their love story on paper.

Kassi thought about him constantly. She hadn't spoken to him since that short, painful time in the restaurant before Ione sent her home. The speed of their disintegration made her dizzy each time she replayed it in her head. In the two minutes he saw Barry in her bed, everything changed. Two minutes!

She missed Clay terribly—missed his touch, his smile, the sound of his voice—but mixed in with the memories and the longing, was also anger. How could he believe she would cheat? How could he think she would go back to Barry, an abusive partner? Worse, how could he yell at her? He practically screamed at her that night in the bar.

Clouds gathered overhead, the rain shifting from a dull, aching mist to fat, sloppy drops. She pulled the hood on her slicker up, stuck her hands in her pockets, and kept walking,

Kassi almost called him a dozen times, always stopping herself at the last digit because he had to apologize. He was the one who broke them, she thought, his anger, his lack of trust.

Still, she wondered if she should go to his house to give him the chance to apologize, but then thought better of it. If she went there, she knew it would be her that apologized, she would succumb to her own conditioning and do what women always do, say sorry even when they'd done nothing wrong. It's what she did with Barry all those years, just to keep the peace.

As she walked, Kassi forced herself to consider another explanation for his behavior. Clay was still in love with Crystal. Maybe she ignored this huge red flag all along because she got drawn into the fantasy of her screenplay about their growing love. Could she have been that blind? The thought that the grand love story at the center of the screenplay was a figment of her imagination was a wound she wasn't sure she could bear.

"Ugh!" Kassi shouted. Her mind was whiplashing, exhausted by the not-knowing. But really, exhausted by the knowing. She always knew her life was too screwed up for someone like Clay to be part of it. And she also knew what came next. Heartache. Loneliness. Life without him.

She looked up, surprised to see she had walked all the way to Peninsula Park where they ate cheesecake and drank Madeira. That was one of the happiest moments of her life. Kassi saw the picnic bench where they sat close together and watched the city below. She pulled down her hood to feel the rain on her face, letting it wash away the tears. It didn't help. Finally, she looked away from the memory and started walking home.

***

Less than five minutes after she disappeared into the neighborhood, Clay pulled his truck into the parking lot of Peninsula Park. The rain was falling harder, so he stayed inside the truck, staring out at the sodden picnic bench through swipes of the windshield wipers.

This was the first time in nearly a week he'd left his apartment other than to go to the gym, the liquor store or The Hideout, even though Mel wasn't happy to see him anymore. Any chance she could, Mel told him what a jerk he was. So, mostly he sat alone in the dark in his house drinking whiskey and watching old movies.

He was so confused by what happened with Kassi, he didn't know what to do, what to feel. He missed her, and Sam too, more than he thought possible. It was nearly a physical pain.

He had overreacted, that was clear. But she knew him,

knew his heart and the ghosts of his past. Shouldn't she, of all people, be able to treat him with a little compassion and empathy? He was upset, his emotions were high. Her ex was in bed with her, which would make anyone angry, and she just shut down with him, like a robot. Total silence. If Kassi had reached out these past few weeks, made the slightest effort, things would have turned out differently.

Clay sighed and looked at the picnic table. That night was one of the happiest moments in his life. Now, he was realizing he might be too damaged to make it work with anyone. The worst part was that he didn't believe his behavior, the anger he showed that day, was really him.

He slammed his palms against the steering wheel. What if it was him? What if he was so fucked up that he could no longer control himself when his emotions were high? A person didn't get through life without emotional extremes. He loved her too much to make her life harder, and that went double for Sam. After everything she'd been through with Barry, he couldn't put her through anything else. It wasn't her job to heal him.

They deserve so much better than me, Clay thought. I should stay out of the way and let Barry, who was clearly willing to do anything, given what he had pulled, to put the family back together again. Barry was an asshole, but he could get help, professional help. They had a history and a kid.

Kassi once told Clay that her life was complicated. She wasn't kidding, he thought, but his life, it turned out, was just as complicated. Except his complications were on the inside and less visible.

The front window on the truck was steaming up and he wiped away the condensation. He turned the key in the ignition. Maybe another trip to the gym would clear his head, help him figure things out.

***

Blocks away, Kassi opened the door to her apartment and stood there, soaked, enjoying the happy scene. "Grammy, you look so silly!" Sam said. She was standing on her step-stool next to the table, and stirring, but mostly eating, the cookie batter.

Gina and Sam were wearing matching aprons, and both were covered in flour.

"Time to make something yummy for your mummy," Gina said, looking up at her soaked daughter standing in the doorway. Sam laughed at the rhyme as her grandma showed her how to spoon out the batter, roll it into balls and place them on the cookie sheet.

"Open your mouth," Sam ordered Grammy, a spoonful of dough at the ready.

"What do we say?" Gina asked.

"Please open your mouth."

She obliged and Sam fed her the batter.

"Oh, you silly adorable thing," Gina said, scooping Sam into a hug as Sam giggled. Kassi smiled, and an unexpected feeling of contentment pushed through the pain. And then it all became clear.

Kassi knew exactly what she had to do. Focus on being the best parent possible to Sam and let the chips fall where they would. Her mother invited them to move back to Pennsylvania until Kassi was back on her feet. It wasn't like her mom was rich, but she had a reliable pension after Kassi's dad died and she owned her house outright. There was plenty of room for them to stay there. Sam could sleep in the same bedroom Kassi had as a child. It was the sensible thing to do. Kassi would go back to school, get training for a good job with a stable financial future.

"Hey ladies, how's it going?" Kassi asked.

"Mommy! We are having so much fun," Sam yelled.

"Okay, concentrate now, Sam. We are going to put this in the oven and it's very hot," Gina said, gently guiding Sam's tiny hands on the tray.

"Mom, I've been thinking about your offer."

"It still stands, darling, you are both welcome anytime. I would love—"

The phone rang. "Hold that thought," Kassi said, picking up the receiver.

"Hello?"

"Kassi Witmire?"

"Who's calling please?"

"Margo Tremane from Tremane Talent Agency in Hollywood."

"Yes?" Kassi said, confused.

"I was a judge for the New Voices competition. Your script came very close to winning. Divided the panel in fact. Didn't divide me. They're idiots. I want to represent you."

"What?"

"You did write *Kitchen Heat*, right?"

Kassi was silent for several seconds. "Did Roz put you up to this?"

There was a pause. "Roz Salishan? Did she approach you? Dammit. She went behind my back. She was on the panel too. I knew she was interested. Listen to me, she's great but you need experience, not enthusiasm."

"I don't know what's happening," Kassi said, "but I'm hanging up."

"Please don't, you'll regret it," Margo said. "As I said, I want to represent you."

"Is this a prank?"

"Do I sound like a prank caller?"

"Kind of."

"I'm dead serious. How can I convince you I want us to make a movie together? Do you want to call me back at my home phone number?"

"How would that help?" Kassi asked.

"My office number, then."

Kassi thought for a minute. "Do you know Brad Pitt?"

"Yes. He's a lovely young man who drinks too much coffee. You want *his* number?"

Samantha and Gina watched Kassi put her hand over her mouth as a look of disbelief spread across her face. She mouthed *Oh my god* to her mom.

"Maybe later. Okay, go on. I'm listening," Kassi said.

Gina picked up Sam and put her on her lap, whispering that they both needed to be quiet.

Kassi nodded, asked a few questions, and nodded some more. She grabbed a sheet of paper, looked around and mimicked panicked writing. Sam jumped off Gina's lap and handed her a red crayon.

Kassi started taking notes with the crayon. Finally, after ten minutes, and just when the timer for the cookies went off, the call wound down.

"I'll be there in two weeks," she said. "Come hell or high water, I'll be there."

She hung up the phone and started happy-screaming, and dancing around the room, then she dropped to the floor, laid on her back and started kicking her feet in a tantrum of joy.

"What on earth is happening?" Gina asked.

"Momma, baby girl, we're going to Hollywood!"

Both Sam and Gina laughed along with her until they noticed smoke coming from the oven.

"My cookies!" Sam cried.

After tossing the burnt cookies in the trash, they started

a new tray while Kassi shared her bombshell news. The Tremane Agency wanted to represent her and the script. Margo was certain she could sell the script, but first she wanted Kassi in Los Angeles to participate in an intensive screenwriting program along with some mentoring.

After that, she would pitch the screenplay and its writer as a strong new female voice ready to take on the inevitable rewrites that the attached producer, director and stars would demand. She knew Kassi would need help, but she had a good feeling and Kassi was suitably young, which in Hollywood-speak meant a potentially long and lucrative relationship.

"It's like a dream," Kassi said, shocked.

"It's more like Hollywood finally recognizing how exceptional you are," Gina said.

Only after the next tray of cookies came out did the rush of excitement start to wane and the financial reality sink in. It was the break Kassi had always dreamed of, but how would she pay for the move?

The cost of renting a truck, moving her furniture, the security deposit and first month's rent for a new apartment, plus finding and paying for daycare and probably buying a car, even a shit one, were all in play.

"I'll take out a loan on the house," Gina said.

"You absolutely will not. I cannot let you risk your financial security for some half-baked dream of mine."

After a long and sleepless night, she was still wrestling with the money question the next day at work as she waited for Ione to announce the section schedule. The restaurant didn't look much different to Kassi after the week of deep cleaning, a bit shinier but basically the same.

Ione came in the back door and posted a one-page schedule on the bulletin board. Kassi was pleased she had the adults-only back dining room today and tomorrow.

That wouldn't solve her long-term money problem, but it would keep her in groceries.

"I was true to my word," Ione said.

"How so?"

"Do you notice any ex-lovers on shift together?"

Ex-lover. That stung.

"I should tell you that I might be giving notice soon," Kassi said.

"Because your little romance didn't pan out? That's a stupid reason to quit your job. Lovers come and go. Make him quit if anything ... wait, do I need a cook or a waitress more? I take it back. You should quit."

"I'm not leaving because of him. I have an opportunity in Hollywood to sell my script and help produce the movie."

"Shit, girl, did you win that contest?"

"That's the crazy thing. I didn't win, but some agent on the judging panel wants to sign me. Get this, Roz Salishan is interested too."

Ione took a few beats to let that sink it. "Roz Salishan? The fucking movie star? I am seriously attracted to her. When's your last day?"

"If I was on my own, I'd hitch down, stay in a hostel or a shelter until I get my first paycheck there. With a kid, I can't take that risk. She needs a home, daycare, so much. I've got to have at least three grand to even contemplate the move."

"Sounds like it's time for one of Molly's famous fundraisers," Ione said. "I'll talk to her."

"Really? I'll seriously owe you, Ione. For this and so much more."

"Someday, you're taking me as your date to the Oscars and you will introduce me to Roz Salishan. That's how you pay me back."

37

INT. ROSE AND THORN RESTAURANT - NIGHT

The restaurant goes all out on a fundraiser for KASSI'S departure to Hollywood. One person is noticeably absent.

Before sending Kassi to Hollywood, the Rose and Thorn brought Hollywood to Portland. Ione sweet-talked, or possibly frightened, a local events company into fitting out the restaurant like an active movie set, with lights and director's chairs and more. It looked fabulous.

Outside, a klieg swayed back and forth, sending a column of light sweeping across the night sky. To top it off, Molly had the reels for two Bogart black and white movies flown in from a Seattle film distribution company. *Casablanca* would screen first against a white sheet hung up across the back dining room wall and *The African Queen* after that. The other walls were covered with film posters and memorabilia borrowed from a local video store.

The servers were competing for a two-hundred-dollar bonus for best Hollywood costume. It was clear to everyone that Kristoph's interpretation of Marilyn Monroe was the front-runner if he could keep the long blonde wig and half-inflated balloons he was using for boobs in place for the full evening.

Even with the short notice, the demand for tickets was overwhelming. It was soon clear this wasn't about Kassi anymore, if it ever was. "Obviously, this town is starved for a real party," Molly said, "and we are sure as hell are gonna give it one."

The deal was that any tickets sold after the break-even point—meaning after Molly decreed the restaurant's costs were covered, including a generous tip for the entire staff—would be directed to the official "Kassi and Samantha Go to Hollywood" fund. Plus, anyone was free to make individual donations.

A crowd was gathering outside. Molly was inspecting the kitchen and dining room, making sure the staff was ready, preparing to open the doors. Everyone was excited. It was all hands on deck. The one person who hadn't shown was Clay. Ione gave him the night off out of respect for his twice-broken heart.

Samantha and Gina were in the dining room for a quick visit to wish her luck before the restaurant doors opened.

"Clay didn't come," Kassi said to her mom.

"Don't let your disappointment show, honey," Gina whispered. "These wonderful people have gone to so much trouble. They love you."

"Maybe he'll come later."

"Mommy, you look weird," Sam said.

"I do?"

Earlier that morning, Kassi raided the Goodwill bins, hopefully for the last time, and dug deep into her closet to piece together a Dracula costume, but she was pretty sure most people would think she was some mash-up of a punk rock grunge stripper.

"You look great," Gina said. "And stay out as late as you want. Samantha and I have a full evening planned."

Kassi gave them both a kiss goodbye and marveled at

the difference in her life when her mother was close enough to help with Sam. It was the only way she could be here tonight with no worries or anxiety.

A few minutes later, Molly and Ione opened the doors and the crowd surged inside. Dave-two was collecting tickets. Kassi and the crew went to work.

The dining room was immediately packed. Right out of the gate, customers started playing drinking games, one of the most popular was taking a shot each time Humphrey Bogart gave Ingrid Bergman goo-goo eyes, which turned into some decent impersonations of the two lovers.

The drink orders started coming in faster than Molly and Ione, serving as bartenders, could fill. They tapped in Jon from the dishpit for help, who was surprisingly good with liquor proportions.

The servers were so busy there wasn't much time for talk, except for "Can you believe this crowd!" or "Be careful, the guy at table eighteen is handsy," as they passed one another delivering food and drinks, clearing dishes and, in one unfortunate case, asking Rob to unclog the ladies toilet.

As busy as it was, Kassi managed to talk for a few minutes to Walter, her big tipper. He was having dinner with a woman, Suzanne, and he introduced her to Kassi.

"I hear you're heading to California," Suzanne said.

"If all goes well tonight," Kassi said, crossing her fingers.

"I'll miss talking with you," Walter said. "I wanted to tell you, it's because of you that Suzanne and I met." Suzanne reached over the table and took his hand.

"Me?" Kassi asked. "How so?"

"A long story, and a good one. Maybe someday you can turn it into a screenplay."

Kassi laughed.

"Let's keep in touch," he said, handing her his business card. "Who knows, I might be interested in investing in the movies. I'm always on the lookout to expand my business ventures."

"I'll do that." She slipped the card into her pocket.

"We left a little something in your fundraising bucket," he said.

"Thank you so much. I'll miss you." She kissed him on the cheek. "Take good care of him," she said to Suzanne.

Shortly after, the food started to run out, the party slowed down and people began to leave, most wobbling toward the exit, some singing movie tunes. It was closing in on ten o'clock.

Kassi took a pee break and checked her face in the mirror. Her black eye shadow had smudged off entirely, and her now-patchy white pancake makeup made her look more like a plague victim than a vampire.

She sighed and shook her head at her reflection. Deep down, she had been sure he would show up tonight, even if only to say goodbye. There was still time, still more than an hour before they finished the clean-up, but she was losing hope.

The door swung open.

"Don't you lock the bathroom?" Ione asked.

"Don't you knock?"

They both laughed. Ione squeezed inside.

"This night is going better than I could have ever imagined. We need to put a film night on the schedule at least once a month," Ione said. "Thanks for moving to Hollywood. Otherwise, I never would have known."

Ione was animated and talking louder than usual. Kassi was happy she decided to relax and have fun. Ione was dressed as Cruella de Vil from *101 Dalmatians*, and with the long gray and black striped wig, she looked both the part and drop-dead gorgeous.

Ione pushed past Kassi to open the stall door.

"Hey, guess what? We crashed through the three grand you need. One person alone gave three grand. Can you fucking believe it?" She let out a sigh as she started peeing. "I've been holding that for way too long."

"Three thousand dollars? Who in the world did that?"

"I promised to never tell, but you can probably guess."

She could guess. Walter as much as admitted it. "I can't accept that kind of money."

"Why do people say shit like that?" Ione asked. "It was freely given. Accept that someone wanted to do something nice for you."

"You should divide it among the staff," Kassi said.

"My fine ass I will," Ione muttered. "I'll treat my three lovers to a Hawaii luxe trip before I do that."

She flushed the toilet and when she came out of the stall she was buttoning up her tight bodice and squeezing her breasts together to get them properly situated. "Don't you forget, I'm your date to the Oscars!" She opened the door to a line of women waiting to get inside the bathroom.

When Kassi walked out, she saw Suzanne in the line. "He really believes in you," Suzanne said, grabbing Kassi's hand as she passed and squeezing. "I should be jealous, but I'm not. Good luck."

"Please tell him thank you. He's so generous."

Molly shouted "Last call!"

Within thirty minutes, the cleaning crew was sweeping the floor, the servers and kitchen staff were happily surprised by the extra cash doled out, and Molly handed Kassi a check for seven thousand two hundred and seventeen dollars.

"I don't know what to say," Kassi said.

"Thank you, maybe," Molly said.

"Thank you. Seriously."

"Remember that if things take off, you can help people here by spreading the word about the Rose and Thorn."

"I will. I promise," Kassi said.

"Good luck, but I suspect you won't need it."

Kassi tried to hug her, but Molly stepped back out of reach. "I don't hug." She spun around and walked back to her office.

38

INT. ROSE AND THORN RESTAURANT - THE
NEXT DAY

It's KASSI'S last day at the restaurant.
It's bittersweet. She keeps it together
(mostly). CLAY is still MIA.

Kassi called the order for her last table at the Rose and
Thorn, a BLT with avocado, and then hung the ticket.

LuRon turned and ducked his head so he could see her
through the window. "It's kind of a dick move," he said, as
if reading her mind.

"What do you mean?" Kassi asked, trying to keep it
light.

"Look, I know Clay fucked up, but that's only because
he is fucked up."

"That's very profound. I mean, really, it is."

"If you want to use that in your movie, you go right
ahead. First one's free."

"Maybe I will. Hey, let me ask you all something. I need
to hear a guy's perspective and you're all I've got."

"Weirdly insulting and sweet at the same time," Gilroy
said, as the kitchen crew turned to give her their full
attention.

"I know Clay got his heart broken. I get that. It's
happened to all of us, right?"

They nodded, and Rob ducked his head to shoot a quick look at Meredith who was refilling coffee caddies with sugar and Sweet 'N Low packets. If she felt his stare, she didn't let on.

"My question is, if you can't get past the heartache, can't get past the betrayal ..." She let her voice trail off before working up her courage again. "If you can't get over someone who hurt you, after hypothetically, two years or whatever, doesn't that mean you probably still love that person? That you don't want to get over them?"

There was a heavy silence in the air.

"I truly don't know," Kassi said, her voice edged with desperation. "I'd like that to not be true because if it is, I really misread things." Still, no one spoke. "Guys, can one of you say something here? I'm flailing a little."

LuRon left the grill, came around to her side and pulled her into a big, deep hug, then leaned against the order window, holding her hands in his.

"I hear what you're saying, and I agree with you mostly, but Clay's not like that. We all knew Crystal was no good for him but Clay believed he could make everything work just from sheer force of will. He did everything right, and it all went to shit anyway. What's broke in him wasn't his love for Crystal, that shit was fragile from the get-go. What's broke in him was his trust in himself. He had to give up on thinking someone could do good and do right and get it back in kind."

Gilroy nodded. "I think Clay lives in a different world, a better world, where if you put in the work, you get back the happiness. Or at least that's where he used to live. We all thought you were pulling him back into that light."

"Kassi, he's not in love with Crystal. He never was," Rob said.

"Nobody's in love with Crystal except Crystal," LuRon

said, returning to the cook's side of the kitchen.

"I appreciate you sticking up for Clay," Kassi said. "You're good friends."

"We're not sticking up for Clay," LuRon said. "He's an idiot. Kicked in the head by a mule when he was little kind of idiot. Man, you two were great together."

"We were all jealous," Gilroy said. "Takes a special kind of crazy to mess that up."

"It wasn't all his fault," she said. She paused. "I might have overreacted. I've been through plenty with Sam's father, and I let that part of me take over." She shook her head, not able to say out loud what she knew to be true. Her life was too complicated for someone like Clay. "It's embarrassing. I threw a drink in his face."

"I hope it was cheap booze," LuRon said. "But that kind of anger, that kind of passion, sounds like you're not quite over him either, so according to your theory ..." He shrugged. "Might be worth a conversation at least."

"Hard to talk to someone who's turned into a ghost," she said.

LuRon slid her BLT order onto a plate and Rob fussed with chips and added an orange wheel garnish with a sprig of parsley tucked into it.

"Is that some backward way of saying the door is still open?" LuRon asked.

"I don't know what I'm saying," she said, taking the sandwich. "I just know that I'll miss you all, and this place. Even the bad memories are pretty good."

She carried the food out. The sandwich was for Walter, her last order. He was alone this time, and she slid the plate in front of him.

"Where's Suzanne?" she asked.

"At work."

"She seems nice."

"She is. I'm happy. You must be too, this being your last day and all."

She nodded. "I am, but it's bittersweet. I'm glad you're my last official order."

He put his hand over his heart and smiled.

"Mind if I sit down?"

"Of course not," he said, gesturing at the other side of the table.

Kassi slid into the booth. "I want to say thanks. For everything. Your generosity, your friendship over the last, whatever, six months. I'm not sure I would have made it here in Portland if not for you. Financially or emotionally."

"I'll miss you. This was the highlight of my day."

"I especially want to say thanks for supporting the fundraiser. It was ... it was far too generous."

He paused, sandwich halfway to his mouth. "It wasn't that much. I would have left more but I didn't want Suzanne to think there was anything weird between us."

She looked at him curiously. "You didn't leave the roll of hundreds?"

He shook his head and took a bite, then washed it down with a sip of iced tea. "No, though now I kind of wish I had."

"Someone dropped three thousand dollars into the bucket. And you're the only one with that kind of money."

"Maybe it was your boyfriend."

"He's not my ... that didn't work out. And he wasn't at the party last night."

"The owner maybe? Sounds like something she would do, based on everything you've told me."

"Probably. I need to go say thanks," Kassi said. She put her hand on his shoulder. "I hope our paths cross again, Walter."

"You've got my contact info. Use it."

Meredith and Roz were standing by the salad bar as Kassi walked over.

"I guess this is it," Kassi said.

"I'm going to miss you, girl," Roz said. "I mean, I won't miss your table-hogging. Or the way you snake all the cute guys."

"I swear I'll leave the new cook for you," Kassi said.

Roz giggled and threw her arms around Kassi. "I'm going to send you something, okay? Some things I've written. Some poetry," she whispered into her ear.

"I would love that," Kassi said.

"Can we come see you in LA?" Meredith asked, taking her turn hugging Kassi.

"Please do, and the sooner the better. I'll mail you my address as soon as I have one."

"LA might be the perfect place to work on my dissertation about fetishes," Meredith said.

"If I meet any leather-clad hotties, I'll put you in touch. But don't write off Rob. That weirdo has it bad for you."

Ione walked up and stood, half glaring and half smiling. "Does anyone who's not quitting feel like working today?"

"I'll miss you too," Kassi said, pulling her into a hug.

"Remember, I'm your Oscar date," Ione whispered into Kassi's ear before disentangling herself. "Seriously, ladies," she snapped at Meredith and Roz. "Get to work. We're losing our best server."

"Hey," Kristoph said, turning the corner. "I heard that."

"Don't worry, you'll be moving back into the number one spot tomorrow," Ione said.

Kristoph slipped his arm around Kassi. "I'll miss you. I always felt like if I couldn't have Clay, you were his next best option."

She patted his arm. "Now we both don't have him.

We've accomplished so little together."

Before leaving, Kassi tapped on the manager's office door.

"What?" Molly snapped. She was working on the computer, typing the dinner menu with her index fingers only. Since she insisted on listing every single ingredient, it was a major investment of time. She looked up. "I thought you were gone. What do you want?"

"I wanted to say goodbye."

Molly nodded. "You did good work, and I'm glad you're getting a chance for something else."

"I'll never forget what you did for me at the fundraiser," Kassi said, moving closer.

"Single mothers don't have it easy. I'm fortunate to be in a position to support your ambitions."

"The Rose and Thorn has been so much more than a job for me, it's more than a restaurant. It's a safe place for all the misfits out there, like me, the misfits who can't seem to find their way. I want you to know, that comes through loud and clear in the screenplay."

Molly looked at her with a flicker of gratitude that was shortly replaced by distraction bordering on irritation. "If there's nothing else, I need to get this menu typed up."

On her way out, Kassi paused by the first aid station where Clay patched up her finger, pretending he was a Vietnam medic. Then, with a sigh, she passed through the back door and stood outside in the parking lot, smelling the old cigarette butts piled high in a coffee can and the barrels of stale fryer grease, and looking out over the Portland skyline.

"Thanks for everything," she said, patting the side of the building, and then she hurried to catch her bus.

At home, Gina and Sam had packed up the place, loading toys, books, clothes, some of the furniture and anything worth taking, which wasn't much, into a small U-Haul truck. Her mom was standing in the middle of the empty room, holding the phone. "Barry," she mouthed.

Kassi took the phone and held it away from her ear as he bellowed that she was not moving to LA with his daughter.

"We've been through this. The attorney can hammer out the details. LA is not that far away," she said calmly. "I have a great opportunity. It's my turn. You can be the one to make it work this time." Then she hung up.

Her mom gave her a discreet fist pump.

"Ready for our big adventure?" Kassi asked, scooping Sam up into her arms.

"I never said goodbye to Cooker."

"Oh, honey, he was super busy but he said to tell you goodbye." She dropped her keys on the kitchen table. "Let's go, ladies. Hollywood awaits."

"What about this?" her mom asked, pointing to the typewriter sitting alone on the edge of the doorstep after they had loaded everything into the truck.

"Leave it," Kassi said. "We're starting fresh. It's beyond time for me to get a computer."

They piled into the U-Haul and pulled away. Gina was behind the wheel, with Sam strapped in between them in a car seat, and Kassi in the passenger seat with an Oregon and California map on her lap. "It's a straight shot down the Interstate."

It started to rain, and beads of water formed on the windshield. At the end of the block, the truck squealed to a halt, then slowly backed up. Kassi jumped out and ran to grab the typewriter, wedging it into the truck's floorboards at her feet.

39

INT. ROSE AND THORN KITCHEN – DAY

(*Two months later.*) CLAY is trying his best to keep it together. His best is not enough. An unlikely ALLY holds the KEYS to his future.

The day was soggy, rain was falling in fat drops, as it had been for nearly a week. The late lunch shift was slow so Clay let LuRon go for the day. Molly was inspecting the kitchen, and while she was always a wild card, so far nothing had stoked her rage. Clay was keeping one eye on her and the other on his work dicing up a crate of yellow zucchini for tonight's soup special.

Molly was rummaging through the dining room utensils, like a ferret on a mission. She stopped, looked at a soup spoon and held it up, triumphantly. "What exactly is this?"

Here we go, thought Clay. He could see even from four feet away that the spoon had a piece of crud stuck to it. Likely a dried-up speck of artery-clogging Hungarian mushroom soup.

"A spoon with some crud on it," Clay said. "Probably your signature soup."

Molly was initially too surprised by the lack of deference to formulate a response, but her reticence didn't last, as

Clay knew it wouldn't.

"Do I need to wash all the dishes myself to be sure it's done correctly?" she asked.

"That would slow things down. So, short answer, no."

Kristoph's mouth dropped open. Rob stopped scraping the grill. Ione stood frozen, her hip propping open the door between the kitchen and dining room, as she determined whether a speedy escape or a clever putdown was in her best interest.

"Slow service is better than dead customers, wouldn't you agree? Dead customers are bad for business, am I right?" Molly asked, her voice spinning up to a full-on hyper-winded shout. "You're in charge of the kitchen, you, you, you." She emphasized each you with a stab of the dirty spoon in his direction. "This is your fault. Your fault. Would you eat with this spoon, would you let a baby eat with it, would you—"

Clay put down his chef's knife and turned to face her. He put up his hand, palm out.

"Dammit Molly, please stop yelling at me."

There was an audible gasp. Clay wasn't sure who it was, but it wasn't him. Or Molly.

There was an unspoken rule at the Rose and Thorn. It was better and easier to let Molly rant and get it out of her system than to talk back to her, even if she got mean, which she did occasionally. Everyone knew she had a tiny screw loose that sometimes got jostled and the jostling led to brief ranting. Most of the time she was kind and generous to a fault. So, why not let her yell until the screw tightened itself, which it always did? It was the staff's way of being kind in return.

But Clay had been doing a lot of thinking about unbridled anger and the damage left in its wake. What Molly was doing, no matter how kind she behaved the rest of the time, wasn't okay.

"No disrespect Molly, but this is a commercial kitchen. Sometimes, rarely, but sometimes, something gets missed. Even with this rare breakdown, either a busser or server would spot it before it got to a table. Worst-case scenario, a customer gets a dirty spoon. They would ask for a clean one." He paused. "Maybe not nicely, someone might lose a tip, you might have to comp a meal, but nobody would die. So yes, I would let a baby lick that spoon because it's been sanitized and I'm pretty sure bacteria helps strengthen the immune system. Now, do you mind? I have to prep for tonight's special."

He turned back to his chopping. Kristoph stepped back into the dishwashing bay, close enough to hear but out of sight. Rob decided he needed a smoke, this instant, and high-tailed it to the parking lot. Molly stood in the center of the kitchen, fuming. Clay could feel the energy radiating maniacally from her, anger lasers pulsating from her eyes hitting him in the back.

Clay expected to be fired.

Ione decided against an exit in favor of an intervention.

"Clay, you haven't been the same since Kassi left," she said, "and you need to stop taking it out on us."

He kept on dicing, the pile of chopped zucchinis looking like an expanding molehill, creeping to the edge of the steel counter, a few falling off. He knew Ione was right. He had been a morose, unpleasant employee since Kassi left as well as a shitty friend, but that wasn't why he said what he did.

Or maybe it was.

"Molly, you know how a broken heart can mess up a person's thinking," Ione said.

Molly twisted her lips, looked at the ceiling for a few seconds, put the dirty spoon in her pocket and slumped out of the kitchen.

When she was gone, Ione turned and whispered to Clay. "The only reason you still have a job is because Molly has her own heartbreak she's dealing with. And in her case, it's recent, not like your crap. It's been two months since Kassi left."

Clay sighed and kept dicing.

"If you ever talk to Molly like that again, I'll fire you myself. Get your shit together." Ione spun around and left.

Rob came back inside, smelling of smoke. Kristoph crossed the kitchen and put his hand on Clay's shoulder. He didn't say anything. He didn't have to.

The door swung open, and Clay expected it to be Molly charging back in to fire him. Instead, it was Crystal.

"Can this day get any worse?" Clay muttered.

She was wearing a leather miniskirt and retro white plastic go-go boots from the sixties, a low-cut red leotard under a Michael Jackson military-style jacket with epaulets.

"I'm busy," Clay said, "and you can't be back here."

"We need to talk," she said.

He put his knife on the cutting board, untied his apron and tossed it on the counter, then went out back.

The sopping rain had turned into a misty sprinkle. Roz was on the far side of the parking lot smoking under an umbrella. She was reading a paperback and looked up, nodded and then went back to reading.

Crystal followed him outside. "You have to stop."

"Stop what?" he asked.

"Acting like a giant dick."

"Please leave me alone."

"You don't want to be alone."

"Yes, I do."

"Then why did you give away your food truck money you big, handsome idiot?" she asked.

He looked up at her, surprised. "How do you know about that?"

Crystal stretched out the moment, casually sliding a cigarette from a retro metal case and putting it lightly between her lips, painted a shade of hot pink. She lit it with an antique silver lighter, inhaled and then blew a thin stream of smoke in his direction.

She smiled. "Ione might have mentioned something."

"She swore to me. Why would Ione do that?"

"Turns out, we have common interests, and I can be very persuasive."

"I don't want to know."

"Oh, don't be a prude. Ione is surprisingly chatty when she's naked and satisfied."

"I said I didn't want to know." He pressed his fists against his temples.

She laughed. "Ione and I have another common interest. Your well-being."

"Does Kassi know I gave her that money?"

"I don't think so. It was very kind of you, silly, but kind," Crystal said. "Ione and I are worried about you."

"Please focus your energy somewhere else."

Crystal took a second pull from her cigarette. "Listen to me, you stupid, sexy beast. Listen closely, because I will never say this again and I'll deny it if you repeat it. I fucked us up, and I'm sorry. I don't regret leaving you. I think we can agree we were never meant to last, but I regret how it happened. You didn't deserve that."

He didn't say anything. This wasn't exactly news to Clay. He'd long ago come to terms with the fact they weren't meant to last, but hearing it from her seemed to partially lift an invisible weight.

"I have a peace offering. Look over there," she said, pointing at the far end of the lot.

"Why am I looking at Roz?"

"Next to her, silly."

It was a red and yellow step van already retrofitted for food service, with a large service window and a collapsible overhang, and the back side was outfitted with a generator rack. It was a thousand times better than the one slowly rusting apart at Townsend Motors.

"It needs some detail work, but it's pretty much ready to go," she said.

"And?"

"It's yours."

"What are you talking about?"

"Look Clay, you gave that unfashionable, plain-looking girl—"

"Kassi. Her name is Kassi."

"Whatever. You gave up part of your dream for her when you gave her that money. That means something."

"Crystal, you can't do this."

"I can. But you have to pay me whatever you can afford, so my silly husband doesn't think I'm sleeping with you again."

"I have seven thousand dollars."

"Make it five. And bring it to the lot. He should see you pay in person." She fished in her jacket pocket and held out the keys, dangling them. "You have to promise me you'll get on with your life."

He reached for the keys, but she pulled them away. "Promise?"

He was silent for a long minute. "I'll do what I can," he said at last.

"Now, for the record," Crystal said, "you know she didn't cheat on you, right? She's not the type and trust me, I know the type."

"I know she didn't."

"Then why did you let her leave?"

He shook his head and tried to explain. "I'm no good, Crystal. The fact that I thought she did cheat, and with someone who had abused her, and then I yelled at her like some asshole. And I couldn't bring myself to say I was sorry when I finally came to my senses, even though I was sorry, really sorry. I was totally unable to do anything to make it right. What does that make me? She's better off with someone who isn't so fucked up, with someone—"

He stopped, his voice choked with emotion.

"Oh, my god, you're human after all. It's almost like you both could have handled things better. How sweet that your dysfunctions align so perfectly. Stop flagellating yourself and just go tell her you're sorry."

She tossed the keys in the air and he caught them.

"I wish it were that easy," he said.

She kissed him on the cheek and walked away, stopping at the far end of the parking lot to yell back at him. "It actually is that easy. And if you do go to California and by some miracle manage to salvage things with that mousy girl, tell her to put me in her movie."

"Kassi," Clay whispered, clenching the keys so tightly in his fist it began to hurt. "Her name is Kassi."

40

EXT. THE THREE PALMS APARTMENTS - THE
SAME DAY

Another sunny day in LOS ANGELES. KASSI
approaches the pool where SAMANTHA plays
under the semi-watchful eye of GINA.
GINA is under the fully watchful eye of
an extremely handsome STRANGER.

"Mommy!" Sam yelled happily when she spotted Kassi
walking toward the swimming pool. She crawled out of the
shallow end, sunburned and raisin-wrinkled from spending
so much time in the water, and ran toward Kassi.

"No running!" Gina shouted. "I've told you a million
times."

Sam stopped dead in her tracks and then pantomimed
a very slow walk, bending her knee and lifting her leg for
each step in excruciatingly slow motion. "Is this better,
Grammy?"

Gina put her hand over her mouth to hide her laughter.

"You little smart aleck," Kassi said, scooping Sam into
her arms.

Gina stepped out of the pool. She smiled and nodded
at the man sitting in the chaise lounge next to them. He
was sipping a beer and enjoying the afternoon sun. Gina
stuffed towels and toys into their bag, including Sam's

rubber ducky. "Wine and cheese after the sun goes down?" she asked quietly.

"I'll be right here," he said.

Gina slipped on her robe, pulling it tight to accentuate her waist, hoisted the bag over her shoulder, gave him a little wave and walked toward Kassi and Sam.

Kassi wondered how it was possible that she hadn't noticed her mother had an admirer. A very handsome admirer, with a strong jaw and thick hair. So handsome that Kassi figured he was probably an actor.

She hoped this meant her mom was beginning to move past her dad's death. Gina was too young to be a widow the rest of her life.

As Kassi continued to hold Samantha, Gina wrapped a towel around the little girl, buffing her dry, and then pulled off the orange water wings from her arms and stuffed them into the already over-stuffed bag.

"Did you find the right location?" Gina asked, running the towel through her own wet hair.

"Who's the guy?" Kassi asked.

"What guy?" she asked innocently.

Kassi rolled her eyes.

"His name is Randy," Sam said. "He's funny but he can't swim."

"You can't swim either," Kassi said.

"I'm a kid, it's allowed."

"Randy is a fellow inhabitant of The Three Palms," Gina said, "and a decent conversationalist."

"Who also happens to be quite easy on the eyes," Kassi said, and her mom swatted her arm. "Are you sure you want to leave after the holidays?"

"I'll be sad to leave you and Sam, but I do have a life in Pennsylvania, which needs some attention after so much time away, I suppose. Or at least my house does."

Kassi took the pool bag from her mother and they walked through the garden to the two-bedroom apartment where they'd been living since arriving in California.

The apartment was in a simple two-story building with a small pool, nearly identical to the cookie-cutter low-rise rentals sprouting up all over Los Angeles, called fondly or pejoratively, depending on artistic viewpoint, dingbats. Their dingbat was pink and named The Three Palms, but Kassi had only found two so far. The hot tub had been out of service since they moved in, the hot water in the apartment took forever and trash pick-up was erratic at best. But it was Hollywood and Kassi wasn't complaining.

"You didn't answer my question from earlier. Did the location work?" Gina asked.

"Yes, it did, thank goodness. It's an old fruit distribution warehouse that they'll outfit to look like a restaurant," Kassi said. "It will be great, and luckily it's not far from here."

"You'll be staying here?" Gina asked.

"Yes, Mom, we will be staying here. It's safe and cheap and people here look out for each other. Like Randy."

"I didn't mean that to sound the way I think you took it," Gina said.

"This place reminds me of the *Karate Kid*, only better," Kassi said. "At least the pool is full here."

"What's *The Karate Kid*, Mommy?" Sam asked.

"A movie. I'll rent the video so we can watch it."

Sam clapped her hands and then rested her head on Kassi's shoulder. The feel of her smooth cheek and her tiny warm breath against her skin sent a surge of love through Kassi.

The sky was turning a pale orange as the sun started its long evening descent. Kassi gazed up through the two palms. They seemed so California, and at night, after Sam and her mom were asleep, Kassi sometimes snuck outside with a glass of wine to stretch out on a chaise lounge and stare up at the moon and stars through the palm fronds.

She always tried to not think about Clay, but never succeeded. In those moments, she found herself trying to imagine what he was doing. Was he looking up at the same stars and night sky in Oregon? Or was he at the gym or The Hideout? She never thought about it for longer than one glass of wine. Sometimes two. Three at the most. It was just too painful.

Better to keep busy.

It had been a whirlwind since arriving in California. Finding a place to live, and diving headlong into the production end of how a screenplay becomes a film. The learning curve had been, and still was, super steep but everyone was so nice. Mostly. The typical asshole guy here or there, but waitressing had taught her a thing or three about deflecting assholes.

Casting for *Kitchen Heat* would finish next week. Right after that, with no break, they would begin filming, what she now knew was the phase called principal photography.

Everyone told her, again and again, that this was a fast-track project like none they'd ever seen. At first, she didn't understand why the studio was putting so much muscle behind getting her film done, but it soon became clear the big cheeses wanted to show their faux support for women in film to offset a lawsuit about sexual harassment.

She was assured repeatedly by the almost entirely white male production crew that she was lucky they needed a good story about women by a woman. Whatever. Her script was good, even with all the edits that had been made by countless people involved in the film. The movie was still going to be great. When more women's voices were heard in films like hers, the more Hollywood would change. She would happily join that chorus.

By the time they reached the apartment door, Sam had fallen asleep on Kassi's shoulder, exhausted from another long and fun day in the pool. Kassi took her into the bedroom and laid her gently on the bed, then deftly pulled off her wet bathing suit and wrapped her in a blanket before tip-toeing out.

"I'll let her nap a little while before we have dinner," Kassi said.

Gina poured them each a glass of wine and they sat down at the small bamboo dining room table. For a few minutes, they were silent, but Kassi could tell her mom had something on her mind.

"I love California wine," Gina said. "This chardonnay is so good."

"I agree. A little oaky, but I can adjust."

"I'm leaving soon."

Kassi nodded. "I can't thank you enough for everything you've done these past few months. I wouldn't have made it through this transition without you."

"I'm proud of you. You've really done it." Gina took a sip of wine. "The nanny will be available, right?"

"Yeah, it's all taken care of. It will be fine." Kassi wasn't certain it would be fine, but she couldn't ask her mother to be her live-in babysitter any longer.

Gina topped off their wine.

"I need to say something," Gina said.

"Okay," Kassi said, reaching for her glass. She expected to hear something about Randy.

"This is such an amazing opportunity, but you don't seem very happy."

Kassi started to speak but Gina shook her head and held her hand up. "Please let me finish. I've been rehearsing," she said. "You've dropped close to twenty pounds that, truthfully, you can't afford to lose. You don't smile anymore, you barely talk, you drink too much and the only thing that seems to bring you pleasure is Samantha."

"Is that so bad? That my daughter brings me joy?"

"Yes. Because trust me, someday she will be on her own and you better know how to take care of yourself when that happens."

Kassi looked out the window. "That's a long way off."

"I think I know what's bothering you, and it's not Barry. Par for the course he's been horrible these last few months, but you're divorced now with a fair custody arrangement. We both knew you would manage the divorce with Sam's best interests as your north star. You have this great situation now, a situation you worked hard to make happen, and yet I'm still worried sick about you."

Kassi took another long drink of wine, then closed her eyes and leaned her head back.

"You know what's wrong," Kassi whispered. Tears welled up and she pressed her eyes shut to trap them.

Gina reached across the table and took Kassi's hand, then offered a tissue. Kassi cried for a few more minutes then blew her nose loudly and shook her head in disbelief. How could she still feel so raw?

"Do you feel better?"

"Not really. Crying is for babies."

"Yet so therapeutic."

"Only temporarily. It has no lasting effect."

"Listen to me, Dr. Spock, you think I don't know how hard it was to pull yourself out of that abusive relationship? I'm proud of you."

"I did it for Sam," Kassi said softly.

"Protecting her was a great motivator, but you did it for Kassi too, because you are a strong woman and a good mother. You did it because it was the right thing to do. No one should be treated the way Barry treated you."

"I'm not really into reliving the past. Where are you going with all this?"

"You were unlucky with Barry, but you weren't unlucky in the end because you have that beautiful little girl now. But those years changed the trajectory of your life. You're getting it back now, and that's wonderful, but your relationship with Barry also messed up your head."

"I left him, didn't I? That took clear thinking."

"Don't take this the wrong way, but because of that situation, you overreact to anger, even normal anger. What happened between you and Barry reset your threshold, any whiff of anger and you shut down, out of fear you'll be abused again."

Kassi sighed. "It's better to be alone."

"Is it, really?" Gina asked. "Love is a wonderful, powerful, emotional thing, and sometimes people in love don't always express themselves calmly and clearly. A little anger in heated situations is normal. It's only when there's too much anger, or it's constant, that you have to worry."

"What are you saying?"

"From what you told me, Clay was a good man with his own special kind of hurt who, in a moment of fear that you were leaving him, acted out of character."

Kassi dabbed her eyes again. "Why didn't he just say he was sorry then?"

"I don't know, but I've never even met him and I still know he is nothing like Barry, and that you're terribly unhappy without him in your life."

"How can I be sure he's not another asshole?"

"You can't, but anger is normal. It's not great, and it will always make you sad, but it's normal. We're humans. Imperfect. Don't let that get in the way of your happiness."

Kassi poured out the rest of the wine evenly between

the two glasses. "Everything sucks."

"Says the woman who not so long ago was struggling to pay rent and now is about to make a movie."

Kassi laughed. "How dare you put my life in context." She took a sip and sighed. "Why is love so hard?"

"Because we get in our own way. That's literally the only thing I can say with certainty." Gina stood. "I'm going to shower and wash this chlorine off me, and then take a bottle of wine and some cheese and crackers outside and sit awhile with Randy."

Kassi smiled. "Your new boyfriend?"

"At least for a little while," Gina said with a wink.

"Scandalous. Maybe you'll come back to visit us sooner now?"

"Maybe I won't leave after all," she said, heading for the bathroom.

When she turned on the shower, the pipes banged and groaned as the hot water struggled to rise to the second floor.

Kassi sat at the table and watched the shadows trade places with the light as the sun dipped below the horizon. She grabbed her purse and fumbled through the stack of postcards she bought last week to send to Roz and Meredith. She pulled one out, a classic image of the hillside Hollywood sign, turned it over and began to write.

41

INT. ROSE AND THORN RESTAURANT - NIGHT

Words matter. Especially when they're written on postcards. And spoken carefully. Weather sometimes matters too.

"Did you see the new waitress?" Gilroy asked, nudging Clay with his elbow.

Clay wasn't biting. He kept slicing roasted red peppers, laying the fragrant strips close together so he could fine-dice them. The special tonight was a gourmet pimiento cheese pasta—cheddar cheese sauce with roasted red peppers and fresh cabbage for crunch along with spinach and green onions for visual appeal.

Molly was still suspicious of Clay for talking back to her last week, but he was gradually regaining her trust. Tonight, she barely berated him for putting what she initially called a Betty Crocker pasta on the specials menu. When she tasted it, she said it would probably never sell but it wasn't terrible. High praise from a still-miffed Molly.

Roz and Meredith were more lavish with their praise as they dug in, expressing such pleasure that eventually LuRon had to try it.

"Damn, that's one of the best things you've ever made," he said. "I know being heartbroken doesn't exactly suit

320

you, but it makes your cooking skills shine."

"It makes him spend more time at the gym too," Kristoph said, sticking his fork into the pile of pasta to twirl up a mouthful. "He's starting to look like that famous bodybuilder …"

"Schwarzenegger?" Rob asked, flexing his undersized biceps and then reaching for a fork as well.

"I was going to say Mike Mentzer because I love his mustache and his little shorts," Kristoph said. "Either way, Clay should write a book about the heartbreak workout and pose on the cover all flexed and oiled up."

"I'd buy that book," Roz said.

"Me too," Meredith added.

The new waitress, Rinza, nodded. "I only just started here, but pretty sure I'd buy it too. Especially if it had the recipe for this pasta."

"I'm not writing a book," Clay said, "and I'm not heartbroken."

"Sure," Ione said, walking in. "Let's talk about that after you read his postcard. Pass this to Clay." She handed it to Roz and then headed back out front.

Roz read it with Meredith looking over her shoulder and then passed it to Rob, who read it with LuRon and Gilroy looking over his shoulder.

"Pretty sure that's addressed to me," Clay said, snatching it out of Rob's hand.

The front was a picture of the famous Hollywood sign. On the back, Kassi wrote:

California is a beautiful place. You would love it here. The weather is always warm and sunny.

Clay read it, then read it again, nodded and tucked it in his pocket. Everyone was looking at him expectantly.

"What?"

No one said anything.

"Can we please get back to work?"

"Fine," Roz said.

Hudson turned on the TV to watch the basketball game just in time to see the last few seconds of a new commercial from Fleet Motors. Crystal wasn't in it.

"Hey, what happened to Crystal?" Gilroy asked.

"She left her car-dealer husband and his commercials," Clay said. "She's moving to New York. Got a role in a theater production."

"Guess Fleet won't be so fast anymore," LuRon said. "How'd she swing that?"

"I didn't ask," Clay said. "Knowing her, she'll make it work, one way or another."

"Who's Crystal?" Hudson asked, angling the antenna, trying to pick up the best signal.

Rob, Gilroy and LuRon looked at Clay.

"Someone from my past."

The game finally came in clearly just as Strickland drove up the court and made a bounce pass to Sabonis for an easy dunk. The kitchen erupted in cheers. Clay smiled, picked up his knife but before he started chopping, he pulled the postcard out and read it again.

LuRon saw it. He took off his apron and caught Clay by the arm. "Come on, man, let's take a break."

"Now?" Clay looked down at the red peppers.

"Hudson, take over chopping up those peppers. We won't be a minute," LuRon said.

"Sure thing."

LuRon and Clay walked through the back door and stood together at the edge of the small parking lot. The sun was setting, and in the deepening shadows, Christmas lights sparkled to life across the street on the windows of

Walter's company, the wholesale gym equipment supply store.

"Sometimes I wish I still smoked," LuRon said, blowing out a stream of frosted breath as they stood awkwardly facing each other. "Just to get outside more."

"I'm freezing," Clay said. "Why are we out here?"

"I wanted to do a quick recap of how things have been going since our girl Kassi moved to California."

"I've got peppers to dice."

"Hudson can handle that. Prison taught him some real knife skills."

"Ironic," Clay said.

"Let's run through the recent highlights," LuRon said. "Phase one: Anger. Drunkenness. Angry drunkenness. Drunken anger. Shitty behavior to your friends."

"I'm not proud of that. I apologized."

"You did. Then came the loner phase. That lasted longer. At least you got some bigger muscles instead of daily hangovers."

Clay nodded. "Not a bad phase. Got pretty strong. I'm benching three seventy-five."

"Don't care. Now you're in phase three. Let's call it the focus phase. You're focused on your food truck. And it's already starting to pull you out of your funk."

LuRon was right, Clay thought. Working on the food truck was helping. He spent all his free time and money on it. He was obsessed, but in a good way.

"I think you're ready for phase four," LuRon said.

"What's phase four?"

"Tell me something. How was that date you went on last week?"

"Elisa? She was nice. Thank Dara for setting me up."

LuRon nodded. "She is nice. Pretty. She liked you. You going to ask her out again?"

"No."

"Why not?"

"I don't, I just …" He shrugged. "Too busy I guess."

"You're not too busy. You're obsessed."

"I like my food truck," Clay said.

"That's not what I'm talking about. Phase four is when you stop fixing your food truck and start fixing your life."

"We both know Kassi deserves better than an idiot who is so royally fucked up. They both do."

"So, you're telling me that you're making some sort of grand sacrifice here? Fuck that, man. That's just lazy thinking." He stomped his feet to stay warm. "Are you the one who dropped that wad of cash into her fundraiser jar without a word?"

Clay nodded.

"You the one who sent a car seat to my baby shower with no name on it?"

Clay nodded again.

"You the one who threw that homophobic customer out the front door when he started yelling at Kristoph?"

"Yeah."

"That's exactly the kind of person Kassi and Sam deserve. The thing is, Clay, that postcard is a door that's still open. A door to a better life."

"You think I'm good enough for her, for them both?"

"Did you ever get a thank-you for giving her all that money?"

"No. Because she doesn't know. I didn't want her to feel obligated. I just wanted to help her out a little. I was worried about her and Sam down there, still am if I'm honest."

"See, when you think about them, your anger and confusion are all gone. All that's left behind is the love."

"What should I do?"

"How the fuck should I know? It's your life. I'm not some Kung Fu master. You've got the food truck all decked out and ready to go, don't you?"

"I still have stuff to do. Finalize the menu, get the logo designed, finish up the exterior artwork. That will take some time. But it doesn't have an interior heater so I can't get started for real until the weather warms up."

"So, what you need is consistently sunny and warm weather?"

"Yeah, exactly, always sunny and warm."

"And?"

"What?" Clay asked.

LuRon rolled his eyes and watched Clay's face as the realization clicked into place, then he reached for the door. "I'm freezing my nuts off out here."

"I'll catch up in a minute," Clay said. When he was alone, he leaned against the back wall of the Rose and Thorn and again pulled Kassi's postcard from his pocket.

42

(Two months later – February 1996.)
MARK'S magazine interview with KASSI is
winding down. Lunch is served.

Kassi was waiting for another question, but none seemed forthcoming. Was the interview over?

"Thanks for spending time with me, Kassi, your candor is appreciated," Mark Hessian said, standing.

Apparently, the interview was indeed over.

"Did I do okay?" she asked. Sam reached out her arms to be picked up.

"You did great," he said.

"When will the article run?"

"We'll hold it until closer to when the film is ready to go so I can add in audience and critical reaction to *Kitchen Heat*."

"I'm so nervous I might throw up." She plopped Sam down on her lap. "Oh shit, I shouldn't have said that."

"That's a quarter for the swear jar," Sam said.

"Don't worry about it," Mark said. "Our interview was officially over. Your cursing was off the record."

Kendra, the nanny Kassi shared with an actress and the first assistant director, walked over to them. "Sorry, I'm a little late but I'm here now and just in time for Sam's nap."

Sam, who adored Kendra, slid into her nanny's arms with hardly a glance back at Kassi.

"One thing to add on the record is that this is not a great town for single moms," Kassi said. "Or any kind of mom, really. Or kids." She laughed, but then grimaced. "Still, the support of other women has been great, at least from most of them."

"I get that," Mark said. "My daughter is trying to break into cinematography and some of her stories about what she goes through are pretty rough. Hard for a father to hear."

"You should write about that. There's enough content for an entire book, maybe even a few lawsuits if we're honest," Kassi said. "This industry has problems. Some bad-behaving men problems."

"Sadly, not many people are willing to talk about that kind of thing. Honesty can damage your career options in this town," Mark said.

Some of the production crew walked by with takeout containers and a waft of savory smells drifted over.

Mark slipped his tape recorder and notebook in his briefcase. "The magazine will send a photographer around next week, okay?"

"Sure, you can connect with my agent to set it up."

More crew members walked by, all carrying sandwich bags and to-go bowls. They were laughing and joking, heading for the picnic seating area.

"I'm going to see if I can grab lunch at wherever those good smells are coming from, my stomach is grumbling," Mark said.

Kassi nodded. "The craft table has been great, a lifesaver this month, but this smells like..." She paused. "I can't quite place it. It smells familiar."

Another group walked by, and one of them with a cup

open spooning a mouthful of soup and smacking his lips. "This is so fucking good."

"What are you eating?" Kassi asked.

"Soup from this new mobile food truck thing out back. Hungarian mushroom."

"I got a grilled cheese sandwich with gruyere and fig jam," his companion said, a young woman wearing a fashionable wool cap despite the sunny and warm weather.

Kassi, heart pounding, was already up and moving toward the door.

At the far end of the parking lot, people were lined up in front of the food truck. It was sleek and painted in bright, bold colors—an intricate design of sandwiches stretching out gooey cheese and steaming bowls of soup and a swirling array of food items: mushrooms, onions, tomatoes, carrots and more. Stained-glass butterflies fluttered above the name: *Thrilled Cheese Soup and Sandwiches.* A smiling octopus held a knife in each arm.

She felt funny and unsteady, and held one hand against the wall for balance. As she got close, she could see Clay in the window, his long hair pulled back. He was wearing a T-shirt with the food truck logo on it. His arms were even more buffed than before, the muscles rippling as he took money and pushed orders forward.

He looked up and saw her, freezing in place as he waited for her reaction.

She smiled and half-waved, and he gripped the counter with one hand and then pushed the money back to the disappointed patrons. "Sorry, I need to take a quick break, back in a flash." He flipped the closed sign in the window, pulled the shutter down and disappeared from sight.

Kassi stood blinking in the sunshine, and then the back door opened and he was standing there. She moved a few steps toward him. He held his hand out and she reached for it tentatively, then he pulled her up and inside the truck.

They stood facing each other.

She looked around the food truck. "I thought you said you would never make that soup again?" she said at last.

"Kassi, I'm so sorry. I knew you would never ... I just ... I freaked out."

She stood on tiptoe to press her lips to his in a soft, hesitant kiss.

"You're here now," she said, pulling back. "You came to me. It took you long enough, but you came. That means something. I should have given you more space to process what you saw and not thrown a drink in your face. We both reacted poorly in the moment. And then we were too stubborn, too entrenched in our own bullshit, to fix it."

"That will never happen again." Clay slipped his hands around her waist to pull her close for a passionate kiss—a planets-crashing-together kiss.

"I've missed you so much," he said. "My life was empty without you."

She slid her hands under his shirt, tracing his muscles with her fingertips. "Wow, you've been working out."

He laughed. "There was nothing else for me to do except miss you, work out and get this truck fixed up."

"What about the Rose and Thorn?"

"I quit." His breathing was ragged.

"You moved here? To California? To be with me, to be with us?"

"If you'll have me. I know we have a lot to talk about, things to work out, and with Sam, but I'm ready, really ready to be the partner you want and deserve."

She leaned her head on his shoulder, surrendering to the joy and intensity of the moment. "I thought I was going to be miserable forever. I knew if I couldn't make it with you, there would never be anyone else."

"This thing between us is so big and good, sometimes it feels a little scary," he said.

She nodded, looking deep into his eyes. "Like the passion and intensity will just burn us up," she whispered. "You know what they say. If you can't stand the heat…"

"Put an air-conditioner in your kitchen," Clay said, tapping the side of his truck. "I love you, Kassi. I believe in us."

"I love you too." She looked over his shoulder at the line of customers watching them curiously through the translucent shutter. "It looks like you have a lot of orders to fill. Let me help."

Kassi reached for an apron.

"And … cut!" yells the DIRECTOR. "That's a wrap. Way to go team. Everyone, thanks for all your hard work, we've got a hit on our hands. I'm sure of it. Take a breather and I'll see you at the wrap party tonight."

The camera pans out for a wide shot of the film set, catching the actors walking toward their trailers. The crew begins to break down the set.

Roll credits.

THE END

ABOUT THE AUTHORS

Kitchen Heat: A Restaurantland Romance is the eleventh book by Clark Hays and Kathleen McFall. They live and work in the Pacific Northwest region of the United States. Please visit the Pumpjack Press website for more information and to sign up for their newsletter.

Made in the USA
Columbia, SC
08 November 2023